H

feathering   ls
of my eye   d
man needing to know who stood before him. I tried *not* to stiffen at his touch, willing myself not to blink, not to release the fresh tears that had begun to pool. He collared my throat with his long fingers and ran a thumb over my lips. "I want my wife back. Come back to me, *Mitawin*," he whispered.

The word on the teacup; the *hallmark* of my deceit. Our eyes locked, and I felt my throat closing and my knees begin to quiver. For a few seconds his grip tightened around my throat, and I clamped my eyes shut with a fleeting thought. *Yes, take my breath...end this tormenting deception.* When he suddenly released me, I could see the pain twisting his face. He turned away and rubbed his chin against his shoulder, bracing both arms on a porch railing.

"My shirt looks good on you, Jess," he said hoarsely. "You always did have a thing for my shirts."

I cleared my throat. "You can't sleep out here," I said after a long silence. "Come to bed."

His shoulders flinched. "Is that an invitation?"

"I only mean...you can't be comfortable sleeping in that chair."

"Are you still wearing those black things?"

I didn't answer. *What has that got to do with anything?* We both started by the sudden hoot of a nearby owl, and like the volume turned up on ear phones, I was suddenly aware of other night sounds: crickets, wind rustling through the sage, my heart bumping in my chest.

Kudos for CJ Fosdick's
THE ACCIDENTAL WIFE

This novel began life as a short story that placed in several contests in 2013.

The Accidental Wife

by

CJ Fosdick

This is a work of fiction. Names, characters, places, and incidents are either the product of the author's imagination or are used fictitiously, and any resemblance to actual persons living or dead, business establishments, events, or locales, is entirely coincidental.

The Accidental Wife

COPYRIGHT © 2015 by CJ Fosdick

Cover Art by *Debbie Taylor*

The Wild Rose Press, Inc.
PO Box 708
Adams Basin, NY 14410-0708
Visit us at www.thewildrosepress.com

Publishing History
First Mainstream Historical Edition, 2015
Print ISBN 978-1-62830-846-4
Digital ISBN 978-1-62830-847-1

Published in the United States of America

Dedication

With eternal gratitude to
D.G., my writing inspiration,
S.L., my Fort Laramie connection,
"K.G., the model for every great school teacher,"
and E.L., the green-eyed love of my life
who keeps me and my laptop humming.

Time is linear.

Doors close, windows open—change is inevitable, marking milestones, forcing choices, jigging dreams. Childhood, Career, Family, Death. We slip through the changes with joy and tears. Only in books can we travel through time, go back to a simpler era to learn missed lessons in love. Impossible passages?

Not always…

Chapter One
The Legacy

Torrington, Wyoming
May 2012

"Damn!" The blade was dull, but the force of it snapped against my finger, drawing blood as I wedged the dinner knife into the locked drawer. I had been in the basement many times, ignoring the antique desk in the dark recesses of the stairwell, but now, any locked drawer in my late grandmother's house was fair game.

The drawer finally splintered open to reveal a metal strongbox—also locked. Whatever possessed Granny Lou to hide something under double locks must have been greatly valued—or greatly feared. The mysterious key I was given at the reading of her Last Will opened the box. Expecting to find cash, jewelry, maybe an amendment to the Dead Sea Scrolls, what I found was wrapped in musty cotton wool...a blue and white teacup, identical to one I broke when I was ten years old.

I remember Gran's bony fingers shook uncontrollably when she picked up the broken shards. Her face was white as frost, matching the tone in her voice when she scolded me for being careless. I had run to my room in tearful shame, confused by her unexpected anger. She had never raised her voice to me before, and it wasn't like her to set such store in a stupid cup.

Holding the twin up to catch a streak of light drifting through squat basement windows, I examined it carefully. A blue pastoral scene wrapped around the cup with tiny birds webbed in the design. I could tell it was porcelain. When I examined the bottom for a hallmark, "Mitawin" was painted there in bold indigo letters. *Oriental?* I didn't recognize the company. Neither did Google when I checked on my laptop.

After carefully repacking the cup, I set it aside to suck my bloody finger while surveying the shelves lining the walls. Driftnets of dust highlighted boxes and bulky shapes draped in sheets yellow with age. *All mine now.*

Gran's Last Will had specified the little Torrington bungalow and everything in it was mine. The rest of her possessions, including her town car and stock in the Holly Sugar Refinery, went to her only grandson, Jake.

Our common ancestor, great great-grandmother Jessamine Gallagher, had also lived long. Long enough to outlive three husbands and insure her literary talent had spiraled down her female line. So far, *only* down the female line. As Jessamine's great great-granddaughter by her second husband, I belonged to that select line of Wyoming women empowered with a sense of history that needed telling.

"Witches!" Jake once laughingly called us. By mouth, pen, and eventually laptop, we recorded that history in diaries, journals, and scrapbooks, stored in boxes labeled by Gran's spidery hand.

"No web of magic there," I had snapped back.

When Gran took her final breath, just days after her

one hundredth birthday, I became the official heiress of the family journals and the mysterious Calling Stone of our illustrious ancestor. The story went that Jessamine found the red buffalo-shaped stone in a Black Hills riverbed in the 1870s. Indians thought it to be a talisman, meant to call their vanishing commissary. When the thundering herds disappeared, the stone's magic shifted to lesser specifics of prosperity and love.

The charm had worked so far. None of our female ancestors who inherited the stone ever died poor, untalented, or bereft of love. In fact, at age nineteen, Jessamine had set her own benchmark for love, marrying a green-eyed Indian half-breed against all nineteenth century odds. Still single on the eve of my thirtieth birthday, I, Jessica Brewster, had no prospects for love and little desire to find a soul mate of any eye color. *I was mocking the charm for posterity.*

Was it a coincidence that I shared part of Jessamine's name? Gran once told me that I was aptly named *Jessica* since I resembled our unique ancestor. Jessamine and her daughter were also redheads. When I bemoaned the color after being dubbed "firehead" in eighth grade, Granny told me Jessamine had once escaped being scalped because the Indians considered red hair sacred.

"Never, ever regret your color," she had warned. "It meant *life* to our family."

"Anne Boleyn was also a redhead," I argued. "Her hair color didn't save her."

Quick as ever, Granny had quipped, "Cured her royal headaches, though."

Life seemed to be a rare commodity in our family. Besides Jessamine, none of our ancestors married young or had more than one or two children who had the gift of years. Until Granny Lou, nobody—male or female—ever lived to the century mark.

Gran was all I had after my folks died, and I went to live with her at age nine. Her only son was killed in Iraq, and she was already raising her twelve-year-old grandson, Jake. Although Jake and I descended from different grandfathers, Granny Lou showed no favoritism, and as children we dispensed with politically correct half-cousin labels and simply considered ourselves siblings—looking up to Granny Lou as our mother bird. The three of us were a genetic force in the nest, all that was left of Jessamine's Wyoming connection.

"I heard grief lingers only when someone dies young or unexpectedly," Jake had declared after the funeral. I suppose he meant that to console me, as I traveled bleary-eyed and red-nosed through a week of funeral essentials, talking to people through two-ply tissues.

Until she caught pneumonia, I thought Granny was invincible, if not immortal. And once—only once—when she had yelled at me over the shattered teacup, I even entertained the notion that she *could* be a witch.

Perched on a lumpy armchair that coughed up dust when I plopped into it, I fished into a box of scrapbooks and photos. Granny wasn't exactly a hoarder, but some of the things she did save made little sense, and I found myself talking out loud to her.

"Why, Gran, why would you keep a scrapbook of John Garfield, interspersed with old news clippings of the assassinated President Garfield?"

Were the Garfields related? I could see her as a

girlish fan of the handsome actor, maybe meeting him once and blurting out her connecting thought: "Are you related to President Garfield, John?" Of course, she would have called him *John*. Granny never stood on ceremony or felt intimidated. She was on a first name basis with everyone she ever met, famous or not.

As I wiped my eyes and blew my nose in the tissue wadded in my pocket, I could almost feel Gran's ghostly presence around me, her almond scent mingling in musty keepsakes. My heart stopped when I heard the raspy singsong voice.

"Hello, hello, hello, is anyone home?" Jake stood on the bottom step, flicking the light on and off to the beat of Alice Cooper lyrics.

I sucked in a deep breath. "God, Jake, I didn't hear you come in."

"Shoes at the door. Gran's rules." He shrugged. "It's creepy down here, even in daylight." Coming closer, he peered at me. "Crying again?"

"Dust," I muttered.

He looked around, scratching his head. "Why don't you just light a match? There must be hundred-year-old dust in these boxes, not to mention spiders." For such a tall piece of physical fitness, my brawny blond cousin had an irrational fear of spiders. *Hello. Who's your favorite rocker?*

"I'll save you some specimens." I chuckled, playfully crabbing my fingers up his leg as I hissed *I am the spider* in my own off-key version of another Cooper lyric. I had hoped for my own private tour of history, but Jake loved Gran as much as I did. I invited him to join me, picking through a smaller box of photographs.

The oldest ones were labeled in envelopes so fragile the glue had caramelized. We laughed at a sepia photograph of our mutual ancestor, dressed in a billowy costume from a play at Fort Laramie. *Camille lives!* was scrawled across the back with Jessamine's name and the 1875 date.

"My God, Jess, you could be her clone," Jake exclaimed.

Even without the color cues, I could tell she had expressive brown eyes, and her thick auburn hair was as untamed as mine. Her lips were full, the expression as enigmatic as the Mona Lisa's. We had the same boyish figure Jake kindly described as "athletic." In other words, both of us screamed for the need of a padded bra.

In another photo, taken probably ten years later, her pose was stiffer, resting her hand on the shoulder of a bearded man seated in front of her. A young girl in pigtails stood at his right shoulder, one of her shoes noticeably unlaced.

"The girl must be Gran's mother," Jake said. "I can see the family resemblance there, too."

"And that has to be the Indian." I pointed to Jessamine's first husband, looking tan and fit with a crooked smile. Except for his dark hair and brows, he did not resemble what I expected a frontier Indian might look like. No fringe or feathers, he wore suspenders over a Henley shirt.

"Some of these photos might be a great addition to Fort Laramie archives," I mused.

"You might get more for this stuff at an estate sale."

I shrugged. "This is hands-on history, Jake. If I

didn't like history, I might have felt bruised taking a job at the fort at half the pay one could expect for someone with my teaching credentials."

"So you admit that now," he said, laughing. "With all your degrees, you could have gone into engineering or geophysics, like me—instead of education. Just think, surrounded by more testosterone, you might have picked up an M-R-S degree along the way."

Smirking on the outside, I burned on the inside at the tired old joke. Granny had not married until she was thirty-five, and approaching that age, Jake was still single, if you discounted his divorce years ago. Was time edging out the promise of a new generation for both of us? Perhaps our ancestor's cherished artifacts would someday be relegated to an exhibit at a national historic site like Fort Laramie. *The thought was conflicting.*

For hours, Jake helped me separate trash from treasure, and by five o'clock, we had most of the basement divided into three basic zones: trash, Goodwill, and keepers. We hauled Goodwill upstairs.

"I may have to make several trips with all this and most of the stuff in her room," I said. "My hatchback will never hold it all at once."

"That car has to be the most impractical purchase you ever made. With all the cars you've dented, you should be driving a tank. Besides, hybrids are a fad that will never survive the Wyoming terrain."

I bristled at the insult, blowing a rude noise through my lips. "Have faith. It's a dealer model, so I made an offer that couldn't be refused." Driving a sporty red car had been on my bucket list since high school. Of course, in negotiations, I had to pretend the

Honda C-RZ was too small, too red, and the instrument panel engineered for a time traveler.

His laugh was exaggerated. "Sounds like you're driving a mid-life crisis, Jess."

"Bite me," I snapped. "Midlife is forty, Jake. I will be thirty on Tuesday."

"Okay, smart ass, what are you doing for your birthday?"

"Working. The fort is expecting the first busloads of students this week, and I've been recruited for living history skits."

"No evening date, I take it?"

I gave him a baleful look. "Not unless you want to step up and take me to dinner."

He stepped up. "We can commiserate over our empty love lives with a bottle of bubbly. I'll pick you up Tuesday night at six."

Bubbly? Jake knew what a single glass of dinner wine did to me. Life without Gran...new job...new car. Oh hell, maybe I *was* at some kind of crossroads? Bubbly sounded good.

"No, I'll pick you up," I said. "That way, I can *throttle* you with my new drive."

Chapter Two
The Tea Party

"I don't recognize the design or the hallmark," my supervisor told me, tipping the teacup upside down. "Maybe it isn't a company name. Have you Googled it?"

I nodded. Besides cataloging books and donations at Fort Laramie, Stella Lowry was a flea market sleuth who knew all about antiques.

"*Mitawin* sounds like a foreign word. It almost looks like a hand painted addition, not a stamp. If your grandmother added this, it would certainly devalue the worth of the cup."

Puzzled, I shook my head. "This isn't Granny Lou's hand, and besides English, she only knew a few words in Lakota. She *did* have a Sioux ancestor," I muttered, tracing my index finger over the word. Granny always referred to him as "the Indian."

"Only half Sioux," I used to correct her, thinking maybe "Indian" or "half-breed" was too derogatory to be politically correct in our enlightened age.

"The Visitor Center sells a small English-Sioux dictionary." Stella shrugged. "Worth a look, anyway."

"So you think the cup is definitely antique?"

She nodded with some hesitation. "Unique design, though. I've never seen one like this—so many birds. Most of the really valuable cups are gold-trimmed, or the design is hand-painted. And without a matching saucer, this one would probably not be worth more than a tank of gas these days."

I decided to donate the cup to the prop room. Vintage clothing and antiques were often included in the restoration sets or the museum displays. Besides the library, the old cavalry building had several rooms on the top floor dedicated to props and storage. At noon, I was scheduled to join the interpretive staff for the 1880's tea party in the parlor of the old Burt House.

My costume was a blue dress with lace trim at the high neck and cuffs—an original dress typical of something worn by an officer's wife, but it was tight around my neck. How petite nineteenth-century women must have been! Many of the original dresses had to be lengthened at the hemline and let out in every seam from the waist up. I tied my hair back and pulled on a pair of white, crocheted gloves.

Since I was the first to arrive at the Burt House, I fired up the cast iron kitchen stove and set the teakettle on the burner. Because the interpretive staff decided to be as authentic as possible, we used local dried leaves instead of tea bags. When the teakettle whistled, I poured the hot water into a large pottery teapot, over a measure of dried mint flakes, then arranged a bowl of sugar and vintage teaspoons on a tray and carried it all to the parlor.

Small by today's standards, the front parlor was still the largest room in the old house, containing a wicker settee, a piano, a few carved wooden chairs around a small central table, and a black pot-bellied stove in the corner. A large open archway led to the adjoining sitting room with additional seating and small tables covered in linen doilies anchored by painted globe lamps. A bookshelf hung on the wall between two deep-set windows displaying an array of books with similar musteline covers, including many by Mark Twain, who was an acquaintance of the Burt family, according to Stella Lowry.

Family photos in an accordion frame dominated one table. I set my teacup down to study the face of Lieutenant Colonel Burt in his braided uniform. Even without the streaks of gray in his coarse hair, he had the look of great authority. His wife, in counterpoint, had shiny dark hair with umbrella brows. Two boys and a girl in the linking photos had their father's fair coloring but the same complacent mouth of their mother.

With Granny's teacup filled, I settled in a tapestry rocker and sniffed deeply of the minty concoction while absently running my finger around the cup's rim. The hum startled me. Like the deep whine of a bee, it called up vivid memories. I had often seen Gran circle the rim of a glass half-filled with water. She always laughed at me when I tried it. I rubbed harder, faster, slower, changed glasses or cups, varied the levels of water, and still—always failed to produce a single decibel. *Did this talent finally pass on to me?*

It was a strange hum, lower than the whistle of a teakettle, dissipating like wind soughing through the trees in a stiff evening breeze. Suddenly light-headed, I was transfixed by the sound and fingers that seemed to glide the rim of the cup with a will of their own.

So transfixed, I barely noticed three other women had joined me. I didn't recognize any of them, but then I was still a recent hire, and the Park Service always added extra part-timers for the summer season. I had only filled in with interpretive history once before, and was not familiar with all the scripting. Basically, we were tour guides, pretending to be historic characters in little vignettes meant to showcase history more than any acting skill. The fort's busiest tourist season always began in May when school buses delivered Wyoming children in year-end field trips.

I set my cup down on the lamp table beside me and smiled. "I'm pretty new to this, but I did start the tea already." I gestured at the teapot I had covered with a quilted cozy to keep warm, and rose to introduce myself. "I'm Jess…"

The brunette image of Elizabeth Burt interrupted with a wave of her hand. "I know who you are"—she smiled slowly—"and I do thank you for fixing the tea. I only meant to take a short nap after Andrew left for drill. I must have drifted off upstairs."

I followed her glance toward the hall stairway. The upstairs bedrooms were also staged with period furniture, including a tall bedstead with a horsehair mattress covered by a turn-of-the-century patchwork quilt. Before any of the interpreters passed the grade for living history tours, we had to learn the history of the house and furnishings, names of the past residents, and even a few of their personal quirks to spark interest.

I had been told that Reynolds Burt, the youngest son, was still living when the Park Service restored his former home. On a nostalgic visit to Fort Laramie in 1961, he had donated some of the actual furnishings, describing where everything was placed when he lived here as a boy. Reynolds also served in the military, earning the rank of Brigadier General by the time he died in 1969.

"You must be Elizabeth Burt," I said, amazed by her uncanny resemblance to the photo.

She fixed me with a squinty eye and nodded. As the hostess she was portraying, she invited the other two women to sit while she took command of the teapot and poured three cups. One of the women was quite heavy, but well-fitted to her costume, her hair fashioned for the times with a neat part in the middle and pulled back into a bun at her neck. The hostess called her "Sadie." The other woman was younger, with a double braid crowning her head, her eyes dark and shiny as polished onyx.

"I'm fairly new here myself," she said. "There are so many names to remember." She smiled as she blew on the hot tea. "Hattie Sandercock, Miss. I do remember you, however. There aren't many redheads here, even among the soldiers."

I laughed. "You ladies are quick, but we need an audience before we fall into character."

Elizabeth Burt squinted again. "An audience? Well if you mean the children, they have already left for school, and the men are all at mess. It looks like we may be the only women today who'll substitute tea for dinner."

"I still need to lose some baby weight," Hattie sighed, resting a hand on her stomach. "I am happy to skip a meal now and then to do so."

"How is little Meade?" Sadie asked.

"Alas, he has a low constitution, seems to catch the ague easily."

Alas and ague...Wow! These women even studied the language of the time. I rose to pour myself another cup of tea and nearly tripped over the length of my dress. When I pulled my skirt up, I could hear the intake of air suck around me.

"What are those?" Sadie pointed, and all eyes converged on my feet.

"Oh crap, I forgot to ditch my Crocs." I met the stares and gasps head on. "What?" I peeled the purple sandals off my feet and held one gingerly in each hand. "They do mold to your feet."

"Where did you get those?" The hostess backed away as if I held two dead mice.

"A bootery in Cheyenne has some in neon colors this spring, perfect with beachwear, and great to wear washing your car...I mean your horse." I chuckled.

Sadie pulled a lacey handkerchief from her bosom and dabbed at her neck. The other two ladies carefully examined a sandal, each turning it over and over in their hands, sniffing it while they glared at me, dumbfounded.

"What are they made of," one of them asked, as if she had never seen such footwear before.

"Why, rubber, I guess, or some kind of synthetic."

"Sin...sin-thetic?" Hattie's dark eyes were round as ripe olives.

"Where are your stockings," Sadie scoffed.

I lifted my skirt to my knees. "You don't wear stockings with Crocs." I wiggled my red painted toenails.

More gasps and grunts filtered through the air. I looked from one shocked face to another. "You've never heard of Crocs? They've been around for years now." *What the hell was wrong with these women? Were they playing with me? An initiation for newbies?*

Flustered and confused, I slapped the Crocs back

on, picked up my teacup, and marched to the front door, craving fresh air...and tourists. Several costumed soldiers passed on the boardwalk, heading for their historic stations, no doubt, at the oldest military building in Wyoming. Just two doors away, Old Bedlam was more than one hundred sixty years old now, the two-story, white-washed building reminding me more of a mansion seen in the Civil War South than former bachelor officer quarters.

I did a double take, clutching the porch pillar when my knees began to quiver. A *boardwalk* replaced the gravel tour paths. The sturdy ash trees bordering the parade grounds were gone, replaced by spindly trees and bushes pulled inside grass yards with picket fences. *Picket fences?*

I stumbled to the gate and shielded my eyes to look down Officer's Row. Two more homes now stood between Bedlam and the surgeon's house next door, and south of the landmark, three large identical buildings had replaced the limestone ruins. Across the parade grounds, I could see more buildings where none had stood an hour ago, more trees and picket fences and tall lanterns that looked like old-fashioned *gaslights.*

To my left, a group of costumed children chanted a song, ringing hands with two soldiers. Horses were tied to a hitching rail in front of the trader's store, and two men in Indian costume lingered around the entrance, talking to a tall man dressed like a cowboy. *Horses? Cowboys and Indians?* What happened to the parking lot...my red Honda...the Visitor Center?

I closed my eyes and could feel my body sway in the wind. Only there was no Wyoming wind. The air was unusually stifling and still. A woman stepped out of the Trading Post and opened a parasol. She followed a little boy headed in my direction, thrumming a stick along the picket fence. I stopped the boy with a hand trembling on his shoulder.

"What...what day is this?"

The boy stared at me blankly, until I squeezed my fingers. "F-Friday," he stammered.

"No, no," I cried. "What year, I mean, what is the year?" He shrugged my hand off and ran to his mother, now close enough to catch the worry in her face. "The year," I screamed. "What is the year?"

Dizzy, I leaned heavily against a sturdy fence post, dimly noticing tea stains on my dress and fingers clamped around an empty cup. In a blur, I saw the tall cowboy turn and run toward me in slow motion. The little boy was yelling something at me. I saw his mouth move, and the words shot at me like bullets slugging through air thick as honey.

"Eighteen...eighty...six!"

The last thing I heard was the scream of the teacup as we both smashed against the fence post.

Chapter Three
Emerald Eyes

"Jess, are you all right?" The deep voice came at me through a tunnel. I blinked at the shadowy face backlit by the sun. The cowboy cradled my head on his lap, loosening my neckline with calloused fingers that smelled of leather and wood smoke. "Jess, look at me," he commanded in a voice edged with worry. "Are you hurt?"

I struggled to my elbows, shaded my eyes from the sun, and looked into the whiskered face of a handsome man with eyes the color of emeralds. I recognized the face from the old sepia photograph. In living color, his eyes were mesmerizing.

A little girl dropped beside him...on her knees...grabbing my hand. "Ma," she cried. Her red pigtails were banded in pink ribbons, her eyes wide as pennies. Green pennies...*His eyes?*

"What's wrong with Ma?" she cried in a tiny, frightened voice.

My stomach lurched. I turned my head and retched into a clump of weeds poking through the boardwalk. Tears prickled my eyes and blurred the new faces that surrounded me. An overture of voices buzzed around me. I recognized only those of the tea ladies.

"Did she faint?"

"Loosen her stays."

"Take her to Doc Brechemin."

I could feel his arms supporting my back, my knees, lifting me as if I were light as a sunbeam. For a second, he tipped me toward his chest and bent his head toward mine. The brim of his hat sheltered us, and I could feel his breath, warm on my face. "Mitawin," he whispered, kissing my brow. "I'm here."

Mitawin? The word inscribed on the bottom of the teacup. The Lakota dictionary I checked out at the Visitor Center said it meant wife...*my wife!*

Everything went black again.

****

They say before you die, the last thing that goes is your hearing. I strained to hear the final whispered words. My eyelids seemed to be stuck shut, and my head was throbbing. Someone was pulling off my gloves, fingering my wrist for a pulse.

"She just collapsed you say?"

"I tried to get to her before she hit her head on the fence post."

"Has this happened before, Mitchell?"

"My wife is strong. She doesn't faint."

My wife. There it was again. My wife! I groaned when I felt a hand cap my head.

"She has a lump on her head, and her pulse is racing. Women sometimes faint with a tight corset, or if they are carrying. Is that possible?"

"She doesn't wear corsets, and if she were with child, I would know."

"Would you?" The doctor snorted. "Most men are blind to the signs; they have to be told."

There was a pause, a throat clearing into a low response. "She's had misses."

"How old is she now?"

"Thirty, come fall."

"Not too old yet. She seems healthy enough. A mild concussion will not set her back long. Rest and light meals. Willow bark or pennyroyal tea will help ease a headache. Her thinking and memory may be muddled for a while, and her sleep and mood patterns may change, but that should be temporary."

"Can I take her home then?"

Home? I forced my eyes open and blinked at the two shadowy men at my bedside.

"Fish Creek's only a couple hours away," the taller figure said.

Fish Creek? *I knew that place.*

CJ Fosdick

Chapter Four
The Homestead

The wagon ride did nothing to lull my aching head. I was bundled in a red blanket with a grain sack for a pillow. Burlap and cotton sacks were packed firmly around me in a spring wagon loaded down with kegs and things that creaked or groaned against each other. A wire cage held two chickens that cackled with protest whenever the wagon hit a bump. The girl with the pigtails was braced between the cage and a small keg, trying to read a book. When I joined the chickens protesting another wagon jolt, she reached over to absently pat me like a dog.

When the wagon finally stopped, the driver turned in his seat and pushed his hat back to wipe the sweat line from his forehead. "We're at the crossing," he announced.

I could tell by the sun it was late afternoon, and I wondered how I got into this wagon and why I felt so sleepy. Was I drugged? Then I remembered bits of conversation in a doctor's office. *Concussion...sleep patterns...Fish Creek.*

Fish Creek. At least I knew where that was. About twenty miles west of the Laramie National Parksite, it was known for its good fishing. My high school biology class had taken several field trips to campsites there. I pulled myself up and peered over the wagon lip. I could

20

see a barn and corral, a few outbuildings, and surrounded by woods on the gentle slope of a hill, a small log cabin with a covered front porch. The girl ran ahead and opened the door as *he* carried me over the threshold.

"Seems we keep repeating this tradition, wife." He kissed my head as he carefully lowered me into a rocking chair in front of a stone fireplace that dominated the room.

I winced, probably more from the address than his contact with the goose egg on my head. *Wife again.* Automatically, I checked my left hand. No ring. No memory of a wedding. *How does one become a wife without a wedding?*

"Tallie," he said, "make your mother a cup of tea while I unload the wagon."

The girl lit the stove with fingers practiced to the chore, and within minutes I was enveloped in a familiar mist of mint.

"How old are you?" I asked, studying her as I steadied both hands around the steaming cup she handed me.

She gave me a look that curled her brows. "Ma, you know I am nine." She seemed smaller than most nine-year-olds, had hair the color of mine, and definitely—her father's eyes.

"Oh, uh, I know that...uh, Tallie...you just seem to be so...grown up. It surprises me."

I never liked surprises, unless they included chocolate.

Her quick smile lit up her face, blooming with a pair of dimples. "I hope you feel better soon, Ma. Pa bought more seed to plant in the garden. Flower and vegetable seed, just like you wanted."

I could feel a lump grow in my throat. "I...I'll be good as new when my head stops drumming." *Next week, maybe.*

Hopefully, I'd be gone in a few days, and I wouldn't have to deceive a nine-year-old who obviously confused me with her mother. What worried me more was passing, until then, for *his wife.* Even if Jessamine and I were identical twins, there had to be noticeable differences. Married couples would surely know the difference, if not by sight, by a lot of other senses I didn't want to think about.

When Tallie left to check on the new chickens, I finished my tea and toured the cabin. It was solidly built, but less than half the size of my Torrington bungalow, with a crowded room dominated by the fireplace on one wall. A trestle table and benches divided the room: a kitchen with a cast iron stove, dry sink, and cupboard on one side, a bookshelf over a narrow work bench on the facing wall. A large bearskin rug covered the puncheon floor in front of the fireplace. A couple of well-placed oil lamps on small tables, like furnishings at the Burt House, promised evening light.

Steep half-log steps led to a loft where, I presumed, Tallie slept. Another bedroom, no bigger than a frame lean-to, had obviously been added to the main structure on the right side of the cabin. A pine log bed with a low dresser at the foot dominated the tiny room. A paned glass window beside the bed was framed and curtained by a woven swag. Women's clothing hung on several wall pegs above a modest array of footwear. Vaguely, I wondered if any of them would fit me.

Oh God. My Crocs! I pulled them off and shoved

them far under the bed, then assessed my red toenails. How do I get rid of nail polish that wasn't invented for forty or fifty years yet? I padded back to the fireplace, found a sharp piece of charcoal, and scraped my nails until my toes were smudged black and the hearth was peppered with red flakes. With my fingers, I swept them under the hearth logs. Charcoal now smudged my hands and feet.

God bless whoever invented paper towels and liquid soap, I thought, after I located a rag in the dry sink.

There was no bathroom, but I knew that indoor toilets were a bittersweet novelty that became less rare by the turn of the century. One of the buildings outside must have been the designated outhouse. *Wrong century for marble vanities and porcelain commodes!*

He interrupted my tour, carrying a flour sack and small containers to stack on the kitchen table. "These supplies should see us through a month," he muttered in my direction. He had removed his shirt, and I could see muscles flex in his arms and back under the weight he carried. I knew he was several years older than Jessamine, but there wasn't any wasted flesh that could give away his age. He must be over forty, but he could have passed for a fitness trainer. For a man of his era, he was tall and broad shouldered, and he wore his long hair pulled neatly back and tied with a leather thong.

When he came toward me, I could see his face better in the low light and noticed his nose was long and narrow, and his crooked smile was directed at me. Tiny crow's feet around his eyes and between his brows may have given away his age, until I locked onto the sparkle in his green eyes. I wasn't used to seeing men sporting sideburns and whiskers, but on him it looked appropriate. *Hot even.* Perhaps from the sun—or from his native blood—his skin was deeply tanned, moist with sweat and the musky smell of a man.

"Feeling better?" He searched my eyes as they lingered way too long over his muscular chest and a puckered scar that looked like a third nipple. I backed into the wall when he reached out to swipe at the tip of my nose, then puzzled over the charcoal residue he examined on his finger.

"No...I mean...Yes," I said a little breathlessly, rubbing my hands into the folds of my skirt.

"I think you should rest. Tallie and I can make do. Are you hungry, Jess?"

I blinked under his steady gaze, feeling suddenly weak. He knew my name. *Oh, snap!* His wife was Jessamine—probably also called Jess for short.

"Nooo, just tired." I sighed. *Scared shitless, to be honest.*

"Then you belong in bed. Doctor's orders." He nodded toward the small bedroom, turned me around, and deftly undid the tiny buttons that closed the back of my dress.

"About time you got a Sunday dress. You look good in blue." Though his lips felt like a hot brand, I shivered when he kissed me on the nape of my neck. He chuckled as he patted my backside, dismissing me like a child. I breathed a sigh of relief that he didn't follow me into the bedroom to tuck me in.

I hung the "Sunday dress" on a wall peg and slipped under a colorful bed quilt, still wearing the costume shift I had pulled over my own black lace bra and panties. The feather mattress was a far cry from the memory foam I was used to, but it *was* comfortable, and I *was* eager to give up the circus in my head to the blessed oblivion of sleep.

How does somebody trade places with their great-great grandmother? Was Jessamine having tea with the interpretive staff of old Fort Laramie, charming visitors with her uncanny knowledge of the nineteenth century? Did we pass into some alternate universe—exchange students traveling through time—or was this all just a very bad birthday nightmare I would wake from in the morning? I pulled the quilt over my head and bit off a quick prayer, then wondered if I was praying for the right thing.

Tomorrow. Everything would be clear, come tomorrow. Happy Birthday, Jessica Brewster!

Chapter Five
Cocks, Cows, and Corsets

I woke disoriented, thinking I heard the sound of a rooster cock-a-doodling in my ear. I tried to focus on a square of light dancing on the wall in front of me. The window to my left was half-open, and there was no screen. Nothing to stop the noisy perpetrator from hopping on the sill to make sure I wasn't deaf to his alarm. I could hear birds chirping their morning song, and the rustle of bedding beside me. *Beside me?*

I must have screamed when a large hand reached out to touch me. I was not alone in the bed.

"Jesus, Jessamine," he grumbled, "you competing with Frank?"

"Frank?"

A dark head popped up before me, hair mussed, new whiskers shadowing a face dominated by sleepy green eyes. "The rooster doesn't need any help."

I pulled the sheet to my chin and gaped at him. "The rooster? You have a rooster called Frank?"

He rolled his eyes. "You named him, didn't you? You and Tallie name everything with a face around here, including the cock of the farm, and all in his harem."

"Harem?"

"The hens he presides over, lucky cock."

I could feel the blush creep up my neck, and it

didn't escape his notice. He grinned. "I know what you're thinking." He fished under the sheets for my hand and guided it to his torso.

I jerked it back when I touched warm flesh, and with a little squeal, examined fingers that felt as burnt as my face. He was sleeping commando. I, who never spent a night in bed with any man, woke up on my thirtieth birthday in a small bedroom in a wilderness cabin with a rooster crowing at the window and a naked man beside me. Not just any man. I rolled over with a groan. *Oh Lordy, this wasn't a dream. I was in bed with my great great-grandmother's first husband!*

I inched away, preparing to leap off the bed.

With a hand on my shoulder, he pulled me back to face him. "Jess, we need words." He must have seen the anxiety in my eyes, for his voice softened almost to a whisper. "You're confused. Doc asked me if you were carrying again. He said it was a common reason for women to faint. Is that possible?"

I wagged my head vigorously, biting my lip.

"Well, I didn't think so, but we've been down this road before. Maybe we need to retire the worry. We have a beautiful daughter. You don't need to feel it is your mission to give me another son."

Another son? I suddenly remembered what Granny had once told me. Their firstborn was early, Jessamine was alone, unable to save the child. The baby was buried in a hidden canyon in the Red Wall of Wyoming. Granny even thought it could have been where the famous "Hole in the Wall" gang of outlaws hid from authorities in the late 1800s.

"I remember what you said when we buried him. 'No more children.' You didn't want to wear down like

27

your ma, with losses that drove her mad. You avoided my love for months, and then, then Tallie got started."

He reached for my hand again and gave it a squeeze. "I didn't know your ma, but she raised a strong woman, Jess, and you're raising Tallie the same. I don't need sons. I need *you.*"

With his thumb, he blotted an unbidden tear from the corner of my right eye, then leaned in for a quick kiss. Though his lips felt warm and comforting, I stiffened, holding my breath. He pulled back and searched my face, then sighed deeply. "Don't shut me out again," he said. "You know I am a patient man...if you need time again. But I am your husband. Never forget that."

I shook my head, relieved, but unable to make eye contact as I twisted a corner of the quilt between my fingers. *Yes...time.* How do I wrap my head around what I knew he was suggesting? It was wrong. *Incestuous?* No, God, no. I wasn't *really* related to him. *My* great great-grandfather was Jessamine's *second* husband. Besides, if this was 1886, this birthday girl was not born for nearly one hundred years yet.

He sat on the edge of the bed, hands clasped on his knees. I sensed he was groping for words that didn't come. Finally, he rose and took a pair of trousers off one of the pegs. He shook them out and turned so I could see him pulling them up slowly, taking his time with the buttons at the crotch. I sucked in my breath at the sight of him, unable to deny the disturbing little flutter in my chest. *Holy Chippendale!*

He was built as well below the waist as above; narrow hips, long legs, muscled thighs, and what fell between them cleared the sleep from my eyes. I had seen male anatomy only in one dimension—on a black and white page in a biology book. In 3D color, the leap to reality must have heated my face enough to fry an egg on it. *Was he deliberately teasing me?* Well, to be fair, teasing who he *thought* was his wife.

Having never had a steady boyfriend, much less a husband, I wondered if all men became unapologetic nudists behind closed bedroom doors. Maybe Wyoming Territory didn't get the news that this was still the Victorian Age, when limbs were barely acknowledged, much less exposed, even among civilized men who—I was almost certain—still wore nightshirts to bed in 1886? Well, maybe not on the frontier, or maybe, just maybe he was used to...uh...teasing intimacy with his *real* wife.

Oh God! I closed my eyes and buried my face in the pillow, listening to his deep chuckle fade as he left the room.

I was grateful the cotton shift I wore to bed concealed my own lacy bra and bikini panties. Even if the Victorian Age was not given a nod on the frontier, nineteenth century men and women would have to be scandalized by such scanty underwear. Nobody, I vowed, was ever going to see these *scanties!* Certainly not my new bedmate, if I could help it.

The little dresser held Jessamine's plain and practical underclothes: cotton bloomers, stockings, chemises, two nightgowns, and a linen petticoat. Though I distinctly remember him telling the doctor his wife didn't wear corsets, I found one shoved in the back of the drawer—a white twill contraption with whale bone stays and lacings. I could imagine how uncomfortable it must have been when laced tightly to cinch in the waist and push up the breasts.

It reminded me of the corset I found in one of Gran's basement trunks. If I look enough like Jessamine to be her twin, she probably didn't even wear a bra. Like my padded bra, though, a corset may have given her a better silhouette, *if* she cared. For some reason, I felt she would have always sacrificed beauty for comfort, convenience over vanity.

It had been years since I skimmed through one of Jessamine's journals, but I remembered the feeling it inspired. Like Granny Lou, she was comfortable in her own skin, strong willed, quirky, yet likeable; someone I might have treasured for a friend.

Finding long pants in the bottom drawer didn't surprise me, though I wondered if wearing trousers in her era might have poked her for cross-dressing, like transvestites in modern times. I suspected she was brave enough to ignore aversive labels—or whatever anyone thought of her.

Reflected in a wall mirror above a small table holding a washbowl, pitcher, and cloths, I studied my appearance after dressing in Jessamine's clothes and pulling on boots that pinched my toes. I brushed and combed my hair with her dresser set, working it into a ponytail tied with the blue ribbon that had matched my Fort Laramie costume. Scrubbed free of any residual makeup, my face was pale. There was a subtle difference, I thought. Was I looking at Jessamine's face, in Jessamine's mirror, after using *her* brush, wearing *her* clothes? I pinched my cheeks and bit my lips, bringing forth some color and stuck out my tongue at the face in the mirror.

A jar on the table held a bunch of green willow

30

sticks with frayed ends. *Toothbrushes?* I found one that looked unused and gave my teeth a dry brushing that did nothing to whiten or refresh. How did they manage without toothpaste or mouthwash? Halitosis and missing teeth must have been epidemic. Frontier dentistry was probably little more than a toolbox of pliers. I noticed *his* teeth, however, were quite perfect—even and still white as a row of opals when he flashed a smile. *Thank heavens, my gold tooth had been replaced by an implant last year.*

The smell of fresh coffee led me to the kitchen with some enthusiasm. Tallie and her father were laughing over something when I joined them. I suppressed the urge to spin and preen in clothes that were just a little snug. The warmth of their smiles energized me, and suddenly I was *very* hungry. Tallie carefully poured me a cup of black coffee while her father scooped some scrambled eggs onto a blue enameled plate.

"I like your hair like that." He gave my ponytail a brief tug as he handed me the plate.

The eggs were so light and creamy, I couldn't help but moan with appreciation.

"You must be feeling better." He chuckled.

"Are these fresh eggs?" I mumbled around a mouthful.

"Fresh this morning. Fresh every morning," Tallie chimed. "We do have good layers. Even one of the new hens gave up an egg this morning. I put the extras in the springhouse, Ma, in case you want to make biscuits later."

Me? Make biscuits? Last time I did that, Jake made a sport of lobbing my burnt offerings into our backyard compost bin. "Will you help me, Tallie?"

She nodded happily, offering me a glass of warm milk that tasted like cream compared to the skim I was used to drinking.

"Is this cow's milk?" I poured a little into my coffee, getting a double look that felt rehearsed for its similarity.

"What other kind is there, Ma?"

I looked from one pair of green eyes to the other. "Oh, well, it could be canned milk, couldn't it?"

"Ma, who buys canned milk when they own a cow?"

Good point. "Well, certainly not us," I chortled, wondering if Jessamine took her turn at milking. *They have a cow. And chickens. And horses. Holy fudruckers! Had I bought into a zoo?*

Well-fed and fortified for more surprises, I announced with more gusto than necessary that I needed to pee in the outhouse.

Again, I was given the double look and stare. "I think she means the privy," *he* interpreted with a condescending nod to his daughter.

Okay, so I was going to have to watch my twentieth century terms if I was going to pull off this charade. I knew there were books written by historians and students about life in other centuries. Even Fort Laramie had one in their library, useful for writing living history scripts. I had thumbed through *Everyday Life in the 1800s* a few times, checking out words and descriptions commonly used then. Apparently the lingo didn't stick in my jarred memory bank.

Tallie rolled her eyes, then leaned in to whisper something to her father as I left them.

Chapter Six
A Snake Named Freddie

Privy, latrine, outhouse! What did it matter how it was named? I always called them outhouses, even the portable fiberglass booths that dotted construction sites and parks. Port-a-potties were just a modern version of the old-time outhouse with the crescent moon door that seemed to hold a place in history as the *butt* of many jokes.

My chuckle turned into a scream when I opened the outhouse door. Coiled between two holes, a large snake dove into the bigger hole with a loud splash. Halfway back to the house, I collided with my bedmate. He grabbed me by both arms.

"A snake, there's a snake in the outhouse!" I sputtered, once I caught my breath.

"What did it look like?"

"Beady eyes...a big snake."

He shook me a little. "Markings?"

"A pattern, it had a pattern."

Tallie tugged on my shirt. "Was it brown and yellow, Ma?"

"I think so."

"Fred-dieee!" she screamed, bolting toward the outhouse.

He relaxed his hold on me and let out a long sigh. "Her pet gopher snake. It isn't poisonous."

"Pet! She has a pet snake named Freddie living in the outhouse?"

He scratched his head. "Normally it nests under the front porch. Maybe it found a mouse?"

"Oh great. Does the mouse have a name, too? Maybe Felix or Francis?" The corner of his mouth twitched a little when he stared at me. I was probably milliseconds from a bout of hysterical laughter when we heard Tallie's piercing cry, and we both sprinted to the outhouse.

She was kneeling on the bench, her head bobbing over the hole. "Freddieeee," she yelled, her hands cupped around her mouth and nose like a megaphone. "Pa, we have to save him," she pleaded, her eyes wide with horror.

He picked her up and set her firmly on the floor. The outhouse was a two-seater, but there was little floor space for three standing people. We bumped heads, jockeying position to peer into the pit. It was deep and dark down there, great camouflage for a yellow and brown snake.

"Well, something is moving down there," he choked. His face shuttered with effort—either to hold his breath or to keep from laughing. "We need a long pole or a tree branch. Unless he's happy down there, he may appreciate a way to climb out."

Tallie shot like a missile into the yard. "I'll find one, Pa."

"Freddie looks pretty fucked to me," I muttered, staring into the hole.

"What did you say?" He gaped at me with dark furrowed brows.

Holding my nose, I squeezed around him and

lunged for a gulp of fresh air. Giggles were bubbling in my chest, testing my weakened bladder. He followed me outside, still glaring at me before he grabbed a hatchet stuck into a tree stump. I watched him march after his daughter, then managed to get my pants clear before relieving myself over the smaller hole in the outhouse.

"Sorry, Freddie." I peered into the hole beside me. "I really didn't mean to scare you."

Chapter Seven
A Horse of a Different Color

I left the snake rescue to Tallie and her father while I toured the rest of the farm. The barn was older than the house, almost as big, with a loft that held loose hay and straw. The smell was stronger than fresh mown grass, earthy and sweet and sour all at once. A large black and white cow gave me a mournful assessment from her stall. She had a huge udder that must have been massive when filled with morning milk. I patted her gingerly on the rump, avoiding the whip of her thin tail when she acknowledged my greeting.

I supposed it was neatly arranged for a barn, some empty tie stalls on one side, the wagon and hitches, traps and miscellaneous tack on the opposite side, with inside access for nesting chickens along the back wall. A narrow door led to the backyard. The chickens had a ramp that funneled into a wire-fenced enclosure outside. The red rooster with the resounding voice was sitting on a fence post, observing one of the new hens, obviously preening before him. *Frank* had a discriminate eye focused on a speckled hen with a solid-colored behind. *Fanny?* I chuckled.

I counted more than a dozen chickens, red and white and speckled hens clucking in groups, scratching the ground, a few basking in the morning sunlight, heads tucked into their wings. "Lucky cock," he had called the rooster. It was hard to tell if roosters had more than one expression, but the one on Frank's face told me he knew he was cock of the roost. *Luck had nothing to do with it.*

Five horses were also pastured outside. Three of varied shades of chestnut and two spotted—one a miniature of the largest, most beautifully marked horse I had ever seen. I thought it might be an Appaloosa or Paint. They were separated by a rail fence, probably by gender or age. Two of the red horses looked young. What I knew about horses I eagerly learned from several summers of riding lessons, at least enough to saddle up, ride without intimidation, and take the correct lead.

Maria Schmidt, my German riding instructor, once told me I had a natural seat. That was after my horse—appropriately named Buck—tried to dump me when he spooked over a windblown plastic bag. He bucked across the arena, stopping inches from the fence. I was nearly impaled by the saddle horn, but I still clutched the reins in my fists and a mouthful of mane when someone pried me out of the saddle. What I also had—besides a severe loss of composure—was a bruised bottom for a week afterward.

Buck did not escape any consequences, either. Ms. Schmidt tied the plastic bag to a riding crop and instructed me to "de-spook" him by rubbing him with the bag from head to hoof, shoulder to tail, before every subsequent lesson. Eventually, he lost his fear of plastic bags, at least.

When I whistled softly, the larger red horse perked up and ambled toward me. I ruffled her forelock and let her sniff my hands.

"You must be Jessamine's horse," I whispered. Her mane was dark red, silky to the touch. She had wide set eyes—a sure sign of equine intelligence. When I stopped petting her, she nuzzled my arm, sniffed my pants pocket, and pawed the ground.

"Looking for a treat, are you?"

I looked around for a patch of grass and pulled up a handful. She ate daintily out of my hand, tickling my palm with her velvet tongue. She was obviously well-fed and cared for, probably very attached to her owner and vice-versa. I felt a tug of hope. *Perhaps?* Just one ride before I left?

Over the fence line, the large spotted horse watched us with the possessive intensity of Frank the rooster. His white coat was covered by random ink spots, and both black mane and tail were long and thick. I knew at once who rode him, if he was ridden at all. He strutted along the fence line with a slight limp. When he came closer, I saw that his tired eyes looked almost human, confirming what I knew about the Appaloosa breed. This horse had already seen a lot of life.

The dry pasture was dotted with scattered tree stumps. The farm was on the edge of a stand of tall pine trees, with Wyoming's cottonwoods typically lining the creek. Off in the distance, I could make out the scallops of the Laramie Range, the border of my world—a western edge that anchored my life. Beyond them, Yellowstone Park had been the farthest west I ever ventured.

I shaded my eyes with my hand and tried to pick out any differences in the horizon. Wyoming wind and weather could be fierce, but a hundred years probably wouldn't alter much more than a treeline even though I knew Fort Laramie had set up mills to harvest wood from the mountains and often hired contractors to go beyond fifty miles or more when their needs for timber and firewood were greatest.

Happily, a lone bur oak had survived any lumber pillage in the yard. Already as tall as the barn, its canopy of branches dripped with bunches of spring catkins, like citrus-colored seed pearls. A gnarled tree like this dominated our Torrington yard, providing food and shelter for the birds and squirrels Granny liked to watch from the summer porch. A neighbor in the forestry business told us the tree had to be two hundred years old, hinting it could soon become a good source of white oak lumber. Granny was horrified, and thinking the man had designs on her tree, she paid for expensive root feedings every spring just to keep it alive.

"It was here before I was born," Granny once chortled, "my old friend will be here long after I'm gone." She had poked a finger into my chest for emphasis. "Think of the taproot, Jessie, long as our family history."

A huge garden beyond the barn was partially tilled and sporadically dotted with new weeds. I recognized the woody tangles of raspberry bushes bordering the far edge, while rows of dried corn stalks still needed to be pulled or pulverized. It was a perfect spot for a garden, sheltered by a windbreak of trees, yet open to the sun, and close enough to the creek to make use of some kind of irrigation.

I remembered the joy our little backyard garden gave us, producing all the juicy tomatoes, onions, and cucumbers we could eat in one summer. One year, we even planted zucchini and were amazed at how much produce came from six little plants. We clipped zucchini recipes from magazines and experimented with cakes, bars, and casseroles, and we still had a surplus of vegetables the size of small bats to give away. Gardening always gave me a larger appreciation of fresh produce, miraculous for turning little seeds into anything superior to food in a can.

Tallie mentioned she had seeds to plant. Maybe I could help with that. City girls, like me, had little knowledge or curiosity of how a farmstead worked, but I could feel a tug of pride, even relief, knowing my ancestors lived off the land with little or no waste of time or resources. Going organic was not a choice for them. They ate what they grew and bartered or traded service for other needs. A healthy system, it apparently worked well in a time before power drinks and supplements.

Chapter Eight
"F" Words

Still mired in the pit, the snake showed no interest in climbing the sapling strategically angled before him, even with axed stubs of branches giving him ladder-like access for the ascent.

"He has a way out now," *he* explained to Tallie, as we all headed back to the house after another call of encouragement to Freddie.

"But what if you hung onto my ankles and I could reach down and grab…"

"No, Tallie. It's his choice, not ours. We showed him the way to choose life."

"But what if he doesn't choose that, Pa?"

He stopped to hug his daughter to his side. Over her head, he winked at me. "Well, then, maybe we can only hope that there's storage in his little head for a brain."

I was beginning to feel sorry for Freddie. Both of us had fallen into a position we didn't choose, but at least *he* had a clear way out!

To take Tallie's mind off Freddie, her father took her fishing while I used up the fresh eggs to make biscuits and test my use of an old iron woodstove. I made myself some tea, happy to take a break after searching through the cupboard, taking inventory of all the utensils and supplies I had to work with. Unlabeled jars held a variety of spices and powders I recognized only by smell or taste when I stabbed a finger into them.

I found a handwritten recipe book on the bookshelf, and I thumbed through it while sipping my tea, marveling that its biscuit recipe was identical to the one Granny always used. *Another thread linking our generations?* Tallie was Granny's mother, after all. Maybe Jessamine got these recipes from *her* mother, or her German grandmother? The thought gave me *goosies*. My head was beginning to throb anew, realizing that even in great change—some things remain the same.

****

While her father cleaned and fried the fish catch for dinner, Tallie gathered spring fiddleheads and watercress from the creek for a salad I found exceptionally crisp and tasty. I had set our placings over a clean tablecloth crowned with a small basket of beautifully browned biscuits. At least they looked beautiful to me, once I scraped off the burned parts.

While they were fishing, I had also checked on the snake. No progress there, not even a nod of thanks after I threw two burned biscuits down the shaft to him.

The purple and white wild flowers I arranged in a glass jar looked festive on the table. Tallie led us in table grace, adding a little prayer of hope for Freddie. I caught *his* eye, and we both smiled a little over her heartfelt sentiment.

After a final checkup on the snake before bedtime, Tallie's lower lip quivered when she reported that Freddie was not using his little brain, but she held back her tears, asking her father for a bedtime story that might have been a ritual with them.

I danced my fingers over the spines of the books on the parlor bookshelf: a very large German Bible, *Leatherstocking Tales*, children's readers, and a book I was very familiar with. Jane Austen's *Pride and Prejudice* had always been one of my favorites, and I was delighted to see some of the passages were marked, pages even dog-eared. *It must have been a favorite of Jessamine's, as well.*

It was two hundred years since the book had been published. The author had probably acquired her greatest fame and recognition in *my* lifetime with all the Jane Austen fan clubs and websites, as well as a battery of Austen wannabes who published books about Lizzie and Darcy's romance and what happened *after* their wedding. I thought demure Jane would have blushed over some of the wannabe books, but she might have been pleased with several movies inspired by her most popular book.

In Regency books, manners and misunderstandings were a common thread. Romance was simple and sentimental. Sex was never described and rarely hinted at; a far cry from the graphic elaborations of sex and violence in books of my era.

"Are you reading that again?" *He* sauntered into the room, pulling off his shirt, and poured some water from a pitcher into the bowl on the stand. After swishing a willow stick in the bowl, he ran it over his teeth, chewing on the stick like a cigar while he washed his hands and ran a wet cloth over his face and around his neck. I couldn't help peeking when he ran the cloth under his arms and over his broad chest, dampening the dark hair that ran like a "T" down to a wisp at his waistband.

"I...I never get tired of this book." I scooted closer to the kerosene lamp on my bedside table, thoroughly distracted by the testosterone explosion in my peripheral vision. "The language is such a war of words...so ironic between educated people with class distinctions."

"Oh really?" He sat on the edge of the bed and pulled off his trousers to drape them carefully over the bedpost. I bent my head to concentrate on the sentence I was reading—over and over again—while he nonchalantly arranged his naked body beneath the sheets and stretched out, clasping his hands behind his head on the pillow beside me.

"It's funny you should say that. Coming from such an Austen devotee, I would think you would appreciate language befitting an educated wife and mother." There was an edge to his voice that red-flagged my attention.

I shut the book and set it on the bedside table. "What do you mean by that?"

"You used a word in the privy today that would curl Jane's toes. I've heard some white men use it, but if a woman used that word, she probably lived in a whorehouse."

"What?" *He definitely had my attention now.*

He flashed a mirthless grin at me and pointed to my book. "The snake looked *spent,* as they would say in that era."

I suddenly knew what he was talking about. "Well, in my era, he looked fucked!"

"*Your* era?"

"I mean *our* era. That word's been around since people were subject to kings." I made a valiant effort to modulate my tone in logic. "Fornication Under Consent of King is the acronym it represents, I believe."

"Acronym?" He turned toward me, propping sideways on his elbow, with raised brows and a definite edge to his voice. "Just where did you hear that?"

"It's been widely whispered through centuries of history."

"Centuries, huh? And you know that because…"

"Because you can easily find it online."

"On what line?"

Oh oh. I sucked my lip, stopping any further slip. I couldn't defend my lapse by explaining the world had become smaller, webbed by information overload from electronics that were unimaginable in 1886. Anyone with a computer had incredible access to history, including the origin of cuss words. I could feel the color creeping up my neck. *Online* had just slipped out.

My mind was clicking faster than a Google search. "Why, the gossip line at Fort Laramie." I tried to sound convincing. "I overheard some of the laundresses talking about it once…while they were hanging out wash…on a line."

"And where would they come by such knowledge?"

I could see this wasn't going to be easy. He was too sharp, too curious.

"Jeez, I don't know. Maybe some of their 'rougher' clients? Maybe it was just a rumor or maybe it came from one of those…those guys hauling freight?" I remembered one of Jessamine's journals described her journey to Fort Laramie disguised as a teamster.

He fell back against his pillow, making a loud snorting noise.

"Bullwhackers. Well, we both know how they could sizzle bacon with their blue streaks, but I doubt they knew or cared about the origin of cuss words." He threw me a pointed glance. "Most *educated* people don't imitate bullwhackers, do they?"

I suppressed my own snort. *Where was smart phone Siri when you needed her?* In 2012, the F-bomb corrupted movie dialog, TV, books, and regularly burst from the lips of *educated people,* even children.

Nevertheless, I did feel slightly ashamed. "I *am* sorry. The word just...slipped. At least Tallie didn't hear me."

"Well, at least you do yourself credit with a blush and an apology." His mouth twisted in a wry smile. "I thought you gave up that potty mouth, Jess, when you became a mother." He rubbed the side of his nose. "You were rather attached to a few cuss words when we first met, but I've never heard you burn any in front of Tallie."

Bringing Tallie into it made me feel even more remorseful. "And you won't. She's a great kid, and she needs a...a mother to match your good example." *Wow! I even managed that without a shred of sarcasm.*

He softened his tone. "You've always been a good mother, Jess. I wouldn't want our daughter to have any other."

I turned my head to blink away the sudden moisture webbing my lashes. *Who could ever replace a woman so regarded, so easily forgiven?* A heavy silence fell between us, like a barrier down the length of the bed. I blew out the lamp and listened in vain for the breath that told me he had fallen asleep.

"Don't...don't your people ever swear?" I finally

whispered. It was my first reference to his heritage, and I wondered if this was shaky ground. *Was he proud or ashamed of it?* It took him a long time to answer, making me think he might be asleep.

"Body language. We get messages across more with body language," he whispered back.

"So you think...er...other people talk too much?"

I could hear him sigh. "Whites use many words that mean nothing and promise less. Like cussing."

"Oh." I had taken Native American studies at Laramie University and knew there were many words that didn't have any language equivalent and vice versa, but the only Indians I ever talked to were my professor and a school groundskeeper. Both were about as chatty as a cigar store Indian, come to think of it.

He broke another long silence. "May I kiss the potty mouth?"

"I...I didn't brush my teeth."

"I don't want to clean your mouth, just kiss you goodnight." I could hear the smirk in his voice.

Weakened by guilt, I turned my head and pursed my lips. *What could a platonic kiss hurt?* His mouth brushed my lips, lingering long past platonic. Trembling a little, I turned back and ran my thumb over my lips, melting into my side of the bed.

Chapter Nine
Yosemite Sam

Frank had a good understanding of his job, but I truly missed the convenience of an alarm clock with a shut off button. Burying my head under a pillow did nothing to mute the noise. *Did roosters ever get laryngitis?* I silently counted to three hundred before he stopped crowing, hoping also, that was enough time for my naked bedmate to rise and put on some clothes.

I would need to adjust my daily schedule while I was here. What was the saying? *Early to bed, early to rise makes a man healthy, wealthy, and wise?* Ben Franklin had to own a rooster. In Torrington, I rarely went to bed before midnight, or rose before seven a.m. Rising at dawn was a new experience, but without electric lighting, I could see why the days in 1886 were defined by sunlight. Oil for lamps, maybe even candle wax might have been considered a frivolous expense.

Coffee was still warm in the pot, and a few leftover biscuits dusted with sugar and cinnamon were on the warming grate when I sat down for breakfast. I guessed Tallie and her father were still milking the cow and feeding the animals. *Her father. My bedmate, the Naked Man.* Now that I had let him kiss me, I supposed I could call him what Jessamine called him. *"Mitch,"* I figured, was short for Mitchell. Did he even have a first name? Mitchell was not a name I'd ever ascribe to an Indian.

Wasn't it more of an Irish name?

With my coffee mug, I stepped out onto the porch and sat on what looked like a crude precursor to an Adirondack chair. I wondered if *he*—Mitch—was the handy man who built all the wooden furniture—or even the house? Out of necessity, frontier people had to wear many hats. *Necessity, the mother of invention, the father of initiative?*

Perhaps the cabin was already built, and he just bought or rented it? What was his source of income? So many questions and no easy way to get the answers, I mused, staring at the speckled mug in my hands. It was not porcelain, not even ceramic, and looked like something a camper might use. My fingernail, clicking against the side was the only sound it produced, keeping time with the song of a thrush and the drum of hoofbeats. *Hoofbeats?*

Even at a distance, the man had the look of impatience. Rather squat, he leaned forward on his horse, as if he were nursing hemorrhoids.

"Morning, missus." He tipped his hat to me. Like Yosemite Sam, his head rose out of a rusty beard that fanned over his neck. Thick brows sheltered eyes that darted in my direction. "Your husband around?"

I pointed toward the barn with my mug. "You need help with something?"

"Just another neighborly proposition. You've got a stubborn man there."

"Oh, really?"

His saddle creaked when he leaned back. "I've made him some good offers for this spread, even for his broke down stallion. You know, I own most everything that surrounds you, it's only a matter of time…"

I could see Mitch strolling toward us. "Morning, Garrett," he called, pleasantly. "You're out early enough."

Garrett? The name was vaguely familiar. Wasn't there a Garrett in our family tree?

"Can Jess get you some coffee?"

The man touched his hat and started to dismount. I took Mitch's offer as a signal to either get me out of earshot or genuinely play hostess. I hurried into the house to arrange a tray of coffee and sugared biscuits, wondering why a familiar neighbor wasn't invited inside where we could all sit at the table.

"He's almost too old for breeding," Garrett said when I returned. "And probably beyond field work."

Mitch was leaning casually against a post, his long legs crossed. "Then why would you want him?"

"Bloodline. I'm willing to take a chance that he can still produce some worthy get. I have a couple young broodmares, fairly bred. A full-blooded App is rare in Wyoming, even among the savages now."

The muscles clenched in Mitch's jaw. He studied his cup thoughtfully before he spoke—minus the friendly tone. "Jess and I decided long ago that we would never separate either of our horses, for any reason. They've produced enough good colts and fillies to give us some income. You bought one of their colts. Breed *him* to your mares."

"Tried that. They threw a red and brown roan with no muscle. Must be the blood of your red mare dominating."

This man was reinforcing my poor initial impression, insulting bloodlines; first Mitch's, then the red mare's.

Mitch took a long swallow of coffee, then set his cup down, smiling wryly. "My people always respect the dominance of red. I thought I made it clear before, Garrett. This property and everything on it ain't for sale."

"I didn't see any foals in your barnyard last year, or any cattle on your range. You got enough money left to burn a dry mule?"

"We get by. And if there are no more foals to sell, our horses will retire in their ease."

"Hay burners," Garrett sneered.

"We've made a living here so far. The fort buys our excess produce and lumber I can fell."

So that's the income source! Doesn't seem very lucrative—or steady.

"We may get back into the cattle game again—if we fall short of need," he added.

Garrett looked a little startled. "You lost your pitiful herd in the blizzard of '81. Seems that would be plain as red paint that cattle ranchin' ain't your strong suit."

The muscles in Mitch's jaw worked again. "Maybe it wasn't the blizzard that cleaned me out."

"You makin' an accusation here?"

"I'm just saying the dead count didn't add up, but I didn't have any branded or notched, so I have no proof."

Garrett snorted. "It's open range. Without a brand, hard to sort them. I lost as many as you did, Mitchell. Just had more to start with, but I ain't no rope and ring man, and resent the implication. We both know what happens to rustlers in this territory."

"I hear the stories." Stone-faced, Mitch swirled the

coffee in his mug without looking up.

"Two brand artists found butchering a Longhorn on the CY spread near Casper were sewed into the hide and thrown into the hot sun for days. The hide shrunk in the heat and crushed them to death. You hear that one?"

When I gasped loudly, they both stared at me, as if I had suddenly become visible. Garrett looked a little sheepish as he removed his hat and ran a hand through his bushy hair. "Any honest family man would take that warning hard as whetstone, but for thieves and ranchers, the tale does serve its purpose."

After a long pause, Garrett went on, a little more subdued. "My ranch is twice the size of yours, but I have eight mouths to feed, and I'm only looking ahead to what I can do for my boys."

An uncomfortable silence fell over us all. I looked to Mitch and found his expression unreadable, his body language tense.

"What about renting out your place, then? My oldest boy, Jed, is getting married this fall. If you rented to him, you might have enough income to move into town."

Mitch's laugh was more snarl. "Jess was raised on a farm, and I know the value of living off the land only too well." We all looked up when he gestured, seeing Tallie approach, lugging a basket of fresh eggs with both hands. "We want her to learn those values until she makes her own life choices."

Garrett took a sip of his coffee, considering a reply. "Daughters are dutiful, but it takes sons to help run a spread. Mary and I have a daughter *and* five sons."

I took the basket of eggs from Tallie and set them on the porch. She looked from me to Mitch, questioning what she must have read in our faces. Her little hand reached for mine, and I automatically squeezed it to reassure her.

"Girls are always a blessing, Mr. Garrett, no matter what they decide to do with their lives. Without sons, maybe there'll be grandsons, or...or hired help." I felt Tallie squeeze my hand. Even I was amazed at what just spewed from my mouth.

I sensed Mitch's smiling approval, even before I glanced his way.

Garrett coughed, setting his cup down heavily beside him. "Well, I see I am up against a solid front. My new offer was going to be more than fair, considering."

Mitch rose, looking even taller than the six feet I judged him to be. "My wife has said all that needs to be said, Garrett."

"I won't give up on this, Mitchell." He glared at me with a parting shot as he mounted his horse and jerked the reins until the horse spun around with a grunt, baring his teeth.

In silence, we watched him ride off, hunched forward just as he came. Mitch took Tallie's other hand and winked at me over her head. Like a family united, we entered the cabin with the basket of eggs, hungry now for a hearty breakfast.

"Can you sell the younger horses," I asked, supervising the griddle of fried eggs with a spatula in hand.

"You can't sell Freckles," Tallie whined.

Freckles? Of course...Tallie's spotted horse. *I was getting used to her brand of F words.*

"As soon as the red mare comes into heat, we can

breed her again," Mitch said. "The first heat of spring is always the strongest."

"Isn't she too old to, to breed?"

"Sixteen isn't too old for a broodmare, but the Appaloosa is ten years older and showing his wear. That he's still alive at all is your miracle."

"Mine?" *What I knew about treating horses wouldn't fill three lines in a spiral notebook.* I turned to flip an egg, wondering what he meant and how I could find out.

"You saved him Jess. Even I might have put him out of his misery, finding him so wounded on the battlefield." His focus was no longer on me but on some unseen memory of the past that tightened his jaw once again. "He's gone through a lot, Jess. We all did."

Battlefield. What battlefield?

I understood—whatever he meant—may not have been a suitable discussion for a pair of nine-year-old ears. The Civil War had plenty of battlefields in the nineteenth century, but Tallie wasn't even born then, and Jessamine was a child herself in the 1860s. Beyond that time, there were scattered battles out West with the Indians. Surely, Jessamine wouldn't have been involved in any of those.

I was still a girl myself when I skimmed through her earlier diaries, noting she wrote what most young girls write about before they fall in love. However, I realized events recorded on paper could never compare with personal memories tangled with heartfelt feelings that were beyond description. How many young girls, with the exception of Anne Frank, even knew how to eloquently describe what was written in their heart?

Granny had told me stories about her grandparents,

always referring to Mitch as "the Indian." Up close and personal, I was beginning to see that *"the Indian"* may have had many dimensions uncommon to a man in either century. He was certainly well educated. *How was that even possible?*

Aside from Cousin Jake, I had no personal male references in any race. I was Tallie's age when my own father died, and my disastrous high school crush on Jimmy Potter solidified my wariness over future male relationships. Jimmy had turned me into a bookworm— a determined collector of college degrees, with no time or space in my life for *any* man.

Here I was now, adrift in another century, flipping eggs for an uncommon man with mesmerizing eyes and a daughter anyone couldn't help but love. If I started keeping my own diary or journal, I doubt I could put into words the twisted emotions I was feeling now. *Questions?* Those came easy, however. As soon as I returned to my time, I would have to re-read Jessamine's journals for the answers.

Suddenly, it occurred to me. Her journals had to be *here*. They were handed down from generation to generation after her death. But Jessamine wasn't dead, unless history was altered. She had many years and two more husbands to outlive. The journals weren't on the bookshelf or in her dresser, but they had to be somewhere in the house or barn.

I plated and served the eggs, masking my thoughts with a smile that was quickly returned. "I can see why Garrett would want this spread, but why your old horse?"

Mitch shoveled in a mouthful of egg and chewed thoughtfully. "He doesn't know the horse's history. I think all the bloodline talk is aimed elsewhere. Garrett just wants his neighbors all the same color, even while he knows the value of an Appaloosa."

"Well, I caught that much. I didn't realize...I mean I thought there wasn't any, uh discrimination over..." I didn't have to finish. I could tell by the twitch in his jaw he knew what I meant.

He snorted over a swallow of coffee. "The wars are over, the battles, maybe not. We were lucky to get even one hundred acres here, especially near the creek. Prejudice aside, anything that is near a water source that hasn't already been snapped up by cattle ranchers is being sold to sheep men moving northward. If it wasn't for the Desert Land Act, and *you* co-signing with the money you inherited from your Nebraska acreage, we might not have this homestead." He rubbed the bridge of his nose with thumb and forefinger. "Women have more rights in Wyoming than Indians. Probably true all over the country." The corner of his mouth twitched into a weak smile.

I pushed my food around on my plate, until Tallie interrupted my thoughts. "But I'm part Indian *and* woman, aren't I, Pa."

Mitch chuckled. "Only one quarter Indian, Tallie, three quarters white, with your ma's looks. You will probably be able to sign any deed of ownership in Wyoming, and you *will* have the rights of inheritance, as well."

It struck me then; Jessamine was *all* white, like me. Doing the math in my head, Granny would have been one-eighth Indian. Even Jake would have some Indian blood. *Not enough to get a break with college tuition and grants, however.* It had taken more than a century, but there *were* some advantages to the native bloodline. There were still reservations, but living on them was an option now, and some of the tribes actually owned lucrative casinos.

I wanted to share this bit of hope for Tallie, but little good it would have done. If someone had told me when I was her age that in my lifetime there would be a black president and drones would replace military aircraft, I might have thought they were deranged or delusional. Tallie obviously loved and respected both her parents. It wouldn't matter to her if her father's blood gave her an advantage or not. Obviously, she hadn't faced the kind of discrimination that would make it a point, anyway.

Mitch polished off a second helping of fried eggs before he pulled a folded square of paper from his pocket. "I almost forgot, Garrett gave me this note for you, Tallie—from Rachel."

Tallie eagerly spread the note on the table while I stacked empty plates in the dry sink.

"Rachel wants me to come for her birthday, Ma." Tallie painted her finger across each carefully printed word, reading aloud. When she hesitated, I joined her on the bench and was shocked by what I saw. *Can u cum to my hose nest weeken 4 my burtday? It wil be fun to see u agin.* The "R" in Rachel was printed backward.

"Where does Rachel go to school?"

"She doesn't go to school," Tallie said. "None of her brothers, either."

"Where did she learn to write, even like this?" I asked, astonished.

"We showed her, Ma. You and I showed her last year. Don't you remember? She came here once a month with fresh meat or cheese to pay you for learnin' her."

"You mean *teaching* her, Tallie."

"Yes, Ma. That's what I said."

I was shocked...and angry, until I realized that frontier education was probably a minor luxury, limited by proximity to schools or teachers. Even in my era, Wyoming was *still* sparsely populated because of its geography and fewer cities than most states.

"Isn't there a school at Fort Laramie that both of you could be attending?"

Mitch put his hand on my arm. "Jess we talked about this. Remember, we decided it was too far and too dangerous for her to go without an escort, and we both were needed here at the farm. Isn't that why you ordered readers from St. Louis and taught the girls their letters? Are you still confused?"

"I...I must be." I tapped the letter with my forefinger. "This child can't write *or* spell."

"Well, don't feel too bad about that. With all the chores they lay upon the girl, she doesn't have time for book learnin'. Half the time she was here, she just played with Tallie. 'Let her be a kid,' you always said."

"Well, that's important," I said slowly. "Children often grow up too fast, but they also learn at a faster rate when young. That's been proven."

Tallie poured a kettle of heated water into the sink basin and added some soap powder for the dirty dishes. "Rachel says her ma doesn't have time to teach."

"Well, you make time for what's important. Learning is important."

"Not for girls, according to Rachel's pa."

"It's especially important for girls," I snapped.

"Haven't you heard the old saying, 'Educate the mother, you educate the family'?"

Mitch held both hands up when I pointed my fork at him. "You'll get no argument from me about that, Jess. Tallie's been reading since she was four. We both made sure of that."

"How far away do the Garretts live?"

"A few miles. Maybe four or five."

I lit up with an inspiration.

Chapter Ten
The Proposition

I took my cues from Tallie as she saddled Freckles and handed me the bridle normally used for Dolly, Jessamine's red mare. The mare moved sideways when I tried to mount her, snorting a little as if affronted. I let her sniff my hand and stroked her muzzle and face until she stood still while I tried mounting again. She knew I was *not* Jessamine. I knew animals had a sense of smell far superior to ours. It was fortunate for me that Dolly could not voice an opinion of the stiff rider that finally perched on her back.

Tallie led the way, clearly excited by the prospect of seeing Rachel again. No wonder she was more mature than most nine-year-olds. *She was growing up with adults.*

We followed the tree-lined creek as closely as possible, enjoying the serenade of birds that telegraphed our presence. The smell of spring was sharp with morning dew and budding flora. Riding a horse again, after so many years, I felt a familiar exhilaration. There was something about the outside of a horse that was good for the inside of a rider. Maybe like riding a bicycle, you never forget how—or how masterful it makes you feel.

It was going to be warm and sunny all day and with little wind, perfect for planting a garden. If my mission didn't take long, I could help with the planting when we returned. On our right, we passed a scattered herd of cattle grazing on the gray-green bunchgrass that was native to the territory. A loose stone fence kept them contained, with a few breaks for access to a thin stream of water. The creek had funneled into a shallow stream that soon became a dry gulch in long stretches, a telltale sign of a dry Wyoming spring.

Closer to his ranch house, we saw Mr. Garrett and three of his sons plowing and planting their fields. He stopped when he saw us, leaning on his plow with a look that questioned our presence. I waved cheerfully and moved on, ignoring any response.

Mrs. Garrett and Rachel greeted us in their dooryard with contrasting enthusiasm. Tallie barely had her horse tied to the hitching post when Rachel was upon her, both girls holding hands, squealing with delight as they jumped up and down. Rachel's mother and I laughed at the sight.

"Shows visitors are scarcer than hen's teeth around here." She wiped her hands on her apron. "You got Rachel's note, I take it."

I slid rather awkwardly off the mare and tied her to the post with a quick study of the slipknot Tallie had used. "We did, and the note's why we've come."

"Tea then?" She invited me inside the frame home that was probably three times larger than Mitch's cabin. The great room was well-furnished with two facing sofas, chairs, tables, oil lamps, and a carpet runner that marked a worn path to a separate kitchen with cupboards, a pie safe, sink with a primitive pump, and a long plank table surrounded by benches and chairs. She pumped some water into a kettle and put it on a cast iron stove that had six burners and two ovens. Everything looked clean and tidy, even the striped table runner anchored by two bowls of wild berries at either end. When I complimented her on her home, she begged me to call her Mary.

"It's been too long between visits, but neighbors can't let time starch our greetings," she said.

Mary seemed anxious to please, bidding me to sit while she went to the cupboard for cups she hastily dusted with her apron. When she set the cup and saucer before me, I noticed the bruises on her forearms. Fading now to yellow, but still distinct. She followed my gaze and blushed. With effort, I checked myself from asking how she got them and studied her teacups instead. Fine china, they were sprinkled with tiny rosebuds—no birds. I turned my cup upside down and studied the English hallmark.

"What's left of my mother's set." Mary smiled, proud of my interest. "Boston made, shipped by rail, with many of her things after she died."

"They're lovely," I said.

"Well, I don't have much occasion to use fancy out here." She sighed. "Henry says I should jest pack them up again, make space for tinware that don't break easy."

"The frontier can always use some refinement," I said. "Speaking of…"

I was interrupted by a shrill whistle and waited while she ladled a teaspoon of dry leaves into my cup and added the hot water. A tiny bug rose to the surface in my cup. When I fished it out with my teaspoon, she was clearly mortified, her face turning two shades whiter, emphasizing the gray streaks that winged over her ears and disappeared in brown hair neatly tucked into a dust cap. She quickly scooped up my cup and dumped the contents into a basin.

"Let me pour you another." Her laugh was dry and mirthless. "Goes to show you how often fancy gets used."

I patted her hand and chuckled. "A little meat in the morning sets up the day." *It was something Granny always quipped when she fried bacon or sausage.* "I really wanted to talk to you about Rachel," I said.

"Rachel?"

"About her note to Tallie."

Mary smiled. "Rachel worked hard on that note after begging us for a party. Her pa said a party was out, but maybe she could invite Tallie to spend a couple days here if she could get all her chores done ahead of time."

I could hear the girls giggling and cooing over a small pen of new puppies in the back yard. "Tallie would love to spend time with Rachel. I think they need to do what little girls must do before they have to grow up. Did you have playmates as a child?"

"Oh yes, playmates and a sister." She looked over my head, calling up some childhood memory that made her smile drift.

"Rachel also needs some schooling," I said bluntly.

Mary's back stiffened. "That's why she came to you last year. To learn her letters."

"Once a month is not enough. She forms her letters but doesn't put the right ones together. Regular school would teach her how to spell and do figures and learn so much more, Mary."

"Henry says schooling is wasted on girls. He says

all they need to learn is the three c's—cooking, cleaning, and conceiving."

I nearly dropped the fancy teacup I held. *Henry was a caveman, reinforcing my attitude about most men.* I popped a few berries in my mouth to keep from blurting something I would regret in polite company. Mary saw my reaction and picked up her sugar spoon, polishing it vigorously with her apron. I drained my cup and counted to ten before I found my voice. "Do your boys know their sums and letters then?"

She let out a long sigh. "Only what Henry shows them on bills and such. He says they can't be spared much either, what with all the work that comes with a spread the size of ours. Henry wants to expand his cattle business, says it pays more than farming."

I tried a new tactic. "Did you go to school, Mary?"

"Through sixth grade," she said proudly. "I was the oldest girl so when Ma took sick, I had to take on the housework. Before she died, she taught me all I know about smooth-running a household." She bridged the polished spoon carefully across the top of the sugar bowl.

"No matter what *Henry* thinks, girls today need to know how to write and spell and teach *their* children. There's a world of changes waiting for them."

Mary slumped in her chair, then eyed me with some consideration. "What do you suggest?"

"You can convince your husband to let her go to the school at Fort Laramie. Maybe your sons as well."

She snorted. "He would never consent to that, and he'd mock me for asking."

"What if Rachel and Tallie went together, with some of your older boys taking turns driving them.

Maybe Mitch would take a turn, too."

Mary chewed her lip thoughtfully. "I don't know."

I reached out to cover my hand on hers. "Both the girls obviously need the socializing, too. And Rachel could share what she learns with the boys."

Mary snorted. "Rachel rarely shares anything with the boys. She is mute around her father and barely has a voice for me. She does chatter on with Tallie, though."

Just as I could detect a spark of light in Mary's gray eyes, we were interrupted by steam whistle screams, this time coming from outside. We rushed to the source in the backyard. Both girls were scuffling with a tow-headed boy that looked about their age, trying to wrench a small shotgun out of his hands.

"Jacob," Mary shouted. "What on earth?" All three children turned still as river rocks.

The boy began to sniffle and swiped a trickle of blood from his nose. "I didn't want to do it, but Pa told me I had to."

Mary jerked the gun out of his hands and paled when she saw it was loaded. "Do what?" she gasped.

With a trembling hand and blazing ears, he pointed to a feed sack hanging from a nearby tree. The sack was visibly wiggling.

"Are you shooting snakes again," Mary scoffed.

The boy scooted away, scrambling for distance.

Rachel found a voice through her tears. "He's shooting the runt, Ma. He's shooting Pepper's runt."

I marched to the tree and untied the bag. A tiny black and white puppy wiggled out of my hands and began to crawl away. One of his back legs was bent at an odd angle.

"He's a cripple," the boy shouted, tears welling in

his eyes. "Pa said to kill the cripple. He won't be any use to us. He can't even walk."

Mary pulled her son up by his shirt collar and looked at me with a terrible sadness in her eyes. "Take him." She nodded her head at the puppy. "Take the runt away."

Tallie rushed to scoop it up in her arms and buried her face in the ball of fur. A little pink tongue lapped at her chin. "Can we keep him, Ma?"

I folded both girls and puppy into a group hug, and when I saw the hopeful pleading in Tallie's eyes, I could only nod.

Still grasping his collar, Mary marched her son inside the house, then met us as we mounted our horses to leave. Her arms were folded across her waist, gripping each elbow for support. When I put my hand on her shoulder, a smile trembled on her lips. "I will think on what you said, Jess."

I squeezed her arm and thanked her for the tea. When we reached their garden, I turned to look back and saw them still standing in the dooryard, mother and daughter locked together, straight as a pillar. Slowly Rachel waved, and with one hand firmly holding the puppy in the folds of her shirt, Tallie waved back.

Chapter Eleven
A Ticklish Situation

"His leg was probably broken in the scramble for food," Mitch said. "A runt is always overpowered. We could try to set the leg with a splint, but if he doesn't take cow's milk, he might not survive anyway."

Tallie looked him square in the eye. "He will survive, Pa. I'll see to that."

"He'll need a lot of care, Tallie. You want to take that on?"

Dimples popping, she grinned and nodded. "Finn has a bigger brain than Freddie."

I laughed, running two fingers over the furball. "Finn, is it? Still with the F-names."

Mitch glared at me, a slight twitch at the corner of his mouth. We splinted the puppy's tiny leg, supporting it with a two inch twig and a wrap of linen. I followed Mitch to the garden with a small sack of seed when we left Tallie, sitting in the rocker trying to funnel cow's milk into the puppy's mouth.

"She needed a real pet, Mitch, not a snake or a chicken. Didn't you ever have a pet?"

He sighed. "I could count the wolf, but I guess he was more yours than mine."

The wolf was not a mystery. I remembered Granny telling me about the wolf Jessamine trained like a dog when they lived in the canyon. *The wolf had died protecting her.*

"I mean as a child. Didn't you have a pet growing up...a dog or a cat?"

He snorted. "What you might play with in the morning could have been supper that night. My people didn't just name things with a face; they ate them."

"Yuck!"

"What did you say?"

I could feel my face heat up when he gave me a narrow look, and I turned aside to hide the quiver at the corner of my mouth. "Yuck. What did you think I said?"

"What kind of word is that?"

"Well, um, I guess it's mostly a kid's expression, you know, maybe when they don't want to eat something."

The lines in his forehead smoothed over. "I've never heard Tallie say that. She eats everything we put before her."

"Tallie is a rare child." I snorted.

He peered down at me with his crooked grin. "Well, she has her mother's appetite." He put his arm around my waist and squeezed my hip. "I don't understand how you can stay so slim, the way you usually attack food...like a beaver to wood."

"Yuk yuk," I responded, moving out of reach. "That's another version of the word. It's spelled different, but means very funny."

His laugh was deep and pleasant. "I've never heard that expression, either. I think you're making all these words up."

We spent what was left of the day planting several rows of corn and beans, then watering them with buckets of creek water. It was back-bending work I wasn't used to, and I was already stiff from the morning horse ride. There was so much dirt and sand in my tight boots, I eventually pulled them off and regretted it at once. The ground was hard and rocky, painful on tender soles and blistered toes. I was tempted to retrieve my purple Crocs from under the bed but couldn't think of a reasonable explanation for such alien footwear—especially after the reaction I had from the tea ladies at the Burt House.

I was relieved when Tallie coaxed us back to the cabin for an early evening meal. She had set the table with a platter of cheese, pickles, and sausage and even opened a can from Fort Laramie's store. She beamed with pride when Mitch praised her efforts.

"Oysters, you eat oysters out here!" I exclaimed after drinking three ladles of water before I even washed my hands. I was sweaty and tired, with blisters popping on both feet. But I *was* hungry. Fresh air and hard work gave me an appetite that would certainly pose a threat to any slim waistline.

Mitch playfully flicked a little water at me as he washed his own calloused hands and toweled them at the dry sink. "It's a common treat '*out here.*' But I thought we were going to save the oysters for my birthday."

"Your birthday?" I couldn't hide my startled reaction.

Tallie made a tiny squeal of regret. "I forgot, Pa. I know how you like them any time we can get them, but I should have waited another two weeks."

Two weeks then. His birthday was in the same month as mine.

"Well, they aren't such a rarity anymore, now that the price is down. Guess we could get more on the next trip," he said.

The next trip to Fort Laramie? Yes! I knew my ticket home had to be somewhere at the fort. I also wanted to check out the school there, to see if the girls could be enrolled. I wondered if a garrison school closed for summer or ran all year long?

"We'll have fresh eggs to sell. There seems to always be a surplus." I tried to tone down my excitement.

"We may need more seed as well," Mitch added, with an incriminating glance at me. "I think your mother is filling the holes more generously than last year. She may even have mixed up the seed."

"That's easy to do," I said rather defensively. "A lot of them look alike, except for the beet and bean seeds, and of course, the potatoes."

"Well, good to know, we can depend on some solid rows." He smirked.

I knew what beet seeds looked like only because sugar beets were a familiar crop on irrigated land all around Torrington, providing raw vegetables for the Holly Sugar Refinery.

"How is Finn doing?" I changed the subject, before my incompetence could be explored any further.

"He sucked milk off my fingers until they wrinkled." Tallie laughed. She had fashioned a neck sling from a large scarf, and the puppy was sleeping in the folds. "He tried to walk, but the splint was holding him back."

"You may have to carry him around, at least until the bone has a chance to mend," I said.

Tallie nodded happily. "It will mend, I just know it, Ma."

Mitch studied me across the table when I stood up to stretch my back. I winced as I bent to touch my dirty feet. My thirty-year-old body wasn't used to a day of riding, planting, lugging water, or going barefoot on rocky soil.

"Are you okay, Jess? Maybe you need to lay off early," he said. "The doc said you needed rest."

Rest? Right. I smiled wearily. *Kinda antithetical to homestead living.*

"We'll heat some water for a footbath, Jess. Would that suit you?"

A whole body bath would suit me! What was it, a week almost without a hot shower or bath?

As if reading my mind, he added, "Once the planting is done, we can bring out the tub for a whole body bath. Both of us will need one by then, I expect." He winked at me, like some signal between intimates. *Oh God, did they bathe together? Share a tub? What tub?*

"You might find the creek still too cold, though I find it bracing myself." He winked at me again, while I cleared the table.

****

I was beginning to revel in small pleasures. Aloe leaves for blisters, mint tea, a bucket of warm water, and a clean towel was not to be taken for granted. I must have moaned with appreciation, because his eyebrows moved an inch higher when I set my feet in the bucket of heated water. I dropped my head back and closed my eyes, relishing the heat that radiated through my toes and up my calves. Already, I could feel my thighs ache from the horse ride.

His deep chuckle forced me to open one eye. "You like, I take it?"

Before I could censor my mouth, I muttered, "Does the bear crap in the woods?"

He laughed out loud. "You've picked up some queer lingo, woman." He glanced pointedly at the bearskin rug on the floor. "Haven't seen a bear for years, Jess. They're keeping their distance from red-headed sharpshooters, I guess."

I smiled, knowing he was referring to *The Bear Story*. Jessamine was no sharpshooter when she killed the grizzly that wasn't too happy about sharing his cave. The rug was probably the infamous bear, looking docile now, spread eagle on the floor, with claws removed. I knew that with all the little references made about their life together, details might come only from Jessamine's journals once I found them...if I were still here.

I started when I felt him pick up my right foot and dry it in the towel. "Water's pretty muddy." He knelt beside the pail.

When he began to massage my foot, I squealed and pulled it away. "That tickles."

"Tickles? You were never ticklish before, Jess." He looked a little offended as he pulled the other foot out of the bucket and carefully toweled it dry, then set it beside its mate with a little heft. "Your feet have grown." He frowned at the sight.

I wiggled my blistered toes, trying to think fast. Apparently, I wasn't the mirror image of Jessamine after all. Foot massages must have been routine for her, and I already guessed the tight fit of her boots meant my feet were larger.

"They're swollen, going barefoot so early, I guess. Or maybe I'm getting flat-footed in old age?"

"Old and cranky," he said rather sarcastically.

Splashing him was an automatic reflex I might have used with Jake, who would have laughed it off. Mitch, however, grabbed a foot and deliberately resumed the tickling. I squirmed, trying desperately to squelch a reaction that made me want to scream and laugh at the same time. I was no match against the strength that dragged me like a limp rag out of the rocker down to the bearskin rug. I kicked, landing a couple of solid hits that made him grunt and me wince at the painful contact.

Suddenly, I felt his hands slide up my ankles, squeezing my calves, heading for my knees. My shift was also rippling upward, his touch becoming more than a tickle. Encouraged by my sudden gasp, he let go of me and shifted his weight until he had me pinned down by my arms on either side of my head. His green eyes held no glint of humor as they plumbed the depths of my own, asking for something I couldn't give. I tried to stare him down, sending him a wordless message that didn't coordinate with the thump of my heart. We were both breathing hard, out of proportion to the playful struggle.

I twisted my head toward the loft. "Tallie," I whispered, calling her name like the safe word I knew it could be. He loosened his grip on me, then fell back on the bearskin and covered his eyes with his forearm, swallowing a deep sigh.

Tallie had retired early, taking her new pet and a bowl of milk up to the loft with her. If she was still awake, she would have heard us, maybe peeking down to view the tussle below.

I lay still, meting out my own breath, wishing the bearskin could come to life and swallow me whole. Mitch rose slowly and kicked the towel across the room, then left the cabin without closing the door behind him. I looked up at the loft and was relieved to see no sign of dimpled cheeks peering over the rail. *Thank God, he didn't slam the door.*

A buzzing horsefly brought me to my feet to pitch the bucket of dirty water onto a bush beside the porch. I listened for a moment, hugging a porch post, wondering where he could find some comfort in the fading light. A breeze was shushing through the trees accompanied by a sleepy chorus of evening crickets.

He missed *her;* I knew that. They had an uncommon love story, cluttered by nineteenth century obstacles. Because of a magic teacup, I had become one of those obstacles. My big feet were heavy as I trudged back inside the cabin, quietly closed the door, and fell into Jessamine's bed, bone-heavy with exhaustion.

Chapter Twelve
A Kiss in the Garden

I woke up alone, still aching, and a little disappointed to see no rumpled bedclothes or even a depression in the pillow beside me. To my ear, Frank's alarm was more "warning siren" than "start of the day." I dressed quickly and found myself in an empty kitchen with a cold stove. *No coffee, no savory eggs, or biscuits today?*

I found a tin of matches and fired up the burner to boil some water. Oatmeal and tea would be a nice change, I figured. Rummaging through the cupboard, I found a can of peaches to go with the oatmeal.

I was setting the table when Mitch and Tallie came into the house with fresh milk and eggs. I could tell they were surprised to see me up so early, and maybe even a little impressed by my efforts.

He was subdued while Tallie chattered on about the puppy in her sling, showing me how eagerly he sucked the warm cow's milk from her fingers. "It tickles," she said, concentrating on her job.

I glanced at him, but he was concentrating on *his* job, pouring milk and sugar over his bowl of oatmeal. The tease I half expected at mention of *"tickles"* did not come.

"Peaches are always good with oatmeal," I pointed out. "It's one of my favorite breakfasts."

That drew some attention.

"We've never had peaches with oatmeal, Ma," Tallie said.

"Oh, I meant when I was a girl," I added quickly. "My granny always served fruit with oatmeal." They watched intently as I cut a peach half into bite size pieces and folded them carefully into my bowl of oatmeal.

He stabbed a peach half with his fork, popped it whole into his mouth, then gave me a grudging smirk with a bite of defiance. "I thought you were saving these for my cake," he said after swallowing.

"Peach cake?"

"Birthday tradition," he said with unmistakable sarcasm, "you forget that, too?"

"No, of course not." I could feel the heat in my cheeks. "But I thought we could easily get another can at the fort when we bring the eggs, and...and you said we needed more seed, didn't you?"

"We'll have to see how much seed we can stretch today," he muttered. "Rain follows the plow; I can smell it coming, and I mean to finish the planting ahead of it."

He turned to Tallie. "We're going to need your help today. Fill up some empty sacks with all the dried corn husks and ears you can find. We can use them in the outhouse."

"Right, Pa. Finn and I can do that much." She patted her little bundle as if burping him, reminding me of a young mother I had seen in the Torrington Food Mart, who always shopped with her child in a sling at her breast.

I found a pair of worn moccasins that were a little

more comfortable than boots, rolled up my pants legs and sleeves, and pulled an old straw hat over my hair. He surveyed me with a critical eye, then handed me a pair of leather gloves that were also too tight. *Okay, so my hands are bigger, too.*

He punched holes in the soil with some kind of wooden tool, while I followed along the furrows, dropping in the seed after he demonstrated how much to drop and how to cover and tamp the ground with my feet.

We worked in silence, pantomiming or using body language when separated by long rows.

"Is this what you mean by sign language?" I said when we stopped to exchange seed bags.

"I never saw my people plant; they just harvested what nature already provided. I suspect they're learning about crop gardens on the reservations, though. At least on the ones that have any tillable land."

"This is a very large garden." I surveyed the work ahead of us as I stretched my back with my hands at my hips, releasing a loud crick in my shoulders. *An acre at least?*

"Well, with what we sell and you preserve, we barely have enough to get by from year to year. I'll need to add to the springhouse or dig a root cellar to keep more stores." He pushed his hat back and wiped his brow with his forearm. "Let's take a break," he said, pulling me toward the bur oak where we kept a crock of water in the shade of its canopy.

We both took a long drink, and wetting our hands, dabbed at the sweat on our necks and brows. I unbuttoned the top two buttons of my shirt and took off my hat to fan my face. It was hot and humid, hotter still after he pulled off his shirt and blotted his chest, glistening with tiny beads of sweat. "The almanac is predicting a hot summer and a rough winter. We can't always depend on our lucky charm for good fortune," he said with an eye on my open neckline.

"Our lucky charm?"

He gave me a look that was becoming familiar; pity mixed with disbelief. "You've forgotten the Calling Stone, too?"

Ahhh, the famous Calling Stone. And wherever that talisman was, Jessamine's journals might be also?

"Well, I know that clunk on my head must have affected my memory, and you find me confused and...and different, but I can't remember where I hid the stone. Maybe everything will come back to me when I can feel it in my palm again."

"You don't remember where you put it?" There was no confusion over the skepticism I read in his face, brows arched, green eyes probing. He thought a minute, then took me by the shoulders and pulled me against him with a sigh. I decided not to pull away or struggle in his embrace.

"Tehike." He rubbed my back, tempering his voice somewhere between annoyance and consolation. "Aside from the concussion, I know you've been troubled since the miscarriage last year, but my grandfather used to say, *'Don't unravel the blanket to reweave the design you're given.'* We've got design, but the future will always be a mystery."

Not always, I could have argued.

He kissed me on the forehead then and studied me at arms' length until I could almost taste the sourness of deceit in my throat. How could I look into those beautiful green eyes and tell this man that I was not his wife, just his wife's descendant, exchanged beyond understanding. His love for Jessamine was so solid, so constant, it could tear him apart to know he might be duped or betrayed by a *doppelganger.*

I was never one to cry easily, and the unbidden well of tears that filmed my eyes with such regularity was disturbing. I tried not to blink or sniff. I didn't want him to see me cry, didn't want to explain what I couldn't understand myself. Instead, I anchored my forehead against his chest, breathing in the scent of him. My arms hung loosely at my sides, my feet braced wide to keep me from sliding boneless into the ground. He smelled of sweat and soil and something more undefinable.

When he folded me in his arms and bent to take my mouth, I could hardly deny him. He kissed me gently, massaging my lips until they parted in wonder. His tongue probed my mouth, tentative at first, then building confidence, skimmed my teeth with a practiced flair. I could feel my heart flutter in my chest, stop, and start—little bubbles popping into the tap of drumbeats. It had been years since I was kissed by any man. I had no basis for comparison, but if kissing were an art, I knew instinctively that this man was a master.

Breathe, Jessica Brewster. Breathe! Don't think, just breathe. My traitorous arms clamped his waist, and I had to close my eyes to stop the spinning. I wanted to dissolve into the garden soil, hide under the furrows, forget everything I ever knew about denial and guilt, then spring up fresh and green, open to sunshine and rain and the joy of living in an unguarded present.

Chapter Thirteen
Apologies

Only Tallie heard the wagon approach, and her shouts brought us back from oblivion with awkward, mutual embarrassment. It was Mary and Henry Garrett, in a small buckboard with Rachel sitting between them. Rachel climbed down and galloped over the seeded furrows to Tallie, who was clutching the edge of a burlap bag filled with papery corn husks. The puppy poked his head out of Tallie's sling to greet Rachel, squealing when the girls squished him as they hugged each other.

Mitch and I greeted them with less enthusiasm. I had apprised him of my mission visiting the Garrett ranch, and though he agreed with me about the girls needing more formal education, he was pessimistic about any positive outcome. Since there was no school closer than Fort Laramie, he was willing, however, to take his turn transporting the girls—if the Garretts agreed to my proposal.

When Tallie related the scene with Jacob and the shotgun, the muscles in Mitch's jaw had flinched like microwave popcorn. "One of you could have been killed, wrestling with a loaded weapon."

"But Pa," Tallie whined, "Jacob was going to kill Finn. That wasn't right."

"True," he had replied, "but your life is worth more

than *any* animal's."

"More than even the App's?"

"More than that." He took her in his arms. "I'll need *you* to take care of your old pa someday when he's as worn down as the App."

She locked her thin arms around his neck. "Ma's going to take care of you forever, Pa."

He had chuckled, looking at me over her head. "Well, she keeps me sharp, for certain."

Hunched on the wagon seat today, Henry Garrett's smile was stitched on his face, and I figured his wife did the handiwork when she spoke for both of them. "We want Rachel to get schooled at Laramie," Mary announced.

Mitch draped one long arm nonchalantly across my shoulders and winked at me. "Good idea. We were thinking about a trip to the fort when the planting's done. Jess can talk with the schoolmaster there about the girls and let you know what he says."

Mary Garrett's quick smile creased her face when she nodded.

The tension between the Garretts was palpable, enhanced by his silence. With a little nudge from his wife, he finally spoke in a voice so low I strained to hear. "The runt was supposed to be drowned. The gun was Jacob's idea."

"Either way was a barbaric solution to a problem easily fixed," I said. "The runt may walk yet. A little care goes a long way, Mr. Garrett. The children could have been less fortunate had that gun discharged accidentally."

"Hmmph." He fiddled with his hat. His ears matched the color of his rusty beard.

Mitch squeezed my shoulder. "Would you folks like to come to the porch for some refreshment? We can set up a plan for getting the girls to school."

Without looking at her husband, Mary sat a little more erect, her hands folded demurely on her lap. When she dared to look at me, I could see her eyes were bright with triumph and a tight smile played at her lips. My own right hand twitched. In my own time, this would have been a high-five moment of victory.

Chapter Fourteen
"Some Things Can't be Done Alone."

"What is that?" I gaped at the tin boat perched on two wooden cradles pressing runners into the bearskin rug. I could see a cloud of vapor rising from the water in the boat. Tallie held a teakettle with both hands at the prow, ready to add its steaming contents to the water.

"Just what it looks like, Jess. We set your bathing tub up for you. Thought you might like a warm soak to ease your pains."

"A bathtub? It looks more like something in need of oars, or an Evinrude."

Mitch cocked his head, looking puzzled.

"It was Pa's idea," Tallie gushed. "He knows how a hot bath always cheers you."

If you only knew how much! A bubble bath scented with a little lavender oil was always the perfect remedy after a long day at work. I approached the "tub" to test the water with my fingers. *Warm!* It was probably impossible to get it as hot as I liked, filling it from kettles and pots heated in the fireplace or on the stove, but anything would be a luxury after the tepid washes of the past week.

"I knew this would get a smile from your mother." Mitch grinned, looking terribly pleased with himself. "I figured she'd want all of us spruced up for another trip to Fort Laramie."

There was a long moment of shared smiles between the three of us, while I wondered how to proceed. Without the privacy of a bathroom, did people normally strip and just pop in the tub? This *was* the Victorian Age, when baring knees, even ankles would draw a gasp. I was grateful when Mitch announced that he and Tallie still had outside chores to take care of. Finn, who was just beginning to hobble along with his splint, took a long look at me and whined until Tallie picked him up.

I lost no time undressing in the bedroom and with towel, washcloth, and a bar of soap, approached my bathing boat with excitement. The tub had a decorative brown stripe painted a few inches below the rim. Its scratched khaki paint and spotty rust spoke of age and use, but it looked sturdy enough. I settled in and swirled the soap around, lathering a rag until a thin layer of suds skimmed the surface. Already, the water had turned a few shades darker, the lye in the soap giving it a clinical smell.

Leaning against the sloping back, I closed my eyes. With both the fireplace and stove heating pots of water, the cabin felt like a sauna, even with windows open. This must be why pioneers bathed in rivers and creeks and skipped regular winter baths. It had to take time and dozens of water vessels to fill a tub even this size. Stretched out, even half sitting, my toes touched the edge. Still, I couldn't complain.

"What's an *evinrude*?"

My eyes flew open. He stood in the open doorframe with a bundle of firewood in his arms.

"Don't you have some barn work?" I tried to squeeze below the water's surface.

"You craving privacy?"

"That would be nice."

"Damn." He grinned. "I thought maybe you'd invite me to share."

I sucked in my breath. "There's hardly enough room in here for one person."

"We managed before."

I could feel the heat creep up my neck. My cousin Jake told me after years of losing to him in gin rummy that he could predict my moves by studying my colors.

"Like traffic lights," he had described it. "Your eyes light up when it's a go, they grow wary for caution, and flash fiercely for stop...and if that isn't enough, you blush like a chameleon in roses." He had laughed.

Mitch threw me a lopsided grin. "This sudden shyness is amusing. Don't you want me to wash your feet again?"

My knees poked the water surface as I pulled my feet toward my bottom with a splash, transmitting my fiercest red light.

Still grinning, he scratched his chin. "Oh, that's right. You've become ticklish there, haven't you?"

Undaunted, he set the kindling in the wood box beside the fireplace and pulled the iron kettle off the hearth with a leather holder. Pretending to close his eyes, he felt for the tub with one hand and slowly added the hot water while I pressed my chest against my knees and locked my arms around them. At least the thin layer of suds camouflaged what lay beneath the water's surface.

He ran his hand along the rim of the tub until he was kneeling behind me. "Can I at least wash your back?"

I groped for the washrag before he could and threw it at him.

Laughing out loud, he wiped his face with the wet rag. "I'll take that as a *yes*."

Scrubbing my back with a vigor that was not unpleasant must have generated my groan, but when he leaned over to kiss my shoulder, I flinched.

"Tallie…"

"…Is grooming the horses," he finished. "Besides, she's used to our bathing routine."

I glared at him over my shoulder, telegraphing another fierce warning.

He winked. "She's very intuitive for a child...knows her place."

For a second, we locked eyes, and I could tell he was amused and determined to shrug off any warning. He scrubbed the bar of soap between his hands, then began to lather my hair.

"I can do that." I jerked away.

He stopped massaging my scalp instantly. "Does your head still hurt?" Gingerly, he probed my hair. "Lump's gone, Jess. You always did heal fast."

"I…I'm still getting headaches." I pushed his hand away to search for the lingering sore spot with my own fingers. After a few seconds of awkward silence, I could hear his familiar sigh of frustration.

"You can rinse," I conceded tersely.

I scooted sideways when he dipped his hand in the tub and splashed me. "The water isn't that dirty. It sure would be a waste, not getting two bodies washed."

"*Not* at the same time," I growled. "You'll have to wait your turn or use the creek."

"Sure you're clear on that?"

I gave him another look. Still, he persisted, sponging my shoulders and upper arms.

"I'm not a child, you know. I can bathe myself."

I inhaled sharply when his hands slid beneath my arms and his long fingers traveled to my breasts. His mouth was close to my ear when he whispered, "Ahh, but some things can't be done alone."

My own hands flew to push his arms away, but my breathless whimper made him chuckle.

"*Tactus liquescens.* I was beginning to think I had lost my melting touch, Jess." He kissed the top of my head before he rose and reached for the teakettle.

"You, you can't…" I sputtered when he poured water from the teakettle over my hair. Angry tears ran with the warm stream of water and suds that cascaded over my head and shoulders. When he returned the kettle to the kitchen stove, I leaped from the tub, grabbed the towel, and ran to the bedroom, slamming the door behind me.

His footsteps clicked on the wood floor, stopping just outside the door between us. Then I heard Tallie call to him and his response, low and indistinguishable. I rubbed myself dry, quickly pulled on my underwear and curled under the bedcovers like a capped hedgehog. *Home. I must find my way back home.*

Chapter Fifteen
Revelations

It was almost dark when I woke to find my hair dried into thick clumps against a damp pillow. I stretched against the linen sheets, clean, but not refreshed. At the mirror, I brushed my hair until it sparked with electricity. The face in the mirror was somber, sad. Almost unrecognizable. A soft knock at the door stilled my hand in midair.

"Let me in, Jess," he called.

The door opened before I could respond...or pull on a shift. He gaped at me, his green eyes wide with shock.

"What the hell are you wearing?"

Red faced, I looked down at my lacey black bra and hi-cut bikinis and scrambled for the towel, wrapping it around me. He lunged toward me and stripped the towel away with both hands.

"What are those?" His forefinger pulled on the elastic at my hip and let it snap. "Where did you get these?"

"Catalog," I muttered, looking for a way to escape the heat-seeking green missiles trained on my figure. I chewed my lip, searching for something, anything to lock my own eyes onto.

"A catalog! What catalog?"

"Er...Victoria's Secret."

"Victoria, Victoria? Like the English Queen?"

"Not exactly."

It might have been funny if I wasn't so scared. I flinched, and my whole body quivered when he reached out to palm the cup of my padded bra and pluck at the strap over my shoulder, fingering the rayon lace. "What kind of women would wear such things?"

"Modern women." I pushed his hand away.

Visibly shocked, he slumped heavily on the bed, his head between his hands. "What has happened to my wife?"

Good question. I backed up against the pegged wall, trying to disappear behind the blue Sunday dress that hung there. "I'm not your wife," I heard myself mumble.

He looked up at me, dumbfounded and so wounded, my heart clutched.

"Well...I...I don't feel like anybody's wife."

He screwed up his forehead and blinked. "Dr. Brechemin said your thinking could be muddled, but I had no idea. You haven't been yourself, Jess. Even Tallie has noticed."

"What has she noticed?"

"She wonders if you don't love her anymore." He hesitated, and I could see his jaw twitch when he searched my eyes. "We share that thought. You...you even stiffen when I touch you."

My heart clutched again. "I'm sorry. I'm in the wrong time, the wrong place. It was the teacup..." *My damn eyes began to puddle again.*

He stared at me, his face twisted in turmoil when I stopped, unable to continue, unable to hurt a man that so obviously loved his wife, a man surely accustomed to a loving response. I wiped my nose on the back of my hand with a loud slurp. Abruptly, he rose and slumped out of the room, closing the door firmly behind him.

I crawled back into bed, feeling as empty as the space beside me. I had tried to tell him, *tried* to tell the truth. But to him, I was his wife gone mad, the woman he loved and wanted. The woman I could never be. It seemed like hours later I rose and fumbled in the dark room for something to cover my underwear. One of his cotton shirts was hanging on a peg, and I pulled it on and rolled up the sleeves. The bottom fell about mid-thigh. Cautiously, I opened the bedroom door and in the dark let my hands guide me along the wall to the front porch.

There was just enough moonlight to show him sprawled in shadow, asleep on the wooden Adirondack. His long legs were crossed at the ankles, his shirt unbuttoned nearly to his waist. His head drooped on his chest, and in the dim light of the crescent moon, I could see his breath flutter the hair on his chest. One hand was buried in the pages of a thin book on his lap, his other brushed against a leather chest on the porch beside the chair. Even in shadow, I recognized the chest at once. It held Granny's legacy treasures, *maybe* even the Calling Stone.

Carefully, I inched the book off his lap and tiptoed to a pillar beside the steps. In more direct moonlight, I could see the binding had no title, but when I opened it my gasp broke the silence of the night. Written in a tiny script that filled only half the page, the journal entry was dated September 27, 1875.

"Why hasn't he come for me? Can I live without his touch, without those green eyes melting my heart?

Did our blood vows mean nothing? I've been such a fool, rejecting the truth. And now, I'm forced to live a lie, forget the only man I'll ever love."

My heart lurched when I turned to look at him and saw that his eyes were open now and even in the dim light, the green sparkled like demon fireflies.

"Do you remember writing that?" he whispered.

I snapped the book shut and swallowed hard, able only to wag my head.

"Then maybe you need to read it. Read all of your damn journals." I could hear the chest grate against the porch when he shoved it. "They're all here. Sketches and keepsakes, too. Maybe if you go through it, you *will* remember...the way we were."

He rose from the Adirondack like an old man and moved toward me, his eyes fanning me from head to bare feet. He touched my face with both hands, feathering his fingers across my forehead, into the wells of my eyes, over my nose and cheekbones, like a blind man needing to know who stood before him. I tried *not* to stiffen at his touch, willing myself not to blink, not to release the fresh tears that had begun to pool. He collared my throat with his long fingers and ran a thumb over my lips. "I want my wife back. Come back to me, *Mitawin,*" he whispered.

The word on the teacup, the *hallmark* of my deceit. Our eyes locked, and I felt my throat closing and my knees begin to quiver. For a few seconds his grip tightened around my throat, and I clamped my eyes shut with a fleeting thought. *Yes, take my breath...end this tormenting deception.* When he suddenly released me, I could see the pain twisting his face. He turned away and rubbed his chin against his shoulder, bracing both arms on a porch railing.

"My shirt looks good on you, Jess," he said hoarsely. "You always did have a thing for my shirts."

I cleared my throat. "You can't sleep out here," I said after a long silence. "Come to bed."

His shoulders flinched. "Is that an invitation?"

"I only mean...you can't be comfortable sleeping in that chair."

"Are you still wearing those black things?"

I didn't answer. *What has that got to do with anything?* We both started by the sudden hoot of a nearby owl, and like the volume turned up on ear phones, I was suddenly aware of other night sounds: crickets, wind rustling through the sage, my heart bumping in my chest.

"There's a breeze. I don't mind sleeping out here," he said in a tone deep and distant, though he stood within reach, his eyes cast down as he gripped the rail.

I picked up the leather chest and carried it back to the bedroom with me. Exhausted, I sat on the bed with the chest sagging the mattress beside me. The journals made it heavier than I remembered. I wanted to start reading them, but I was too tired to light the lamp, and my head was boiling with a tide of emotion.

The Calling Stone was always kept in a beaded pouch in the chest, separated from the other keepsakes that must have meant something to my ancestors.

"Vitals," Granny had whispered when she first showed them to me, handling each item with reverence while I sat at her knee, begging to blow on the flute and the harmonica. I remember The Calling Stone was warm in my hand, and though it looked smooth as a river rock, it prickled my fingers when I stroked it. She had patted me on the head with a soft chuckle. "Someday, you will understand," she had assured. *Someday. Not today.*

A small part of me wanted to go back to the porch and invite him back to his own bed and damn any consequences that might result. But a larger part of me said it was wrong. What I was beginning to feel was all wrong. He was Jessamine's husband, not mine. I was just her descendant, lost in time. I had to get back to my own century, back to hot showers and flush toilets, my little red Honda and Cousin Jake who understood me so well.

I groped in the chest for the Calling Stone. "A charm" he had called it. I didn't believe in charms or magic, even wishing on pennies thrown into a fountain, but Granny had believed there was something special about this stone...the teacup, as well, or she wouldn't have locked it up so well. Granny was right about most things. *Someday, you will understand*, she had assured me. Would Jessamine's journals clear everything up?

My fingers locked around the little pouch that held the stone, and when I spilled it into my hand, it was warm to the touch. In the dark room, I thought I could even see it glow, crimson as blood. I squeezed it tightly and thought it pulsed a little against my palm, like a tiny beating heart. It felt comforting, and after a while, my throbbing head gave way to the welcome abyss of sleep.

Chapter Sixteen
Tallie's Twist

I was awake, even before Frank's morning alarm. In the gray light of dawn, I more closely examined the contents of the trunk. The stack of thin journals were in a large casing, separate from the familiar keepsakes. I slipped the Calling Stone back into its little beaded pouch and tucked it beside the willow flute wedged at an angle. The lock of hair was baby-fine, tied with a white ribbon that had not yet yellowed with age. One end of the ribbon was also knotted around a gold ring made of something softer than metal. I didn't remember the ring when Granny showed me the lock years ago.

The harmonica was still shiny, no sign of rust, but the little scissors already had a patina of age. It had belonged to Jessamine's German grandmother, my grandmother times four.

I knew the grandparents were killed by Indians in a famous Minnesota uprising when Jessamine was just a child. Granny told me Jessamine and her baby sister survived only because their grandfather hid them in a steamer trunk. Their parents also survived, then moved the family to safer territory in southeastern Minnesota, and eventually to Nebraska after it became a state. Jessamine started keeping her journals in Nebraska when she was a few years older than Tallie.

Wrapped in a piece of stained buckskin, what

looked like an old coin about the size of a nickel was actually a bullet. "It almost killed the Indian," Granny told me. *Of course—the scar on his chest.* I couldn't wait to read about *that* incident in the journals.

The old tintype taken of Jessamine's family was encased in a drab silk folder with Plum Creek Photography marked on the corner. Jessamine and her sister wore large white bows in their hair, and another child I knew to be their younger brother was perched on their father's lap. Their parents sat stiffly beside each other on a settee, with the girls posed on the floor at their knees. Both parents had lighter hair, typically styled in their era; hers neatly pulled back with a center part, his combed flat with more on his chin than his head.

I loved going through Granny's ancient photos, as well as the ones at Fort Laramie, trying to imagine their backstories. Photography must have been expensive and rare in the nineteenth century. Were the dark and somber clothes they wore really their best? Why so many vacant expressions, not even a whisper of a smile? Even among photographs of children. At least in Jessamine's family photo, the parents looked slightly amused, and Jessamine had the far-away look of a daydreamer. She must have been about twelve at the time. I wondered why this photo wasn't displayed on the mantel or somewhere in the house, like most family photos would be.

The bedroom door slowly opened, and Tallie timidly peeked in, carrying a steamy mug of chicory coffee. "Are you awake, Ma?"

I patted the bed and gratefully took the mug before she literally leaped at the invitation, hauling her puppy up beside her. "What are you looking at?" She snuggled next to me on the bed.

"Just an old family photo."

"That's you isn't it?" She pointed to Jessamine.

"That's your mother." I nodded, carefully sipping the hot coffee. "Haven't you ever seen this photo?"

"A long time ago, before we moved here, you showed it to me." She identified the boy and younger girl as Uncle Charlie and Aunt Lizzie, then announced her grandparents were dead. "All of them. I have no grannies or grandpas."

I felt a tug of emotion and gave her a squeeze. "Not everyone has grandparents in their lives." *I was lucky, I thought, to have one that lived a century.* I had been Tallie's age when Granny Lou became my sole guardian.

"What's in the chest," she asked.

"Memories. When you get older, you will own this chest, and then pass it on to your daughter."

She pulled a face. "I'm not getting married. No children for me."

I smiled at her. "I think you will. In fact, I see a very lovely daughter in your future, maybe one with red hair, like yours."

"I don't like boys. They're all mean, like Jacob Garrett." The pup looked up at her with adoring black button eyes when she scratched him between the ears.

"Jacob doesn't represent all boys." I chuckled. "You'll change your mind when you fall in love."

"Like you changed your mind about Pa, you mean?"

I took a long sip of coffee, trying to avert her quizzical gaze. She had her father's expressive eyes.

"Pa told me you were not an easy catch, but he thought you were a brat, anyway."

"He said that?"

"Pa said women with red hair can change with the wind, though, and you surprised him."

I sank back on the pillow, smiling. "Well, people do change when they grow up, but I don't think redheads are always difficult. Do you think you're difficult?"

She blinked at me. "I try not to be, but sometimes it is hard when I'm around mean people, like the Garrett boys."

I laughed. "Not all males are like that. Your pa is kind and thoughtful, don't you think?"

She grinned back at me. "Silly, too. He used to call us his pea pods, because we were so much alike."

"Used to?"

"Well, now he says the wind is changing again, and I have to be careful around you."

"What do you think he means by that?" I took another long swallow of coffee.

Pa says the bump on your head took your memories, and we have to be patient until they return." She looked at me with wide innocent eyes. "Are you looking for your memories in that chest?"

"I guess you could say that." I gulped.

"You won't tell Pa I tattled on him, will you?"

I snapped my mouth shut and made her laugh when I pretended to lock my lips with an imaginary key. "Have you had breakfast yet, Tallie?"

"Pa was up early. I could smell the coffee, and when I came down, he fixed me some oatmeal and told me to let you sleep."

"Where is he now?"

"When I collected the eggs and fed the chickens, he was getting the mare ready to be covered."

"Covered with what?"

"The App, I guess. He said the mare was ready for breeding. Want to come and watch with me?"

I almost choked on my coffee. "He lets you watch that?"

She nodded, tilting her head. "It's just nature, Ma. Sometimes nature needs help in the spring. The App waters the baby horses so they grow in the mares. Pa says it's like watering the seeds we plant in the garden each year. Only with horses, we have to wait almost a year before we harvest a foal. We get a lot of money for the App's babies, Pa says."

"I see. Well, when you put it that way, it sounds very logical. Why don't you just go ahead, and maybe I'll read a bit before I join you."

"I'll tell Pa you're coming to help." She beamed.

"Why don't we just surprise him, Tallie. I wouldn't want him to wait on me."

When she left, I thoughtfully drained my coffee and got dressed. Still wearing Mitch's shirt, I tucked it into my long pants and pulled on Jessamine's tight boots. I gave my face a quick scrub with a damp cloth and ran a brush through my thick, clean hair, pulling it into a tail.

I had never seen horses breed, and my curiosity was perking. I understood the logistics, but horse breeding had evolved into a science of sorts, with the semen of superior horses being bought for thousands of dollars to inseminate quality mares that might deliver the next Triple Crown winner in racing circles. The

Kentucky Derby had to be in its infancy in 1886, but until the automobile displaced them, horses were highly valued for much more than just recreation or races.

Even in my time, good trail, ranch, and rodeo horses were still in demand. After Garrett's first visit, I understood our handsome Appaloosa was historically unique for its color and stamina. If his *get*—as Garrett referred to his progeny—had the App's color, their pedigree would make them exceptional, even financially rewarding. From what I had seen so far, any financial rewards in nineteenth century Wyoming were certainly dependent on the grace of nature.

CJ Fosdick

Chapter Seventeen
The Black Stallion

I could tell he was surprised to see me. He had dark circles under his eyes, but his crooked grin suggested I was welcome. I didn't think many men processed forgiveness as easily as he seemed to. I returned a quick smile as I prepared to sit on the log fence to watch.

"We could use your help, Jess."

I chewed my lip, wondering how I could possibly be of any help. Tallie held the lead rope on Jessamine's mare while he hobbled her back legs with a rope.

"Braid her tail like always." He handed me a piece of twine.

"You want me to braid her tail?"

"To get it out of the way," he said. "You remember how to braid, don't you?"

Like one of Tallie's pigtails, I imagined. I approached with hesitation and patted the mare's butt when she started to swish her tail. Hobbled, at least she couldn't kick me. I divided her thick red tail into three parts, and wove them together tightly, tying the end with the piece of twine.

He dipped a rag in a bucket of soapy water, and pushing the braid aside, scrubbed the area the tail had covered.

"She's been winking for days now," he said. "The estrus is thick—consistent for the strongest heat of the

100

year. We'll have to do this for the next few days if we want her to settle on this cycle."

"Right," I nodded, understanding not a word he said.

"Tallie, let your ma hold her bridle while I get the App."

"I got her soothed, Pa, I can do this," Tallie said, while feeding the mare from a tuft of hay stuck in her pocket.

"Well then, both of you can tend her head, but you'll have to hold tight so she can't rear or I'll have to tie her down."

"We can do this," Tallie answered.

"Right." I echoed a weak affirmation. "We can do this."

As Mitch left to get the Appaloosa, I looked at Tallie. "You seem to know what you're doing. Does the mare try to get away very often?"

"No, she just fidgets and her eyes grow big sometimes."

"Well, that happens when you get scared. Horses are a lot like people, I guess."

"That's what Pa told me. He says Dolly is an easy breeder, though, and has always been a good mother."

I couldn't help rolling my eyes. "Well, if he says so, it must be true, then."

Mitch emerged from the barn with a tight rope on the App's head. The stallion spotted us immediately and curling his muzzle, he jerked his head up and let out a deafening whinny. Before my eyes, I saw him change and grow in stature, like a sword being unsheathed and ready for battle.

The mare's ears perked, and she responded with a

whinny in equal volume. Tallie patted her on the nose and whispered, "Easy girl."

I reached for her forelock and ruffled my fingers through it, following Tallie's lead with more fervent consolation. *Did she know what was coming?*

Mitch circled the stallion when he began to pull and snort, eager now to do his part. With business-like authority, he led him to the mare and loosened his grip until the stallion easily mounted her rump and jockeyed for entry. The mare cooperated with a swish of her tail to the left. As he thrust into her, the mare's eyes grew wide, matching my own, as I heard her grunt with the impact. I could feel a hot blush stain my face when I saw Mitch watching my reaction. I studied my feet while my hands tightened into a death grip on the mare's halter.

When I thought the thrusting would never end, a distant sound pierced the air, high pitched as a steam whistle and all of us looked around to see where it was coming from. The other animals were pastured out of sight, on the other side of the barn.

In my peripheral vision, I saw movement on the far horizon, a band of bright morning sunlight shimmering out of focus, like a mirage. A black dot burst through the haze and bobbled on the horizon a moment, then like a rolling stone, it gathered volume and definition, hurling toward us. The sounds morphed into a shrill whinny, and I could make out a blur of dark legs, churning up a line of dust.

The App backed off the mare, his ears flattened tight against his head, every muscle tensed as he watched the black horse approach. The mare whinnied with agitation and began to shuffle her front feet, lifting one, then the other, and finally both of them off the ground.

"Hold her if you can," Mitch yelled.

Tallie and I put all our weight into preventing her from rearing again, fearing she would topple over backward with her back legs hobbled. We could hear the black horse pounding the ground now, snorting as he plowed toward the garden, closing the distance between us. I grabbed the mare's halter with both hands and twisted her head away from the sight. Her eyes were wide as golf balls, and her ears twitched with anxiety.

"Easy," I cried, trying to rein in my own heart-pounding fear as I could feel my toes leave the ground and the rope halter saw into my grip. I could see Mitch grappling with his hold on the Appaloosa, jerking the lead rope when the App began to puff and snort, arching his neck and wrenching his tail high in the air. In concert with his owner, the old horse's jaw was popping with tension, and I could see his flank rise and fall with every snort. Muscles that had been slack before shifted in his rump, his legs stiffened, and I knew he was preparing to mount a running challenge.

Mitch saw it too and valiantly tried to turn him away, but he was no match against a thousand pounds of determination. The App bared his teeth and let out an ear-splitting warning that made the black stallion slow and veer at an angle toward the woods. Rearing up, the App lifted Mitch off his feet, putting him in danger of being pummeled. With another long shriek, he pawed the air and lunged forward.

"Let go of the rope," I yelled at him above Tallie's screams. But he held on and was dragged for several yards before the Appaloosa sailed over the fence with Mitch flying through the air at his side until we heard both fence and the lead rope snap on impact.

The stallion raced ahead of the App, disappearing into the woods that swallowed up both horses. I let go of the mare at once and was grateful to see her rope hobbles had come loose, and she had sense enough to turn back to the barn, crow-hopping and tossing her head in high anxiety. Tallie and I raced to Mitch. He was writhing on the ground, cradling his right arm at an odd angle, and a spot of blood was blooming on his torn sleeve.

"Oh fuck," I swore under my breath. His dark frown told me his hearing was intact.

"Help me up," he snarled.

I pulled on his other arm while Tallie tried lifting his shoulders to roll him to his knees. We got him to his feet, and for a few seconds he swayed as if he would collapse.

"Use me like a crutch." I propped his left arm over my shoulders as I leaned into him. "We need to get you back to the house."

"Stall the mare," he hissed, breathless.

"I can do that," Tallie cried.

Mitch was starting to sag against me, and I thought he was losing consciousness. I couldn't help them both.

"Put her in the barn," I called after Tallie, "but be careful."

She gave up a signal wave when she reached the barn and threw open the door, barely clearing the way for the frightened mare to rush inside.

With both of us huffing, I managed to haul Mitch into the bedroom before he collapsed on the bed. Using the little scissors in the leather chest to cut away his torn sleeve, we could see a large sliver of wood had pierced his arm like an arrow. He flinched but didn't cry out when I jerked it free before the flesh could swell even more around it. I dampened a cloth in the washbowl and pressed it over beads of sweat that glistened on his forehead.

His arm was bleeding freely now from a ragged two inch cut, soaking through the compress I held against it. *A tourniquet. Make a tourniquet, the panicked voice in my head instructed.* I tore off his other sleeve and wrapped it tightly around his arm above the cut. Tally joined us, and when she saw her father lying so still with the cloth over his face, she began to cry.

"Is he...is he?"

We both started when the body on the bed groaned "Not yet."

"Honey." I smiled, wanting to appear calmer than I felt. "Can you get me some disinfectant and heat some water on the stove.

"Diss...disinfectant?" she repeated.

"Get the jug," the body on the bed ordered.

Tallie was gone in a flash. I could hear the front door slam and wondered where the jug was kept and what kind of *disinfectant* it contained. Did they even know about peroxide or iodine and sterilizing wounds in 1886?

One sniff in the jug Tallie brought told me it was alcohol all right, but not the kind used for cleaning wounds. *Any port in a storm?*

He pulled the washcloth off one eye and peered at the jug before I could saturate the wound and cut makeshift bandages from the remainder of his shirt.

"First things first," he breathed, pantomiming a drink with his good arm and thumb. I propped the pillows beneath his head and tried to help him sit up, but when I touched his shoulder, he winced and looked up at me with eyes dulled by pain. "It's out of joint."

"Oh, fu...fudruckers," I said, catching Tallie's eye.

He took a long gulp from the jug, then two more, and his head thumped back on the pillow, watching me through hooded eyes while I splashed some of the alcohol into his wound and using the scissors like a tweezers, picked off particles of dirt and slivers of wood. I then studied his bare shoulders, looking from one to the other to compare any difference.

"Where does it hurt most?"

He pointed to a spot that was definitely swollen and discoloring already. "You'll have to reset it," he scowled.

"Me? I don't know how to reset a joint. Simple first aid, maybe, but you need a doctor for that!"

He glared at me. "Christ, the only doctor I know is miles away, and the nurse in the room loses her nerve!"

"I'm not an effing doctor *or* a nurse," I shouted in panic.

He groaned. "How hard can it be...pulling an arm back into socket?"

"Oh God. What if I break your arm?"

"That might be less painful." He snorted.

New beads of sweat were popping on his forehead and around his mouth. I knew a limb out of joint could be agonizing. I grabbed the jug and took a long swallow myself, then broke into a strangling cough. It must have been a hundred proof.

He almost looked amused.

"Fff...fortification," I hissed. "I'm going to need some divine intervention to work a miracle here."

"I'll get the Bible, Ma," Tallie offered.

"You sure you trust me to do this?" I asked him.

He rolled his eyes. "I've trusted you with my life before, Jess. Damn it, you always...do what you have to do."

I am not Jessamine, I wanted to scream. Just a weak imitation, feeling sooo much weaker by the minute.

I took another swig from the jug, coughed again, then shoved it back at him and watched his throat constrict with each gulp. I hoped it would bring both of us quick pain relief.

Tallie returned with the old German Bible from the living room bookshelf and self-consciously, I kissed it and said a quick prayer before handing it back to her. She followed my example and looked up at me with the same trust he had shown. *They were both depending on me.*

I picked up his elbow and rocked it a little back and forth, watching for any obvious movement in his shoulder. I didn't want to pull on his wrist and cause the wound to open and bleed again.

He plastered the damp rag over his eyes and growled, "Do it already!"

Tallie leaned over the bed and locked both hands onto her father's left hand. "Do it, Ma," she said in a quivering voice.

Bracing myself, I moved his elbow inward and closed my eyes, visualizing how hard I needed to pull. *Hard enough to hold down the head of a frightened mare?* I could feel sweat beading on my own forehead, and my grip on his elbow was getting clammy. He groaned loudly when I jerked his arm, and the bed scraped against the floor. Letting go of Tallie's hand, he hooked his good arm on the headrail, bracing his long legs against the footrail until it squeaked.

"Try again," he panted, taking a few short breaths.

I wiped my hands on my pants legs, gripped his elbow, and pulled with all my might. A soft pop followed by deep and satisfying moans left me shaking like a leaf.

He closed his eyes, giving up a weak grin. "Feels...better...already." He sighed.

"You did it, Ma," Tallie cried.

I grabbed the bedpost when I felt my knees wobble and stretched each arm to release the tension. My palms were raw and scraped from pulling on the mare's bridle. A single tear rolled down my cheek. *Yes. I did it. Jessica Brewster, who barely passed her CPR course, just set a shoulder!*

Chapter Eighteen
The Ironman

Mitch fell asleep or passed out from the liquor soon after the ordeal, and Tallie and I took the opportunity to go look for the Appaloosa. We didn't have far to look. The old horse was already back in the paddock when we got to the barn, lathered from his run, with his limp more pronounced and several scrapes on his chest and legs.

While he paced before the barn door, curling his lip and whinnying, Tallie and I quickly replaced the splintered rail fence, hoping it would keep him inside the pasture if the black stallion showed up again. It was heavy work, taking both of us to lug another log to slip in the Y posts Mitch had cleverly fashioned from thick tree branches. We found some shorter deadwood to brace against the top log to keep it from popping out of the Y's, and finally surveyed the result with smug satisfaction.

"That should keep him in until your father recovers enough to figure out something better. Maybe we should keep the mare in the barn stall until she's, er, out of danger from salacious stallions."

Tally hooked her arm with mine as we hurried back to the house. "What does salacious mean?"

"Looking for trouble," I told her. "Where do you suppose the black horse came from, anyway?"

"I've never seen him around here before."

"Could he belong to the Garretts?"

"They don't have any black horses."

"A wild horse, then?"

She thought a while, then told me they run in groups. "Pa sees them in the mountain passes sometimes, but they are never alone, and the soldiers from the fort try to round them up when they can and bring them back to train or sell. Rachel thinks they even eat them when game is scarce."

"Eat them! How awful."

"That's what I think. I even hate to eat the deer Pa hunts. He says it's the natural order of things, though. His people always hunted for wild things, but they always valued horses. They never ate things that didn't grow wild. When they come to Fort Laramie now, they *do* trade for food supplies, though. I've even seen their children eat broken crackers off the floor at Trader John's."

I thought about how much we take convenience for granted in my century, able to pick up frozen dinners or fast food we don't have to shoot, skin, or harvest directly from ground to dinner table. There was not a lot of variety in the food I tasted here so far, but most of it was fresh and preparing it worked up an appetite for anything edible after a day of endless chores. Despite the work, there was simple satisfaction about living on a homestead. I didn't even miss frozen pizza or Chinese take-out.

Tallie was still chattering. "I don't even like chicken anymore, Ma."

"I thought you ate anything, Tallie."

"Pa tells me we have to butcher the chickens that

don't lay eggs, but I can't eat my friends."

"Then maybe you need to stop naming them." I smiled.

"But you do that too, Ma."

"Well, maybe we're both closet vegetarians at heart."

"What's a vegetarian?"

"Vegetable eaters with stinky breaths."

She thought about that. "I do like vegetables," she said, "but I hate brushing my teeth."

I chuckled all the way back to the house.

Finn was on the bed, watching my patient like a guard dog on assignment. When I felt Mitch's forehead, it seemed hot. But then, the few times I had any close contact with him, he always radiated heat. I carefully peeked under the bandage on his arm and could see the wound was red around the edges and the bandage needed changing. I found some clean rags in the kitchen and thought I might go ahead and clean the wound again, as long as he was still out.

Half way through the procedure, I could feel his open eyes on me.

"I didn't mean to wake you," I apologized.

"I have to get up anyway and go find the App," he muttered drowsily.

"He's already back. Tallie and I found him near the barn, maybe a little winded, but otherwise safe and sound."

He tried to sit up. "Well, then I have to fix the fence so he won't get back out."

"We already took care of that." I gently pushed him back on the pillows.

His eyebrows inched toward the bridge of his nose,

but I could tell he was relieved. "You sure know how to make a man feel useless, Jess."

"You're going to remain useless for a few days at least. And we may have to make a trip to Fort Laramie and get your arm stitched up."

"Isn't that what nurses do...stitch up wounds?"

"I've never done that, either."

"Oh Jesus, Jess, you have lost your memory." He pointed to the scar on his chest. "You don't remember this either?"

I gaped at him. "I'm, I'm not good with a needle."

He rolled his eyes. "Just get your damn sewing basket in here and pretend I'm a quilt." He grabbed a fistful of the counterpane on the bed and waved it in my face.

Jessamine made the quilt? Was there no end to her talent? I had noticed the stitching on it before. Tiny and even as a sewing machine.

I found the sewing basket under the bench in the living room and grabbed a tin cup from the kitchen. Tallie was rooting through the cupboard, looking for something to eat. "Slice up some sausage," I told her, "and peel some potatoes. I'll help when I finish tending your pa."

"Okay, Ma. I can do that."

Tallie could do more than most children her age, and her "can-do" attitude was refreshing. I was beginning to believe talent could be inherited and felt a little inspired for myself. *Maybe "can-do" was catching here.*

I threaded the thinnest needle I could find and dipped it into the cup of whiskey poured from the jug.

"Seems like a waste of good liquor," he

commented as I cleaned the wound again.

"Sterilizing is important," I said. "Prevents infection."

"Doc Brechemin isn't this thorough."

"Have you been treated by him before?"

"Well, no, but I know any man on that post would never waste good whiskey like this. Not even the Doc, unless it was absolutely necessary."

"This is absolutely necessary. Do you want to finish what's in the cup?"

He stared at me with a look of defiance. "I can do without this time."

"You would have made a good Ironman." I sighed.

"Ouch." He flinched when I stabbed the needle into his arm and began to stitch with a shaky hand.

He didn't cry out again, but his arm muscled when his hand squeezed into a fist, and he closed his eyes, taking quick breaths with every stitch. It took seven uneven pink stitches to close the wound.

"Pink!" He assessed my handiwork. "Did you have to use pink thread?"

"That's better than black. You want it to look like a zipper?"

"What's a zipper?"

"Oh Lord." I took a sip from the cup, swishing it like mouthwash before I let it trickle slowly down my throat. When I again offered the cup to him, he took it this time and drained it in one gulp. His head fell back on the pillows, and I could see his eyes were heavy-lidded and glazed over—a sure sign he was half-bagged and probably free of pain. I wrapped his arm with a clean rag and asked if he had a neckerchief to use for a sling.

"Don' need any damn sling," he mumbled with his eyes closed. "I'm...Ironman."

I chuckled and patted him on the head. "Go to sleep, Ironman, while I help Tallie fix us some supper."

Chapter Nineteen
Fried Moustaches

Drinking a glass of white wine on an empty stomach always made me giddy. Drinking hundred proof whiskey from a jug turned my tongue into flannel when I asked Tallie if there was any canola oil.

She gave me a strange look. "Oil? You mean for cooking? Isn't that hog fat?"

"That'll do." I giggled. She watched me intently as I concentrated hard on slicing the peeled potatoes lengthwise into quarters and eighths, trying not to sever any fingers. I put the spears into a large iron skillet. The hog fat browned the potatoes until they looked crisp enough to transfer to a shallow pan in the oven—after I salted them liberally.

Tallie set the table for three, but when the patient in the bedroom started snoring loud enough to rattle through the house, we both laughed. "Alcohol has remedies and ravages," I told her. "Let Ironman sleep."

She gingerly stabbed a fork into one of the potato spears I put on her plate. "What are these?"

"Haven't you ever had French fries?"

"No, Ma. You never fixed potatoes like this before."

Of course. French fries were probably still a novelty if consumed at all in the nineteenth century.

When I was feeling low, Granny used to fix them

for me with a juicy burger and chocolate milk. It was my favorite meal as a child.

"What's a burger?" Tallie asked.

Did I just say that aloud?

"A burger is the best san-wich ever." I grinned.

"Wasn't your granny from Germany?"

"Yeah voll!" I saluted her smartly. *French fries from a German Granny? Do any details escape this kid or her father?* "Finger food, Tallie." I gave her a demonstration, savoring each bite, even without a dip of ketchup.

After licking the salt off the end, she took a small bite, assessing thoughtfully. "I love it," she finally declared, her eyes rolling with surprise. "Can I have another?"

I laughed, nodding toward the bedroom. "We'll have to save some for the Ironman."

"Do we have to?"

We both giggled, and giving in to my new silliness, I turned one of the fries into a moustache, squeezing it between my nose and upper lip. "Papa bear will be very hungry when he comes out of hibernation."

When Tallie imitated me, I threw a fry at her, and squealing with laughter, she threw one back at me. I grabbed the empty plate laid out for Mitch and used it as a shield. We were laughing so hard, we didn't notice "Papa Bear" watching from the doorway, cradling his right arm at the elbow. He did not look amused.

I hiccoughed, trying to suppress a fit of giggles. "Care to join us?"

He came closer, surveying the table before he picked up one of the fries and examined it from every angle. "Food or weapon?"

"French fried potatoes, Pa," Tallie announced. "Ma made them."

He fixed me with a gimlet eye. "So you eat them?"

I had a sudden urge to shove one into his mouth, but he beat me to it, chewing it with great deliberation before he sat down and picked up a handful. "I could eat a horse," he said. "A black one—skewered over a deep pit."

I poured both of us a cup of reheated coffee and watched him devour the rest of our fries, alternating them with the sausage and daily bread. I could tell by the stilted way he moved that he was still either nursing pain—or just hammered.

"A sling might help." I sipped my own cup of coffee. "Your arm is going to need some support for a few days."

He burped loudly, which sent Tallie and me into another fit of giggles. Swaying a little when he stood, he gave us both a dark look before he headed back to the bedroom. "I do need some help," he muttered with a furtive glance in my direction.

I picked up a dish towel cut from a flour sack and followed him.

He sat on the bed while I fashioned the towel into a sling, tying it behind his neck. Bruises had already surfaced on his shoulder. "I need to pee," he sheepishly announced when our eyes met.

He looked at his crotch, and my smile slipped when I understood what he was asking of me. *It took two hands to unfasten buttons.*

"This is what zippers are for." I averted my eyes from the task at hand. "Can you make it to the privy?"

"Don' think so," he muttered.

I retrieved the pot stored under the bed for such emergencies. "And this is why indoor plumbing is needed," I said half to myself as I turned my back.

When I was sure that he had finished, I turned back and noticed his ears were as red as my face felt. "Just do the top button," he said in a small voice. The corner of his mouth curled into a tight little grin. "Your face matches your hair, you know."

The uncomfortable silence that followed was abruptly sobering.

"This wouldn't happen"—he finally snorted— "with a breech clout."

"A breech clout?"

"No buttons, Indian style. I'll need a cloth, something to fold over...over my waistband." He poked a long finger into his navel.

I swallowed a hiccough bubbling to the surface when I understood his meaning, and offered him a remnant of his torn shirt still lying on the bed.

"You could always go Scottish and wear a kilt." I grinned. Our eyes met again, and we both laughed. *This conversation had to be the liquor talking.*

With only a little convincing, he lay back down on the bed, pulled the quilt up to his waist, and grappled with a pillow to find a comfortable position for his arm.

"You're a lefty," I observed.

He stared at his left hand. "You just noticed that?"

"Well, no," I hedged. "It's just more uncommon nowadays."

"Nowadays?"

"Well, I know my teachers often urged students to write with the right hand. Better for penmanship, they said."

"Umm. Sister Mary Catherine rapped my left knuckles with a ruler when I, when I learned to write. She gave that up when she understood swollen knuckles only reinforced my determination."

"Sister Mary Catherine?"

He closed his eyes and sighed. "Tole you all about her. The convent school...St. Louis...my six years of purga, purgatory?"

So that's where he got his education! No clues, so far, in Jessamine's journals. I really needed to get back to them. I untied the window swag to blot out the waning light and suggested he go back to sleep. "Sleep heals," I told him.

He covered his eyes with his good arm. "Bossy as a nun." He smirked beneath his arm.

Tallie cleaned up the kitchen and washed the dishes while I carried another cup of coffee to the front porch and began to skim through a sketchbook the size of a small school notebook. Most of Jessamine's best drawings were of her family, the ones labeled Charlie, Lizzy, Tallie at various ages, and Mitch of course, with his telltale crooked smile and long hair.

In one of them he was leaning against a tree, wearing nothing but a wide sash gathered between his legs and draped over a cord at his waist. *A breech clout, I presumed.* Muscular arms were crossed over his chest, his chin was down, shoulder length hair loosely hooked behind his ears. She had captured a defiant look in his eyes. *No mistaking his heritage in that pose.* Another had him crouched before a campfire, looking like he was ready to spring off the page. *Paha Sapa, 8/75* was scribbled in the corner.

Eleven years ago. I wondered if they were married

then? A few of the sketches from the same year were of an old Indian with a weathered face, a pretty Indian girl holding a small child, and a tall woman dressed in an elaborate fringed costume with a knife in one hand and a basket in the other. A sketch of the Appaloosa, tethered before a teepee showed a remarkable knowledge of equine anatomy. Jessamine could have been a textbook illustrator.

Scenic drawings of mountains, waterfalls, and rainbows were more primitive, definitely less professional. Jessamine's preference to character study was obvious. I once took a course in photography, and the instructor found my photos unbalanced in composition and focus.

"The eye of love sees infinite detail," I remember him saying.

He liked to compare photography with masterful paintings. Honest depiction like the *Mona Lisa* or Vermeer's *Girl with the Pearl Earring* represented the earliest form of photography, he declared. *Love in the eye of the artist?* I could see that in Jessamine's sketches of her husband and daughter.

I put the sketches back in the trunk and sat for a long time just taking in the scenery around me, smelling the minty beebalm and transplanted lavender that grew among the sage chicks around the porch deck, watching the daylight fade into dusk. The wind was rising, threading its familiar song through the taller sage. The mountains always looked softer at dusk, edges blurred by a setting sun. Even if I had Jessamine's talent, I would never be able to capture the sounds and scents of the peaceful panorama before me. For several minutes, I closed my eyes and painted the memories in my mind, wondering why I never noticed such detail in my own time. There were no time stamps on a sunset.

After using the outhouse, I walked to the barn to check on the animals and scattered hay to those in the dry pasture. I scanned the horizon for any sign of the black stallion, checked the repair on the fencing, and assessed the damage he might have done to anything that had been planted.

If it didn't rain soon, more water would have to be hauled from the creek or nothing more would sprout. How simple it was in Granny's backyard to just attach a hose to the outside faucet and water a small *hobby* garden, compared to an acre that had to yield a larder of real necessities.

The first stars of night began to flicker like lightning bugs when I gave in to the dizzy exhaustion I felt and climbed into bed. In the shadows, I could see Mitch was sleeping on his side, snoring more softly into a pillow wedged under his arm and shoulder.

The room smelled of whiskey and sweat, and a hint of French fried potatoes.

Chapter Twenty
Domesticity

I woke in the first gauzy light of dawn with a pounding headache...and a large hand draped possessively over my hip. Gently, I removed the hand and rolled out of bed before Frank blasted his morning alarm. Grabbing the clothes I left in a pile on the floor, I dressed in the living room, pulling on socks and long pants that could have stood on their own. I was running out of clean clothes, and there was no convenient washer and dryer to fix the problem.

Tallie made her way down from the loft and sat on the last step with the pup, rubbing the dregs of sleep from her eyes. "Why are you up so early, Ma?"

"I don't know. Maybe I just need to, to get ahead of all that needs to be done around here." I sighed, plucking at the stains on my plaid shirt. She came to my rescue when I hinted something about laundry soap.

"You want me to help you haul out the washtubs, Ma? Pa said we could skip washday until you felt up to it. Is your head all better now?"

I gave my temples a two-finger massage. "Not today, but maybe with a cup of mint tea, I'll be able to wash tomorrow if you'll help me."

"I always do, Ma."

I gave her a grateful smile. Tallie made this mothering business so easy. The only children I had ever been around after high school were neighborhood kids Granny hired to mow the lawn or weed the garden on occasion. They were never as respectful as Tallie, or eager to do anything more than we asked of them, even when paid well. I wondered if my new daughter was the exception—or the rule in this era.

Together, we headed for the barn when Frank began to crow. I fed some hay to the mare and helped Tallie collect the morning eggs. The fresh lays were warm and remarkably pliable in my palm. It was like a treasure hunt, as not all of the nests contained an egg or two. Tallie seemed disappointed with the count.

"Maybe they were traumatized by all the commotion yesterday." I shrugged.

"I hope that's all." She frowned.

Chickens, pigs, even other livestock were still commonly butchered on family farms, even in my time. Butchering hens that had a name would be as hard on Tallie as it would be for anyone used to buying skinless chicken wrapped in cellophane or butcher paper in grocery stores.

Tallie offered to make breakfast—"while you milk Flossie"—she added, disappearing before I could close my mouth. *I had never milked a cow in my life.*

I thought I would start by making friends with "Flossie," and gingerly patted her bony rump, positioning myself beyond the reach of her whipping tail.

"Nice girl." I ran my hand over the ridge of her back and down one side. I could see her udder swollen with milk. She assessed me with baleful brown eyes that probably mirrored my own. I found a metal pail and set it strategically beneath her, easing myself down on a three legged stool. I knew the milk had to be squeezed out of the four fat fingers that dangled from her udder. She shifted her weight a little and let out a deep noise that sounded like more moan than moo when I gripped one of the fingers.

"Easy girl. You're not going to kick me now, are you?" She mooed again, looking a little desperate, I thought. The stall was too narrow for her to turn and ram into me, but she wasn't tied to her feeding manger to keep her from backing out.

"Ok, girl, if I feed you now, you will stand still, won't you?"

She answered with a swift kick to the bucket, lifted her tail and dumped a pile of loose, foul-smelling manure into the straw bedding behind her. I gagged over the two shovelfuls I managed to scoop aside and proceeded to fill her manger with hay and secure her rope halter to a large iron ring above the manger. She appeared mildly grateful for the hay. Even more grateful when I took the bull by the horns, so to speak, and squeezed two of her fat fingers.

Nothing happened. I squeezed harder and this time she seemed to flinch and moo even louder.

"Ok, Flossie, you're going to have to help me out here." I patted her on the side. "Just, just relax and let go. You'll feel so much better." I almost fell off the stool when I heard her laugh.

"You won't get any milk like that." Mitch grinned, peering over the stall.

"How long have you been there?"

"Long enough to see that you've lost your touch."

"I never...I mean...well maybe this is just below my pay grade."

He narrowed his eyes. "What?"

"She's not used to me. Isn't this your job?"

He entered the stall and gestured with his arm in the sling. "I'm a little tied down just yet."

Feeling deservedly shamed, I asked how his arm felt.

"Better than my head."

"You too? I think maybe we both had too much pain killer last night. Do you have any aspirin we can take?"

"Aspirin? He gave me the suspicious look. "The only sure cure I know is willow bark tea, and I already asked Tallie to brew up a pot for breakfast." He knelt down behind me and with his good hand enclosing mine, gave me a quick demonstration of how to properly milk a cow.

"You have to pull down on the teat when you squeeze, like so." The milk hit the bucket with a ping, but my hand stung with the pressure, and I sucked in my breath. When I opened my hand, he gawked at the rough red line, then unfolded my other hand and sighed.

"Just rope burns, from holding the mare's halter yesterday," I told him. "Can the cow feel these?"

His eyes sparked a little when he grinned at me. "Most female teats are pretty sensitive. I usually grease them with an aloe spear when they trouble Flossie. Looks like you could use some of that...on your palms." Still grinning, his eyes never left mine as he kissed my palm. "Why didn't you speak up last night?"

"I...I was a little distracted treating Ironman, I guess." *Distracted again by the obvious innuendo, his proximity and the faint mingling of whiskey, manure, and fresh milk.* I dropped my eyes and rubbed an index finger under my nose.

"Maybe I should call you Ironwoman, then? You're never short of courage, Jess, as reluctant as you sometimes pretend to be. You came through yesterday." He kissed my palm again, drawing my eyes back to his.

They were clearer, this morning, the green a little brighter, but not back to the sparkle I had come to expect. I could think of nothing to end the awkward silence between us, until Flossie mooed impatiently, and we both chuckled nervously.

"I can finish the milking with one hand." He returned my hand to my lap and flexed his fingers. "Put some aloe on those rope burns, while I work my *pay grade* here."

****

The willow bark tea was bitterly strong, but it did the job. So did the salve Tallie brought me. More feel-good comfort came from the fresh eggs and warm milk for breakfast, but I was beginning to crave something sweet. Trading washday to satisfy my sweet tooth seemed like a good idea while my hands healed. I eased into the rocker with Jessamine's recipe book at hand.

Despite our protests urging him to rest, Mitch insisted three good limbs were enough to repair any of yesterday's damage outside. He demonstrated his miraculous recovery by pulling his arm out of the sling and grinding out a slow circle that made his face turn a shade gray before he quickly replaced it. "I'll take an afternoon break," he conceded softly.

Tallie fed her puppy a bowl of milk, then began to brush him with a small hairbrush I hoped she wasn't using for her own hair. I could see the pup had already doubled his weight, and the little splint on his leg was

126

no longer an encumbrance, clicking on the cabin floor like a playing card on the spokes of a bicycle. He followed her everywhere, watching her every move as if he already knew his life depended on it.

I scrubbed the wooden table with a salted rag, taking a cue from Tallie who usually cleaned the dishes and table after each meal. "I'll do this if you go and help your father," I told her. "Even if he says he doesn't need help, Ironman will need supervision in case he passes out or starts bleeding again."

She giggled and settled Finn in her sling before running outside. With my last cup of willow bark tea, I planted myself in the rocker and began thumbing through recipes. Jake might have held his sides laughing at my unusual bout of domesticity. Granny usually did all the cooking for us, but I did have a few "specialties" even Jake didn't know about. Besides my talent for opening cans, thawing meat for the grill, and boiling water for boxed potatoes, I could bake chocolate chip cookies and zucchini cake from scratch. Egg salad and a couple of easy casseroles were also in my repertoire.

For years, I did all our grocery shopping, and when Granny began forgetting to turn the stove off, I spent more time in the kitchen. Granny wasn't fussy and didn't eat much, so cooking for two was easy as long as I could open a can or fix microwave meals. Most of the time, we ate supper on trays while watching the evening news or her favorite TV game show.

I found only two cookie recipes, neither featuring chocolate chips, which probably weren't invented for years yet. I was not surprised to find several German recipes, one for *kolachen*, and Irish recipes for *colcannon* and soda bread. Jessamine was German on her mother's side and Irish on her father's.

I finally stopped on the page of a bread recipe that bore the stains of use. The only bread I ever baked was from Rhodes frozen dough popped into a cold oven to defrost overnight. The next morning, I sprayed the risen dough with liquid butter and dusted it with garlic powder before turning on the heat. Granny and I thought it was a better alternative to ready-made packaged bread. With a little recipe adapting here, I could even try making a loaf of sweetbread. How hard could that be?

I made a double batch of dough in a large bowl, then set it on the woodstove to rise. *Proofing the dough,* it was called. Instructions said it would take a couple hours before I needed to punch it down and transfer the dough to bread pans for a final rise before it was ready to bake. With the final step, I planned to add sugared raisins to a third of the dough before putting it in the pan and letting it rise again.

While the dough was proofing, I found a recipe for milk soup and thought that might make good use of the remainder of Flossie's milk, and a good medium for a can of oysters. Would Mitch and Tallie be impressed with my culinary improvisations? *Probably not if Jessamine cooked as well as she did everything else.*

I settled in the rocker with the journals, deciding I wanted most to learn about the keepsakes in the chest. What was the backstory on the scissors and the musical instruments? I knew why the lock of baby hair was treasured and suspected the bullet was retrieved from Mitch. He had alluded to Jessamine stitching him up when he referred to the scar on his chest last night. I was also curious about the stone. When and where was it found and did it truly deserve the magical reverence it was given? Was it somehow connected to the teacup with "*Mitawin*" painted on the bottom? With answers, I would know more about the extraordinary ancestor I had replaced. Better yet, I might find the key to getting us both switched back. I *did* want that, I told myself.

How easy this would all be if the journals were scanned or transcribed to a computer. I could tap the Control and F key and type in the key words: scissors, flute, harmonica. *Easy peasy!* The highlighted words would take me right to the page they were found on. Jessamine's writing was tiny, sometimes difficult to read, with a lot crammed on each page—probably because paper was still a precious commodity.

Many of the pioneer records I read at Fort Laramie were brief. I could see how precious time must have been, and writing in a diary or journal may have been considered frivolous, especially if nobody else was ever meant to read it. *The luxury of leisure time belonged to ruling classes.* Classes of people who had servants who cooked, cleaned, and washed their clothes, milked cows, planted gardens, hunted for food—and served it all up with sweat and a smile.

The bread didn't rise as high as I thought it should, and the milk in the oyster stew burnt the bottom of the pot, giving the soup a scorched taste, but I seemed to be the only one to notice. Mitch had three helpings and Tallie seemed to like the dense raisin bread.

"It's even better toasted." I looked from one face to the other to see if I could detect any dishonest testimony.

"If this is the last of the oysters, we will need to

make that trip to Laramie this week yet." He sopped up the last of his soup with a compact slice of bread. "We'll need more seed for sure. The black stallion trampled a corner of the garden already sprouting, and I think maybe some deer or other animal took out another row."

"What if he...or the deer come back again?" I asked.

"We may have to fence in the garden, or put up something to scare them away. We'll also have to breed the mare and stall her in the barn for the rest of the week, until her cycle is over. The stallion was drawn by her powerful scent...which isn't unusual. I've seen wild stallions fight to the death over a mare in heat."

"Then you think it was a wild stallion?"

He nodded. "Maybe an outcast loner, maybe a stray from somebody's ranch."

"I didn't smell anything," Tallie said.

Mitch patiently confirmed what I already knew about animals having a sharper sense of smell and instinct. "More often, it protects them from danger, doesn't lead them to it," he said. "When I was a boy I noticed the warriors who rode mares often separated them from the rest of the herd each spring, unless they wanted them to breed. A bred mare always required more care until she foaled the following year, and then it was hard to separate her from her colt or filly for months after delivery. That's why most warriors had two horses, or valued a string of them."

Tallie thought about it for a long minute. "That's a lot like human mothers, isn't it?"

Mitch turned to me and winked. "Exactly. Your mother had to be looked after before, and then she looked after you real close until you could get around on your own."

I quietly began to clear off the table and wash the dishes.

Chapter Twenty-One
Time Stamps

Leaving for Fort Laramie a few mornings later, spirits ran high, all for different reasons. Mitch was happy to lose the sling. I had snipped the stitches in his arm the night before and was pleased with how fast he had healed, with scarring that mirrored some of the zig-zag stitching on Jessamine's bed quilt. I coated the site with salve and wrapped a clean strip of cloth around his arm before he rolled down his shirt sleeve. A dark purple bruise had colored his left shoulder and ran down his armpit nearly to his elbow, but he insisted it looked worse than it felt. Like a major league pitcher warming up, he rotated his arm and shoulder frequently during the day. "Oiling the joint," he told me, to keep it from going stiff.

"Use it or lose it," I agreed.

His eyes twinkled when he threw me one of his crooked smiles. "I can agree with that—for most things."

Tallie was thrilled that Rachel Garrett was allowed to join us and sleep overnight. Since Rachel's birthday, the distance between the Garrett farm and ours had begun to close. Mary rode a fat horse over yesterday, with Rachel clamped behind her, her legs sticking out almost at ninety degrees.

Mary saw my eyebrows lift and explained the mare

was going to foal later in the month.

"Should she be ridden, then?" I frowned.

"Henry says she can up to delivery day." She must have read my astonishment. "I know, seems cruel, but it was the only horse he could spare that was big enough to hold us both."

Morning coffee extended to lunch that day with all we had to discuss while the girls played with the puppy, gathered a basket of wildflowers and searched for honeycombs. I showed Mary the set of William McGuffey's readers I found on the bookshelf. With them, Jessamine had home-schooled Tallie so she could read and spell, probably better than most nine-year-olds in my day.

I had spent a few hours reading the contents, surprised by how often they referred to God and the attributes of good character and making good choices. The basic early primers were well done and illustrated with woodcuts. One of the books was devoted mostly to spelling, something I felt would benefit Rachel, especially. I offered to lend Mary the book.

"Oh, no," she demurred. "Henry would probably think I was wasting time, trying to get out of chores at home."

I looked her in the eye. "Are you afraid of Henry?"

She began to pluck at an invisible stain on her dress. "Why, no, not afraid...I just mean to keep him jolly. He works so hard to give us what we all need. We have a good solid roof over our head, plenty to eat, enough clothes to wear. What more could any wife want?"

What more? Hot running water and indoor toilets came immediately to mind, but other words came to my mouth.

"What about respect...and love?"

She sighed heavily. "I've been married twice as long as you, Jess. The bloom is off the rose when the children are as growed up as ours."

"But you must have married for love? Doesn't everyone?"

She chuckled. "New love is jest desire of the flesh, before it turns into bedroom routines necessary to breed sons to work the farm and feed the ego. I suppose love...I don't know. I haven't really thought about that for years." She looked at me quickly, with sadness in her eyes that spoke volumes. "I wish I could speak my mind, like you do, Jess. It's always been easy to see your husband respects you and listens to you. If that shows love, you are blessed."

My throat went suddenly dry. I finished my tea and caught myself absently rubbing two fingers along the rim of the tin cup. I was never exposed to many married couples, never thought about what makes a happy marriage. I remembered before they died how my parents were just there for me. I got my share of hugs and kisses but rarely saw a display of affection between them. *But then, aren't all children self-absorbed, rather oblivious to emotions that don't concern them?*

This practice run as a wife and mother was forcing me to reexamine the notions I had about what I needed—and didn't need—for my life's journey. I gathered up the books on the table before us and told Mary I would see if the school at Fort Laramie used McGuffey's or something even better. There couldn't have been many choices for schoolbooks in this century. It wasn't like they had a National Book

Depository. The nation was still incomplete. In 1886, as progressive as it often seemed, Wyoming was still a territory—four years shy of statehood.

Mary hugged Rachel and squeezed my hand when she said goodbye. "I know you'll take good care of my baby," she said with a note of warning or regret in her voice. I knew better than to ask her to join us on our trip. Sadly, Mary was an indispensable servant in her own home. I wondered if that were true of all pioneer women. They worked hard and died young. In 1886, forty-something Mary Garrett was already at the threshold of her life expectancy. With less work and better health care, I probably had at least fifty years ahead of me yet. *Fifty good years back in my own time!*

Two little girls giggling in the loft above me was a pleasant distraction that night as I paged through the McGuffey readers more thoroughly. I had always missed the companionship of a best friend as a child. My mother, then Granny Lou, were my constant companions. As a spoiled, only child, I was an adult before my time, giving in to the fantasies of childhood only through the books I read. I hoped it would be different for Tallie, hoped she and Rachel would remain lifelong friends. I was beginning to see the value of having a close friend, or at least a sibling. I never had either, unless I counted Cousin Jake, who *was* more like a brother.

Mitch had spent the day reinforcing pasture fencing so the horses and cow could all be kept outside while we were at Fort Laramie. I could tell he had overdone it when he retired early with a fleeting smile and little to say beyond "goodnight, girls."

The kerosene lamp was beginning to smell, and the

dim light was straining my eyes when I heard him
snoring, and I wondered if he had taken some liquid
pain killer that day. The jug, I learned, was kept cool in
the springhouse—for emergencies only. I had formed
an opinion about the consequences of drinking after my
disastrous senior prom, when I came home drunk,
disheveled, and full of remorse. I wasn't a teetotaler,
but traumatic life lessons had limited my drinking
thereafter to an occasional glass of white wine. *There
was definite value in self-control.*

****

After Flossie was milked and the chickens fed, the
cow, red mare, Appaloosa, and Tallie's pony were led
to pasture. Mitch and the girls hitched the wagon to the
remaining two horses while I packed a lunch basket for
us. I stuffed another bundle deep in the basket, beneath
a layer of towels and six dozen carefully wrapped eggs
we meant to sell at the trading post. Mitch threw in the
wagon some handmade rope leads he thought he could
also trade for more seed and nails.

We added the portable chicken cage to the wagon
to contain the puppy. Subdued by yesterday's bee sting,
his nose was swollen and red. He had led the girls to a
hollow log containing an old honeycomb that was not
yet abandoned. We worried about him poking his nose
into more trouble at the fort if he wasn't contained.

I sat beside Mitch on the wagon seat while the girls
braided their hair and continued their giggle fest for
most of the ride.

"What can possibly make little girls carry on like
that?" he asked.

"I imagine *gigglespeak* is more a commentary on
how they feel being together," I replied.

"Were you like that with your sister?"

"My sister? Oh, uh, yes," I answered, remembering the photo with Jessamine and her younger sister wearing matching hair bows.

"We haven't heard from Lizzie or your brother for a while. Maybe the postmaster at Laramie will have a letter for you."

"Yes, that would be nice." I clasped my hands on my lap. I wished I had read more of Jessamine's earliest journal spanning several years. The changes in her spidery handwriting and obvious quality of writing instruments required more concentrated reading. There were dark smudges and unmistakable spots of ink over many of the pages. *Were pencils even in common use when she was a girl?*

"If it's okay with you, I thought I'd check at the mill to see if there's any need for an extra load of wood." Hunched over, holding the reins loosely with arms braced on his knees, he looked sideways at me. "We could use the money."

I frowned at him. "Chopping down trees? With your arm still on the mend? That's rather like chopping at logic."

He took both reins in his right hand, flexed his left hand, and circled the questionable arm. "It feels fine, Jess. I had a good nurse." He winked.

"Well, I think you should have that checked out by Doc Brechemin, as long as we're there."

"He could check us both out. Maybe determine if your concussion did any permanent damage?" He eyed me carefully. "Your memory, I mean. You seem to have misplaced it."

A bubble rose in my throat. "Don't, don't

memories grow dull with time?"

"I imagine they do when you're seventy-five. You have a long way to go before that happens, Jess." He transferred the reins to one hand and covered the fist in my lap with his free hand. "I want you mended, too."

I understood his concern. I could try to tell him once more that I was an imitation, hardly the *real* woman he knew and loved. But Tallie and Rachel were sitting behind us, petting the little pup who seemed to appreciate *their* concern over his swollen nose. This was not the time or place, and soon—maybe even today—I would find a way to switch places with Jessamine and give him back the woman he truly desired.

Maybe I'd find all the answers I needed at Fort Laramie. I gave him a weak smile. "I…I just need time. Everything will be right again with time." *It wasn't a lie, at least. I was truly out of sync in time.*

Chapter Twenty-Two
Theatricals

Without a watch, I could only guess the time of day by the position of the rising sun. The easy drive to the fort must have taken two hours, more or less. Our arrival was heralded by the strident sound of a bugle mustering the soldiers to attention in front of their respective barracks. Finn added his howl of protest to the noise when Tallie put him back in the chicken cage. Mitch parked our wagon near the Trading Post and settled the horses.

I purposely wore the same blue dress I had worn the day of the tea party at the Burt house, thinking maybe I would need to return to my time exactly as I left it. Used to wearing tailored slacks or skinny jeans for almost every occasion, the long skirt hampered my agility, making me feel a little helpless...and though loathe to admitting it—maybe a little feminine. Long skirts definitely stood out among all the trousers at the Garrison, outnumbered as they were. Of course, it was the style of the era, as impractical as it seemed, but I wondered if it somehow gave women cache to use their femininity to advantage, inveigling a little gallantry from all the men on hand.

"Thank you, sir," I heard myself say when Mitch easily swung me from wagon to ground.

He curved his good arm firmly around my waist

139

and leaned into me. "Guard mount." He nodded toward lines of men marching to the parade grounds after a second bugle call, accompanied now by drum and fife players. "The girls might enjoy the ceremony."

We followed Tallie and Rachel, quick to join a few children already sitting cross-legged on the boardwalk. I noticed a photographer was among them, angling his tripod and black-draped camera at the field action, exchanging glass plates with an assistant, who quickly covered and sorted them in another black box. The photographer had his own audience, both children and adults, who were probably immune to a daily dose of guard mount. I divided my attention between both demonstrations, having seen neither one before.

Though it was only May and Wyoming weather was still unpredictable, I noticed the noncommissioned soldiers wore their white summer helmets and dark blue campaign shirts tucked into light blue kersey trousers, all with a dark stripe running down the side from waist to boot.

"Infantry," Mitch commented, clearly more impressed by the action on the parade ground. "There aren't as many yellow stripers left here, even with the new cavalry building."

When the details had squared up around the American flag, several formalities were observed before men with triple striped chevrons on their shirts marched down the lines inspecting guns while each soldier remained sober faced and ramrod straight, robots with moustaches, presenting arms. Nearly to a man, every soldier sported some sort of facial hair. Finally, the most impeccable robot was chosen from the lineup and marched toward the flag where the musicians and a few officers stood.

Mitch leaned into me again and whispered, "That must be the orderly of the day—for the post commander."

I figured the post commander was the soldier with the fountain of gold tassels cascading from the top of his dark helmet. Silver eagles decorated his shoulder insignia.

Beside him stood the man I recognized from the photo in the Burt House, wearing the same double breasted uniform with gold braid on each shoulder. *Lt. Andrew Burt in the flesh.* I looked around and spotted Elizabeth Burt in bonnet and light shawl watching proudly from her gate.

A guard was then formed out of the ranks and marched to the front of the guardhouse across the grounds from us, where after more robotic formalities, a new line of guards relieved the old. Once this was accomplished, all the soldiers were formally dismissed for duty and began to stream across the grounds, able now to relax and chat on their way to new destinations.

Impressive. I wondered if this was a typical routine, or embellished for the sake of the photographer. Had Jessamine ever watched a ceremony like this? *Well, of course, she would have.* Her journals placed her at the fort for nearly two years, living in the home of her now-retired Uncle Leo, who had been the long-time ordnance sergeant here. With the four Schnyder children and her brother and sister, Jessamine must have found it to be a cozy arrangement in the smallest house on Officer's Row, the one with the stone magazine behind it. I had read that much but began to regret my new habit of skimming the entries that didn't mention Mitch.

I could feel him watching me, waiting for a reaction at the end of the ceremony. "Just as impressive as always," I pronounced.

His eyes brightened a shade. "You remember this, then?"

"How could anyone forget such pageantry?"

He gave me his lopsided grin. "You've seen it more times than I. You always said how easy it was to tell the time of day by the bugle calls."

"A great convenience without a watch." Automatically, I checked my wrist, remembering that my Fossil watch was in my purse, along with my street clothes, in a locker on the top floor of the cavalry building back in my own time. *Did they even have wristwatches in 1886?* I could tell that the long cavalry building was the largest—and one of the newest on the post in 1886. I made a mental note to check out the second floor if there was time.

When the girls rejoined us, Mitch announced, "We'll leave for home—at the very latest when they call drill. Four thirty, isn't it?" he asked with a cursory nod to me. "That should give us enough time to get everything done here. The next bugle call will be for dinner at noon. Meet back at the wagon for our basket lunch when you hear that signal. Just remember, none of you wander off the post, for any reason."

"Are we in danger?" I looked across the river toward the small subdivision of teepees we had passed on our way here.

He followed my gaze. "You know the so-called Laramie Loafers pose no threat, Jess. With all the firearms around here, you're safer in this post than home in bed."

I scowled at him, trying to decide if this was another intentional innuendo.

He smirked back at me, removing any doubt of innocence. "Fort Laramie is the safest post on the frontier. Never been under attack as far as I know, but it is a big garrison, with a lot of traffic. The stage line and Hogle's Rustic Hotel isn't far off, and the river usually runs high this time of year." His green eyes grew more serious, directed at me. "I'd feel better if the girls stayed within calling distance to one of us."

"Of course." I nodded absently, my eyes shifting to the sights around us.

Surrounded by houses and humanity, the fort seemed to be thriving—more so, I imagined, than any burgeoning frontier town. Staff training for the restored Laramie site had included a history of the fort's longevity from its fur trading days in 1834 to its ghost town status by the end of the century. As park employees, we were told that railroads had been the death knell of the Western Post Network. When trains instead of wagons began transporting pioneers, towns sprouted like weeds along the rail routes. With Indians being herded onto reservations, their threat to any settlement was diminished. The original intent of western posts like Fort Laramie would soon be obsolete in the rush of Manifest Destiny.

Once considered the gem of all forts, Laramie had been a central oasis, a filling station for thousands of hopeful settlers. Its soldiers had patrolled the surrounding territory, safeguarding their wagon journeys. But the fort's days were numbered. A few more good years before the buildings were auctioned off for paltry sums, many stripped for lumber and windows.

The girls followed Mitch to the trading post while I looked around, my mind cataloging the buildings I knew from the restorations, and those that had been empty lots in my time. The Burt House looked brand new, Old Bedlam looked remarkably the same, and the roof of the long stone Trading Post was not yet buckled, though I knew it was one of the oldest buildings on site, along with the old guardhouse on the opposite side of the parade ground.

A sudden chill went through me. *How was this possible?* I had seen photos of the fort, even studied maps and diagrams of the site when I trained for my job, and here I was—lost in time more real than *déjà vu*. I leaned against the picket fence when I felt my legs grow weak and my heart skip a beat.

"Why, Jess Mitchell," the voice behind me called.

It was Elizabeth Burt, who grabbed my elbow.

"Are you all right? You look about to faint, again."

I summoned a smile. "Elizabeth. Yes, I'm fine. The wind must be picking up."

"I've been wondering how you fared since our tea party?" She stepped back a little to assess me. "You look thinner and nearly as pale as you did when your husband carried you off to Doc's."

"Oh, I'm fine now. We, we just arrived here to get some supplies, and check out a few other things. Did you, did you notice anything strange about that day, our tea party, I mean?"

Her dark brows dipped into a vee. "The only thing strange about our tea party was the shoes you wore to it...and your red toenails." Her gaze dropped to my feet, and I obliged her curiosity by lifting my skirt to expose Jessamine's worn gaiters.

"My teacup. Did you see what happened to my teacup?" I asked.

"Your teacup?" She gave me a fish eye. "Someone picked up the pieces and probably dumped them in the latrine. The cup was useless, you know, after your fall."

She followed my gaze to the faded tea stain still on my skirt.

"One of the laundresses might still be able to remove that," she pointed out.

Self-consciously, my hand closed around the stain. She stared at me with a mixture of pity and curiosity.

"I...I was hoping to find the schoolmaster," I said, ending the awkward silence.

"Sergeant Henderson? He would be at the new administration building where school is held nowadays." She pointed across the grounds. I shaded my eyes, taking in the large concrete building that replaced the grassy lot I was familiar with. It had five separate entrances alternating with numerous paned windows.

"It's all-purpose now," she added, "theater, chapel, library too, along with the post adjutant's office. It even has an indoor latrine."

"*That* modern?" I smirked.

"Well, Doc Brechemin has been pushing for better sanitation, and the sutler is taking orders for indoor facilities. Many of the homes have them now, you know." She smiled warmly. "Can you join me for another cup of tea?"

I thanked her for the invitation, promising I might stop by later. She gave me another quizzical look when

I told her I had business with Sergeant Henderson.

"He may be diverted," she said. "There's a photographer here this week from Cheyenne who once worked with William Jackson."

It was my turn to elevate a brow.

"William Henry Jackson, you know, the man who photographed Yellowstone. Anyhow, his apprentice has set up a little studio in the theater and is making cabinet cards for a dollar. Most every family, and the soldiers who can afford it, are having pictures made."

"What a nice idea," I said.

"Tom Sandercock convinced Colonel Merriam that Fort Laramie needed some good site photos taken for the archives, and well, the portrait studio was just a bonus."

"Tom Sandercock...Hattie's?"

"Husband, the post engineer," she finished for me.

"Yes, of course." Not daring to ask, I had to guess Colonel Merriam must be the post commander, the one with the silly gold plume spouting from his helmet at the ceremony. I thanked her with a broad smile, and lifting my skirt with both hands, dodged a few gopher holes to cross the parade grounds.

Miraculously, the first door I entered on the far left of the new administration building led me straight into the theater that must have doubled as a chapel, judging by the number of benches and odd chairs facing a stage. A settee and some pillars were strategically placed amid a scenery backdrop on stage, and the photographer was adjusting the tripod of his draped camera while an officer in full regimental dress preened before a mirror, licking his fingers, then smoothing his hair and moustache.

Two rows of blue waited their turn on benches below the stage. Apparently, all these soldiers could afford the price of a photo. A boy with a wave of dark hair covering his forehead sat at a table to the right, beside a pudgy, owl-faced soldier wearing a high-collared jacket with three chevron stripes on the sleeve and the number seven. I figured this meant he was a sergeant of the 7th Infantry.

"We aren't taking women or families until this afternoon," he announced rather loudly when I approached the table.

"Are you Sergeant Henderson?"

"Yes, ma'am, William Henderson, but like I said…"

"I'm not here for a picture." I quickly bent over the table and lowered my voice. "I was hoping I could speak to you about your school here."

He blinked heavy lidded eyes at me. "My school?" He made no effort to lower his voice.

"That's right. I have two new students for you, if you'll take them."

"New students on the post?"

"New girls."

"Girls?" He blinked again, then glanced at the boy beside him.

His repetitions were annoying. *We were both speaking the same language.* "You are the schoolmaster here, aren't you?" I snapped.

"Temporary master, until the new one arrives."

"I see. Well, can you tell me if classes will continue this summer?"

His laugh had the timbre of a hoot. "I highly doubt there is any interest for that. Who wants to know?"

"I do." I held out my hand. "Jess, er...Jess Mitchell. I have two nine-year-olds who would like to attend classes here."

He looked from my hand to my face and back again, before limply taking my hand. "Is your husband a new enlistment here?"

"He isn't a soldier."

"Ahh. Post civilian, then?"

"No, we homestead near Fish Creek, but you have the closest public school to us, and we can provide transportation."

"Public school? I'm paid to teach only the children of the personnel who live or work at Laramie, Mrs. Mitchell."

I could see I had to play an ace. In my peripheral vision, I noticed the row of soldiers turn their heads in unison when I argued that my *uncle* was Sergeant Leodegar Schnyder. "I believe he may hold the record for the longest enlistment here, doesn't he?"

"German Bloke," one of the closest soldiers overhearing us said. "How's he takin' retirement?"

"Uh, very well, thank you for asking." I smiled. *Just don't ask me where he retired to.*

Wanting to change the subject, I boldly asked how the school was funded. "Who pays you to teach?" I amended. "Who administers?"

The owl swiveled his head to blink at the boy beside him. "Toots' pa is the CO here."

Toots? A boy named Toots? Gaping at me with furrowed brow, the boy was perhaps no more than eleven or twelve. He held a hand over his mouth and whispered something to the owl. After a few whispered exchanges, the sergeant stood to address me with an obvious tone of dismissal.

"Toots thinks you need to speak to his pa, Colonel Merriam. The adjutant's office is at the far end of the building. You can set up an appointment with him there."

I smiled sweetly and bobbed a little curtsy. *Did women still curtsy? They did in Jane Austen's time, but this wasn't Regency England, and it occurred to me that western posts in America were probably less formal.* Suppressing a few latent giggles, I strutted past the rows of waiting soldiers, who seemed to regard me en masse with some amusement. *The theater setting was so appropriate.*

My own curiosity drove me to peek in the windows I passed on the way to the adjutant's office, and when a windowpane separated my eyes from a paper missile, I had to check it out. About twenty active children filled a room bordered with bookshelves, some of them quite empty. The books—not the noise—told me I had found the library.

Only a few of the girls were reading books. Two boys were sailing paper airplanes at each other while a group of older girls huddled around a fashion magazine open on a table. The youngest girls on the floor—some with bare feet—were tying and untying a gaggle of shoes. In the corner, several raucous boys were flipping pennies against the wall, yelling heads or tails like Vegas croupiers. In waves, the room fell silent when they noticed me.

I smiled and introduced myself.

"Are you the new teacher?" One of the older girls asked.

She sighed heavily when I told her I was just

checking out the new library.

"Sergeant Henderson sent us here to check out books while he helps the photographer," one of them explained.

"Well, I don't want to interrupt your selections." I smirked.

The little girls scrambled to recover their socks and shoes. One of them, looking a little shamefaced, explained, "Kitty was learning us how to tie double knots."

"You mean she was teaching you." I chuckled. "Where does your teacher normally hold classes?"

Mostly in the theater, I was told. "Sometimes in the library or outside when it's warm enough," the tallest croupier explained.

They all seemed willing to feed my curiosity. "Where do you keep your papers and books?"

They pointed to a shelf at my right, and I turned to a jumbled mess of baskets containing papers and jars of pencils. A few of the textbooks caught my eye: Webster's Spelling Book, outdated New England Primers, a Boy Pioneer Scrics, and even some of the McGuffey series I recognized from Jessamine's collection. With additional library books to read, I felt the school at Fort Laramie had adequate resources in the hands of a good teacher. *Did Henderson fit that bill?* After meeting him, I had my doubts. Without knowing his background or qualifications, I was pretty certain his resumé didn't include multiple degrees in education.

Slowly, the children returned to their diversions, ignoring me while I scanned the library bookshelves. A frontier teacher must have had to juggle a few balls to keep students interested, considering the age range. I guessed Henderson's charges were probably four to fifteen years old. Too many to get individual attention in the few hours a day that school was in session.

Deep in thought, I drifted to the door and made an inconsequential exit.

Chapter Twenty-Three
The Ghost of Fort Laramie

Happy with his trading, Mitch surprised us with a celebratory quart of sarsaparilla to wash down the egg salad sandwiches I had packed for lunch.

"The trader gave us more than the usual amount for our eggs," Tallie chirped.

"Commerce rules the day to our advantage." Mitch smiled. "The photographer seems to need egg white albumen for making photographs. We were able to trade for more seed potatoes, two pounds of nails, and all you had on your list, Jess, even some extras." He winked, pulling something out of his pocket. "It's the last bar of milled soap in stock. The sutler said it came from riverboat trade by way of New Orleans."

I held the bar up to my nose and breathed deep. Not exactly roses, but without the sharp scent of lye, it would do nicely. I returned his smile, touched that he had thought to please me. After lunch, we split up again, Mitch off to the sawmill, the girls charged to keep an eye on the wagon with our new purchases tucked under a canvas drop. While the girls played with the puppy, I fished in the basket for my own package to trade with the sutler.

John London was a thin man with a long, poor-soul face and a voice tinged with an eastern whine. I watched him from the far end of a long wooden counter that bridged the dry goods section of the store to the grocery end. Besides crockery and kettles, shelves on my end were crammed with bolts of cloth, striped blankets, shoes, shirts and pants, accessories like ribbons, stiff collars, and a stack of straw hats and bonnets. A buffalo robe was draped over the counter end, a ready camouflage for what I had to trade. While his son measured out a transaction of coffee and beans to a civilian in buckskin, the poor soul headed my way.

"What would I do with these?" He gasped, when I lifted the buffalo robe to expose my trade.

"You wear them," I said, "on your feet."

"Where did you get these?"

"They are all the rage...down South. Swamp protectors," I embellished, talking fast. "They call them Crocs, kind of appropriate, don't you think? My brother sent them to me."

He pulled off one of his leather brogans and managed to stuff a foot into one of the sandals. I sighed with relief when they seemed to fit. *More evidence that my feet were large—or his were quite small.*

"They mold to your feet," I hastened to add, "and are as waterproof as any of those." I pointed to a pair of pointy-toed rubber shoes on the shelf. "They won't jam your toes, either."

Wiggling his toes, he replaced his other shoe with the remaining sandal and took a few steps.

"I've never seen the like," he mumbled. "But purple?"

"The South does wonders with Indigo dye."

"They *are* comfortable," he admitted, bouncing a little on his heels. "What would you want for them?"

I pulled a scrap of paper from my gaiters and laid

out my list.

"I can do the chocolate and powder, even the brushes, but your last item is still rather new and pricey." He stroked his moustache. "What size would you need?"

"Your size," I said quickly, assessing his height. "Maybe longer."

"I don't know, Mrs. Mitchell. Would your brother be able to get more of these—Crocs you call them?"

"Possibly," I hedged, giving him my brightest smile.

He seemed to be wavering, and when his eyes rolled toward the ceiling, I knew he was calculating financial risk.

"Tell you what, Mr. London, if you agree to the trade, I can promise you a new supply of soap to sell."

"Some of the laundresses here make their own soap, and I get occasional shipments of Pears or Castile soaps. Little need for…"

"Scented soap? I know a lot of wives on the post who would pay dearly for soap that smells like lavender or mint."

Deal struck, we shook hands, and I raced back to the wagon to hide my new package just before the girls returned from a short walk, accompanied by a boy in a crew cut, wearing suspenders and short pants.

He tipped his short brimmed hat to me. "Louis Brechemin, Jr., ma'am. I seen you in the library this morning."

"His pa's the doctor, here," Tallie explained. "He could look at Finn's leg."

"I'm sure the doctor has more important things to do—with two-legged patients," I said.

"Oh, he takes care of sick animals, too," the boy assured me. "He birthed a cow once and sewed up Sandercock's pig when she got in a fight with a coon over a corn cob."

"Well, that certainly gives him veterinarian credentials." I laughed. "If he isn't too busy, we could see what he says."

"He ain't busy this afternoon, unless Mrs. Hall decides to give up her babe. He released Private Wolfe from the hospital this morning. Finally sober as a judge, Pa says, until next pay day. Almost cut his own throat, Wolfe did, when he passed out with his head between fence pickets last week."

"Well, I'll bet Private Wolfe was pretty grateful."

"Pa said the Wolfe wasn't gonna howl again. He can barely speak above a whisper now."

I chuckled all the way to the Brechemin home, next to the Burt house.

The doctor recognized me at once and rose from a wicker chair on his veranda to offer me a seat. Introductions made all around, I remembered his calm and pleasant voice, coming out of my faint a few weeks earlier, but his face had been a blur. Square, like his son's, but with a dark moustache that hid his upper lip. Was it a military thing, I wondered, or some kind of fraternal rite?

I once read the Amish distinguished married men from bachelors by growing beards. Maybe, like shaved legs and underarms, facial hair in this century was counter to a woman's preference in the next. Mitch was an exception, keeping his whiskers close to the surface, shadowy, but never long enough to comb. But perhaps that was more genetic than preference? I had never seen an Indian—in picture or person—sporting a beard.

"How do you feel now, Mrs. Mitchell?" the doctor asked.

Automatically, I felt for the missing lump on my head. "No worse for wear," I chirped.

"Glad to hear it. Your husband stopped by earlier with a few questions for me."

"Questions?"

"Well, he was concerned about your memory loss. Wanted to know if I thought it was permanent. I told him a bad concussion can take memory for months, in some cases, even years. Young Solace Coolidge stopped a baseball with his head last summer, and he hasn't been quite right since."

How very comforting to know. I glanced at Tallie and smiled when she rolled her eyes. All the children were uncommonly quiet, as if they were in the presence of great authority.

"May I?" He reached out to probe my head when I nodded.

"I don't think you struck your head hard enough for that kind of loss, however." He looked into my eyes, checking for any dilation. "You'll be fine," he pronounced, "barring any other worries."

Moving to sit on the porch rail, he crossed his arms and legs and peered down at me, like he expected a litany of "other worries." My memory was good enough to recall strange bits of conversation overheard when I was coming to consciousness at our first meeting.

"She's had misses," Mitch had said.

"She's still young enough," Dr. Brechemin had responded.

My muddled mind hadn't computed their meaning...then.

"As a matter of fact, we may have another patient for you to look at," I said quickly. The three children handed Finn down the line, like passing a basket of rolls at a dinner table. "His leg was broken soon after birth," I explained. "I set it with a small splint, but he still limps. Your son tells me you often take on patients with more than two legs."

He laughed heartily and clapped his hand on his son's shoulder. "I don't advertise that."

The pup licked his hand when he felt his leg bone, then looked up at me with uneasy eyes.

"His leg feels solid, but he may never lose the limp. A knitted break often shortens the limb." After a brief glance at Finn's swollen nose, and my bee sting explanation, he returned the pup to Tallie's eager arms. "Animals adjust better than we do to insects *and* fractures that handicap, however."

Tallie brought the puppy to her shoulder, patting him like a baby before she set him on the ground to demonstrate how well he moved.

"No worse for wear." The doctor laughed, as all three children came to life, running after the limping puppy, through the gate and clattering down the wooden boardwalk.

I was about to follow them when the doctor's wife and daughter joined us on the porch and more introductions were made. I recognized daughter Lillian as one of the older girls scanning the fashion magazine in the library. Susan Brechemin, a small woman with a kind face, took my hand, though acknowledging that we had already met at least twice before.

"Mrs. Mitchell is a practicing bone setter," the doctor told his wife. "On puppies and her own husband."

I looked at him sharply.

"Your husband showed me his arm...neatly stitched, I might add. His shoulder, too, was properly set."

"I'm sorry, but it, it seemed the right thing to do at the time. He was in such pain and didn't want to make the long trip here."

He dismissed my apology with a flip of his hand. "You did what any dutiful wife would do for her man, Mrs. Mitchell. It just amazes me that a woman of your size had the strength to reset a joint. What pulled it out?"

"We were breeding—a horse," I clarified when I saw his brow inch upward. "A black stallion came out of nowhere, probably scenting our mare..."

"A black horse," Lillian interrupted. "A lone black horse?"

Her mother looked at her and sighed. "It's just a cautionary tale meant to scare you children."

"Did the horse have a rider, dressed in green?" Lillian persisted.

"No rider that I could see. It veered off into the woods when our Appaloosa challenged it, pulling Mitch's arm out of socket when the horse reared up with Mitch still attached to the lead."

"Another sighting." Lillian crossed her arms over her chest.

I looked from one to the other. "Is there a black horse missing from the post?"

"There was," Mrs. Brechemin said. "Many years

ago, long before any of us were even born, if you credit the legend."

The Doctor snorted. "The monotony of life on a post with no real commission is diverted by baseball games, poker playing, and brewing up ghost sightings."

"The sightings may be doubtful," his wife countered, "but the *legend* that started them *was* documented in post records."

"That's true, Papa," Lillian said. "Carrie Merriam said the colonel read that when Fort Laramie was just a fur trading post, the agent in charge brought his daughter from the East to visit. She enjoyed riding her big black horse, even when her father made her promise never to leave the compound without an escort."

"Good advice then, even good today," Doc Brechemin interrupted.

"Well," Lillian continued, addressing only me now, "the girl slipped out anyway, in a fine green riding habit, and two soldiers chasing her couldn't keep up. Horse and rider were never seen again."

Lillian's wide blue eyes sparked with a challenging nod at her parents. "Everybody knows it's true." She turned back to me. "Why, every seven years since then, a girl in a long green riding dress with a jeweled quirt is seen around the area, riding a big black horse."

The doctor laughed tersely. "Everybody, Lil?"

"Papa, you told me yourself about the soldier who was struck by her quirt as she galloped by. Didn't a former surgeon write in his records that the man was bloodied by the cut and had a gold button to show for it, the kind of button found on a woman's fine riding habit."

Brechemin twitched his moustache with both

hands. "Well, even doctors embellish their reports now and then. We are not immune to drama, or even a hiccup of fun—to document for posterity." His voice trailed after his daughter as she huffed back into the house, slamming the door behind her.

Clearly embarrassed, the Brechemins exchanged a grim look.

"Have there been any other notable disappearances around the fort?" I asked.

Mrs. Brechemin shook her head. "None that we've heard of, if you don't count the soldiers who take the grand bounce, but there are other tales of unexplained bright lights and ghosts in uniform, some of them quite unfriendly."

Her husband chuckled. "Aren't all ghosts considered unfriendly? They might be dismissed as guardian angels otherwise."

I thought of the warm presence I felt in Granny's little bungalow. *Her spirit comforting, guiding me through my grief?* Now, a phantom horse, ghostly appearances and disappearances, traveling through time? I didn't *want* to believe in ghosts, but I wasn't ready to make fun of the possibility anymore. I clasped my hands together, pinching the flesh that covered my knuckles. What was reality? How could I, Jessica Brewster, who wasn't born for one hundred years yet— be conversing with people who were long dead, people who were a footnote in the history of Old Fort Laramie. *Maybe I was the apparition here.*

Chapter Twenty-Four
Photographs and Letters

Tallie begged us to pose for a family picture when the boy named "Toots" began hawking the opportunity outside the administration building. I hoped the photographer was tipping him well; the kid was a natural salesman once he raised his voice above a whisper.

Mitch shared my reluctance to have a picture made. He had worn a coarse Henley shirt with suspenders and didn't think he was dressed well enough for a formal portrait. Tallie was persistent, however, and I was beginning to understand how much sway she held with her father when he relented, then sided with her to convince me. I was a harder sell, until I realized the photograph might be scripted fate. In a bright flash of actual memory, I visualized one of the old photos Jake and I found in Granny's basement. It was a casual family grouping, Tallie with a shoelace untied, Mitch in suspenders, and Jessamine standing stiffly at his shoulder, looking pale and enigmatic. *Was that Me? Jessamine's doppelganger?*

The photographer had a clean-shaven face and a gap tooth that I thought might not have been as noticeable if he *had* sported a moustache. He had a slight whistle when he spoke, trying to convince Tallie a puppy would not be able to sit still long enough to

---

hold a pose for the count.

With nobody waiting behind us, he kindly took the time to answer her "why not" questions and show her the process that went into making a picture. A table against the wall behind him was spread with rows of small white papers about the size of a typical four by five inch photo. He explained the papers had been coated in a solution of albumen and salt, then left to dry before each paper was dipped into a silver nitrate solution which made the surface a little shiny and sensitive to glass plate negatives.

Another long table set beneath a window streaming sunlight held "negative and paper sandwiches," he pointed out. "The light eventually exposes darkening images on the paper, and when we see the best result, we give them another bath to fix the exposure against further darkening before the last toning step in the process."

Tallie gaped at him, trying to take in the science of it all. I gaped at him, trying to take it all in as well, feeling suddenly very appreciative of my pocket-sized Olympus camera back home. Whatever my twenty-first century dollar was equivalent to back in 1886, I thought the price of one of these little pictures had to be a freakin' bargain.

An older woman in a canvas apron and a bright kerchief covering her hair sat at another table gluing the dried finished photos to cardboard. "Cabinet cards," she explained. "Smaller versions of these have become popular as calling cards. *Cartes de visite,* the French call them. The French have romantic words for everything, don't you think?" She laughed. She seemed to have a system going, with names and numbers of the photos on a list beneath a cash box.

"Ma knows how to make *French* fries," Tallie blurted, before I shuttled her along.

Most of the photos taken of soldiers in the morning had already been picked up. Some of the family photos were still drying. I recognized the Burt family at once, along with a photo of Hattie Sandercock from the Burt tea party, holding her new baby, with two other youngsters flanking a rather thin man I took to be her husband. I also recognized Lillian Brechemin dramatically posing with the same three library girls who were entranced by a fashion magazine.

Tallie turned the pup over to Rachel and stood beside her father seated on a small green velvet bench. I stood a little behind him with my hand on his shoulder, as directed. As the photographer counted, Finn squirmed away from Rachel long enough to run to Tallie and pull on her shoelace. A whistled curse escaped the black hood on the camera, and after a small consultation with his assistants, the photographer slipped a new glass plate under his hooded drape and began to count again. I clenched Mitch's shoulder to keep from shaking. *Maybe history couldn't be changed!*

****

We crossed the King Bridge on our way home as the bugle call for drill began. The same bridge declared "unfit for use" in my time was still solid and stable, with steel bows and oak treads. I hadn't paid much attention to the fort's location before, but nestled in the right angle of the Laramie River on two sides, the site had been well-chosen for any defense.

The girls fell asleep in the wagon bed before we were out of sight and sound, bookends to an equally tired puppy. Having discovered nothing that would help me return to my time, I was contemplative, and Mitch noticed. He fished in his pocket and pulled out a crumpled envelope.

"This may cheer you up." He handed it to me.

"A letter?"

"Probably from Lizzie or your Aunt Julia."

I tore it open cautiously and checked the signature before reading the contents. "It *is* from Lizzie." My finger shook as I followed the lines of script, reading quickly. "She says the farm is doing well, the winter wheat was a bonus cash crop, giving them enough money for George to add a frame addition to the house, and buy more beef cattle. She's expecting again. She says Charlie is coming to Wyoming to look for summer work and hopes we can put him up. Maybe, she writes, between the two of us, we can save Charlie." I looked at Mitch. "Save Charlie? What does that mean?"

"I have no idea, but a visit from your brother should cheer you up. It's been years since we saw him last."

"Years," I mumbled, calculating how old Jessamine's little brother must be now and wondering how well he knew his older sister.

"When is he coming?"

The letter was dated nearly three weeks ago. "I have no idea." I gulped, trying to quell the sudden panic I felt.

"We'll have a family reunion." He nudged a weak smile out of me. "That was good news about your sister breeding again. She had a slow start but seems to be making up for lost time with three of them, isn't it, in the last five years?"

After another long silence, he nudged me again with his leg. "What did you find out about the school?"

I pulled myself out of my fog long enough to answer. "Well, the school master is temporary, appointed out of the ranks just recently. The last one died of brain fever, and so far, no civilians have applied for a permanent position. Summer school is wishful thinking, as well as the possibility of the girls getting educated there."

"Disappointed?"

I nodded. "But I can see their point. They already have over twenty children, all ages, which makes it hard to teach when the trend is for smaller classrooms and better curriculums. With mixed ages, a teacher would have to be pretty good at multi-tasking."

"What's a curriculum?"

"A curriculum is the study course. I spoke quite a while about that with Colonel Merriam."

"The commanding officer of the garrison?"

"That's right. Colonel Merriam told me I could apply for the teacher's job if I had the credentials."

"You graduated from high school in Nebraska. Isn't that enough?"

I wanted to laugh and cry at once. If he only knew how many degrees I had framing my bedroom wall in the Torrington bungalow.

Patting my hand, he assured me I had done well educating Tallie. "You have curiosity that doesn't quit and a joy about sharing what you know. I could easily see you teaching twenty kids at a time."

We rode on in silence for a short while before he added, "Maybe you just have to be content teaching our children." *Our children? Yeah, right.*

The dust the horses kicked up from the road dried my throat, and the exhaustion I felt made me wish I could join the girls and just fall back into the wagon and go to sleep. Maybe conk my head and go for a *lasting* coma this time. "I stopped in to see Doc Brechemin." I finally sighed.

He nudged me with his leg again. "So did I."

"I know. He told me of your concern."

He threw me a sidelong glance. "Doc was impressed when he looked at my arm. Said you would make a good nurse. I told him my wife has many talents, once she calls up her confidence."

"We talked about ghosts," I said, feeling a sudden knot in my throat.

"Ghosts?"

"Have you ever heard the legend of the girl in green, riding a black horse?"

"Who hasn't? Surely, you heard that one, too."

"I...I've always avoided gossip, but...a black horse?"

"You thinking about the black stallion?"

I nodded. "An odd coincidence, don't you think?"

"It was a riderless horse, Jess."

"From a distance, it appeared so. Did you ever find any hoofprints. I know you looked."

"No, but that wouldn't be odd with all the moving dust and tumbleweeds sweeping the plains in a dry spell this time of year."

"What do you suppose happened to the girl? How can someone just disappear like that, without a trace?"

"The speculation, if you even believe the story, has always been that she was abducted by Indians or desperados, killed and buried in some cavern or mountain crevice."

"Do you believe the story?"

He shrugged. "I think it may have been contrived to keep females from leaving the safety of the garrison. No men have been known to disappear without a trace."

"But Lillian Brechemin says every seven years there are sightings of a girl in green, riding like the hounds of hell are after her."

He snorted. "Lillian Brechemin and the other teenage girls at the fort love to romanticize everything. She was well cast as Joan of Arc in the play we attended there last year. Have you forgotten that, too?"

When he noticed the tear roll from my eye, he abruptly pulled the horses up, wrapped the reins, and pulled me against him on the wagon seat. "Jess, forgive me. I just hate to see you like this, so fogged up and weepy. If you never get your memory back, I can live with that...as long as we make new memories...together."

He bent to fit his mouth over mine and kissed me with such tenderness, I felt another warm tear sting my eye and run down my cheek. He pulled back to look at me strangely, then took my hand in his and ran a finger across the palm that was still faintly striped with a pink callus.

"I see a tall, dark stranger in your life. It isn't your brother. This one has green eyes...and he wants to make love to you." His eyes searched my face, looking for a sign I could not give.

I blinked, releasing a fresh spill of tears. He pulled a handkerchief out of his pocket and shoved it at me with a deep sigh, then clucked to the horses as he took up the reins. Wagon wheels creaked, horse hooves pounded the ground, and the ever-present Wyoming wind chuffed through the brush and solitary trees we passed, but silence fell between us the rest of the way home.

Chapter Twenty-Five
The Birthday Deal

"These are in fashion?" Mitch modeled his birthday gift from me. "They seem rather tight."

Not even close, I thought. I could see the early versions of Levi's were certainly cut fuller, with a higher waistline, and on a tall man like Mitch, they barely touched his ankles. "Jeans are supposed to fit close to the skin. Think of them as leg gloves."

"Leg gloves." He laughed, picking at the rivets and sinking his hands deep into the pockets. "What are they made of?"

"Denim. Very durable denim. They will last forever."

"John London stocks these at the trading post?"

"Not many. He said Levi's were catching on with miners and carpenters, though."

"Well, they seem well made"—he ran a finger over the double stitching—"but I doubt they'll catch on with anybody else."

"You might be surprised."

"How did you pay for them?"

"We struck a deal for some scented soap."

"Scented soap?"

"I promised to make some for him to sell to the ladies at the post."

He made a clucking sound and shook his head.

"You have some strange ideas, Jess. London must have really wanted to get rid of these."

I felt a little wounded. "You don't like them?"

He gave me a slow grin. "I'll wear them if you strike a deal with *me*."

"What kind of deal?"

"You model those black things I caught you wearing after your bath."

My chin dropped. "You...you called them scandalous."

"Well, they are, but I've been thinking about them a lot lately, and...well, maybe if you just wear them in our bedroom." His mouth twitched into his telltale grin. "Behind a closed door? Maybe with a new bolt...from the inside?" He cupped his chin, stroking it with a thumb. "I wouldn't mind if you sleep in them, either."

I chewed my lip to keep from laughing. Lacey lingerie must have been a turn-on for men in any era. "I'll give it some thought." I crossed fingers behind my back before he insisted we shake on it.

"I'm liking these leg gloves more and more." He held my head with both hands while he planted a loud kiss on my forehead. "At least you remembered my birthday."

****

While he and Tallie finished planting the last of the seed we bought at the post, I started a cake, using up a whole can of peaches—improvising to use the sugared syrup they were packed in. Remembering his birthday wasn't hard with Tallie's constant reminders and the date circled on the wall calendar.

Except for the calendar and Mitch's shotgun hanging over the fireplace, the walls were bare. With all of Jessamine's artistic talent, I wondered why there were no sketches or pictures decorating the room. I added our Fort Laramie cabinet card to the mantel, along with the old tintype of Jessamine's family. With brother Charlie coming soon, I thought he might be pleased to see the tintype displayed. It was probably the only picture the family had of parents who died too soon.

According to Jessamine's journal, both were in their forties, and without going into much detail, she had mysteriously recorded them dying together. *Unexpected? Maybe violent?* Perhaps Charlie would give up some details without being directly asked.

I made a pot of tea while the cake was baking and settled in the rocker with the old German Bible and one of the journals on my lap. Family births and deaths were recorded on the dedication pages that followed Revelation. Charlie had been born in 1863, which would make him twenty-three years old today. His parents had died in 1874, the summer of Nebraska's grasshopper plague, also noted in the Bible.

Jessamine had rented out what was left of their farm and with her siblings, joined a company of freight wagons headed for Fort Laramie to live with her father's sister, Aunt Julia, and Julia's famous husband, Sergeant Leodegar Schnyder. Disguised as a boy, she had managed the hazards of the trail with the help of a green-eyed half breed with a single name—*Mitchell.*

With scant mention of sister Lizzie or brother Charlie, journal entries along the trail had been short and disciplined. Daily mileage covered, sights seen, hazards noted. There were a few small sketches of some amazing landmarks along the Platte River Road:

Chimney Rock, another she named *The Castle,* and *Scott's Bluff,* as well as a turbulent river crossing and the views from a steep mountain descent.

Entries became more interesting after *the Indian*—as she called him—saw through her disguise. The obvious thread of prejudice and frustration that ran through the rest of her entries and into 1875 at Laramie surprised me. True love for Jessamine and Mitch was a trail as bumpy as the one that tossed them together. I was even beginning to feel sorry for "the Indian."

Because I hadn't read the whole Fort Laramie section, or anything beyond it, I didn't know when, exactly, they married. I was never one to read the end of a book first, and with this particular story, I wanted to savor the journey that led to such obvious happiness. So far, I thought their "courtship" might have made an adventurous historical romance. An American version of *Pride and Prejudice*—without the manners, of course.

I wondered if any of my ancestors reading this before me had considered writing their story down? Then I remembered that Jessamine actually outlived many of her descendants, and only then the journals would have passed on to Tallie, and then Granny Lou when Tallie died.

Granny was never a romantic...or long with words, verbal or written. But she liked to read, and I once heard that voracious readers were secretly stunted writers—of the genre they preferred, of course. Granny always preferred non-fiction. I, on the other hand, loved a good fantasy or historical romance. I had to admit that most of what I knew about romance, I had learned from books like *Pride and Prejudice* or *The Outlander.*

Classic love stories with more than a sweeping touch of idealism, besides characters you could relate to.

I returned the Bible to the bookshelf and the journal to my bedside table, before checking on the cake. I have the gift of years ahead of me, I mused, and with my credentials in education, I'm ahead in the grammar game. *I* could write Jessamine's story—maybe as a memoir. I'd have to fill in the holes with fiction, however, speculating on how she truly felt.

"Write what you know about," an English teacher once told me. Beyond one silly high school crush, I had no real romantic experience. *So scratch that!* Thirty years old, and the romance in my life was a fictional footnote. It would be like writing a book about parenting without ever having children.

****

Tallie's birthday gift to her father was a cross stitch of the Appaloosa, done on an empty salt bag. I thought it showed some real talent and was happy to see Mitch gush over it.

"We will have to frame it." He gave her a big hug.

"I think we could use a little art on the walls"—I smiled, tweaking her dimpled cheek—"from a little artist with a lot of natural talent."

Still wearing his new jeans, Mitch brushed a patch of dust from his thigh and thanked us both for his "fine clothes and fine art."

"Gertrude Stein said 'when you are not rich, you either buy clothes or you buy art.'" I smiled.

"Who's Gertrude Stein?" they said in unison.

"Oh, uh, just a witty writer, I read about. How about some cake?" I asked, eager to change the subject.

A college course in literature had introduced me to

Gertrude Stein, an American who had achieved her greatest fame in the 1920s with a salon in France that promoted artists, authors, and free thinkers. Granny had a black and white framed print on her bedroom wall of a naked woman, legs crossed, sitting deep in a big upholstered chair, in a room softened by light from a fireplace. Plants and paintings decorated tables and walls surrounding her, and the quote from Stein was the tagline on the print border, *"When you are not rich, you either buy clothes or you buy art."*

The print was Granny's only souvenir brought home from San Francisco, the last vacation she took before I came to live with her. It was a great embarrassment to me. A naked woman with two drooping breasts surrounded by art made me wonder if Granny was a deviate or a candidate for dementia. But eventually, I found humor in her art choice.

The cake was also a big hit, and I warmed to every compliment. With no frosting, I had pounded sugar crystals almost to a powder and sprinkled it over the warm cake. I was beginning to see the appeal some women had for creative cooking. With no fast foods and limited supplies, pioneer women were forced to improvise. Without birthday candles, I found three large tapers to light, and Mitch insisted we each blow one out.

"Can you make this for my next birthday, Ma?" Tallie asked.

I caught myself before asking when that would be, mentally noting I had a "go to" source in the old Bible. *What kind of mother—even a substitute mother—would forget the birth of her child?*

Tallie cleaned the dishes while Mitch poured the

last of the tea into our cups and guided me out to the porch.

"There's going to be a glorious sunset tonight," he said.

"And how would you know that?" I smiled.

"I know about sunsets. I've seen forty-three years of them now."

"Well, I guess at such an advanced age, you might qualify as an expert. The only thing I know about them is the old seaman's prediction. *Red sky at night, sailor's delight; red sky at morning, sailors take warning!* In your expert opinion, does that ring true?"

"Sometimes." He grinned. "Some think if you see a haze around the moon, it means tomorrow will be bright and sunny. There are always exceptions to riddles and rules, you know. Do you remember what I once told you about sunrises and sunsets?"

With my hands on the rail, wanting to divert attention from my memory deficiency, I ignored the question. "Can we even see a sunset from here?"

"With the house facing slightly southeast, we're more likely to see a sunrise. Let's take a walk." He took the cup from my hand and set it on the step. I took the hand he offered without my usual reluctance. It was his birthday, and like his hand, the evening was unusually warm and inviting.

We walked in a comfortable silence past the barn, toward the garden. Raspberries were budding, and the seedlings from our first planting had already sprouted, fragile and thin, almost blue-green in the waning light.

"Do you think they'll survive," I asked.

He shrugged. "Maybe half of them will. The rest will go to deer or rabbits, or maybe a drought if it doesn't rain soon. I'm going to have to work on getting some irrigation channels from the creek this summer."

"How will you live without, without food from this garden?"

He caught my pronoun at once. "How will *we* live? Like *we* always have so far; under nothing short of our blessings, Jess. We've been open to new opportunities, adapting to changes, yes, but there's something more working for us. My people always believed in signs and superstitions, even charms like our Calling Stone." He squeezed my hand. "Maybe it's as simple as that; put your faith in a talisman and believe it will work for good. Didn't you say your Aunt Julia put great faith in a string of rosary beads?"

"Irish Catholics still believe in charms and legends, I think."

"Well, they've suffered from famine and prejudice, as much as my people have. Maybe suffering breeds hope—as well as a need for charms?" He stopped beside the wooden fence that I fixed and tested a foot against one of the rails, then gave me one of his lopsided smiles. "I think you're the charm that makes our life work, Jess. All of this was your idea. You're the strength that feeds us, come what may."

When he looked at me, my heart tripped with the unexpected wish that I *was* the incredible Jessamine, and when he took me in his arms and longingly gazed down at me with a backlight of tangerine sky, I was lost in the ambience. I closed my eyes and surrendered my mouth.

He kissed me with a growing intensity I could never have imagined. His tongue probed my mouth, forgoing the gentle approach he had taken before, and wonder of wonders, my own tongue took the cue and joined the dance. His arms tightened around me, and my head rolled back, exposing my neck with a mewling sound that came from one of us. He pulled on my lips with his teeth, then fastened his mouth on my throat still supporting me with one arm. His other hand traveled to the curve of my hip before it moved to my butt and pulled me hard against him. My arms chained his neck, fingers threading in his hair, and my back arched against him when his mouth found a spot behind my ear that made me wince.

"Just as I last remembered. You two could never keep your hands off each other."

With a loud mutual gasp, we broke apart and stared at the man behind us.

"Charlie?" Mitch huffed.

Even in the spangled light that bathed us, he must have seen the fierce blush I could feel radiate from every inch of my exposed skin. I held my hand on my heart, trying to still the beating of a double shock while I caught my breath. Brother Charlie looked at me with an equal mixture of embarrassment and mirth. "Evening, sis." He removed his hat. "Can I get a hug, too?"

I gave him a weak smile and awkwardly reached out to shake his hand, then pulled it back and went for the hug. "Charlie, you've grown," I squeaked into his ear as he closed me in a vise-like grip that only exacerbated my pounding heart.

"That happens." He released me to grab Mitch's offered hand.

"Well, you certainly have good timing. I was just enjoying a birthday kiss." Mitch looked a little flustered when he glanced sideways at me.

"Your birthday? Well, I am sorry to bust in then."

"No intrusion," I nervously chirped. "We were expecting you any day."

"I could have bunked at the fort overnight, but I wanted to beat the rain tomorrow and didn't want to arrive smelling wetter than a sheep dog."

"Well, that would have been fitting. Last time we saw you, you were what, just a kid, still wet behind the ears." Mitch chuckled.

"I put my horse in your barn and gave him some hay. I hope that was all right."

Mitch nodded, throwing his arm across my shoulders as we headed back to the house. "We must have just passed you, then."

"Who told you it was going to rain tomorrow?" I thought to ask.

"The sutler. Ain't that where we always got the freshest news, Jess?"

I bit my lip before I could say Channel Six News. "Whoever has command of the almanacs, I imagine."

"Well, the man must be new, because I didn't recognize him at all. Who was the trader when we lived there?"

"I don't recall." I blinked, happy for the sudden diversion when Tallie charged through the door to meet us.

"This can't be Tailing Tallie," Charlie cried when she stopped before him with a dimpled smile that lowered her chin. "You were jest a toddler when I saw you last, in Nebraska. You used to trail along after me when I did my chores. Remember how we played hide and seek in the barn, Tallie?"

"I think so. You always found me under the saddles."

"That's the only place you ever hid." He laughed. "We'll have a lot of catching up to do."

"Yesss, a lot of catching up," I murmured under my breath, as I followed him into the cabin.

Charlie gobbled up everything that remained of our supper, as well as two pieces of cake, washed down with a quart of milk. I couldn't help glancing at the tintype of him as a small boy on his father's lap. Even with the sepia coloring, I could tell the boy had grown to favor his father, sandy haired, with light colored eyes, short beard, no moustache. He followed my glance and lifted the tintype from the mantel.

"How well I remember this," he said quietly. "Pa had deep pockets that day. Besides this picture, we all got money to spend at the Plum Creek Mercantile. I burned for the tomahawk you chose, Jessie, and traded your brief ownership for my licorice drops—one at a time. I think you got the better end of the deal. You ended up with some of Lizzie's choices, as well, didn't you?"

I nodded dumbly, wondering what that could have been.

He turned to Tallie. "Your ma was always a wheeler-dealer. With Lizzie's notebook, she started writing about our trail ride to the homestead. That was the start of your journal writing, weren't it Jess?"

I nodded dumbly. I could feel Mitch watching me, perhaps wondering if I truly remembered.

"Well, that reminds me. Lizzie sent along a new photo made in Plum Creek this year. It's in my saddle bags." Tallie tailed after him, the pup tailing her when

Charlie loped out the door.

"Is your memory returning," Mitch asked, when we were alone. Nonchalantly, he rested his chin on his palm as he sat at the table.

"Some of it." I wiped off the table. "That all happened so long ago. Every child must remember things differently. Do you remember your childhood?"

"I remember more about the feeling I had then. No anxiety. We weren't rich by any measure of today, and we sure didn't have clothes or art. We had moveable shelters, and we ate whatever the earth offered up in any given season. But I had few days that didn't keep me entertained."

"An ideal childhood, then."

"Idyllic memories, anyway. I hope Tallie can say the same when she's grown."

"I'm sure she will. Loveable children probably reflect their beginnings."

"We *are* doing right by her, aren't we Jess?" When he looked at me, I had to swallow the knot in my throat and could only nod dumbly.

I wondered how Charlie viewed his childhood. With the grasshopper plague and parents dying when he was only a little older than Tallie, it couldn't have been ideal. Jessamine had to fill their shoes, just as I was filling hers now, playing the mother card. Brief as my role would be here, I couldn't help feeling a weight of responsibility. Jessamine must have felt the same, looking after her siblings.

Lizzie would have been about twenty-six when her cabinet card was made. She looked older, with her blonde hair pulled back and parted in typical style, but it was harder to guess the age of her husband, sitting beside her with a child on each knee. He had the large square hands of a farmer, looking uncomfortable in a dark suit with a starched collar. Lizzie held their youngest child, in a long white dress; stepping stones, all of them maybe a year separating each child. Charlie pointed to the eldest child wearing a sailor suit and went down the line. "That's George, Jr., Patrick and Lizzie's got Ethan."

"All boys?" Tallie asked.

Charlie nodded. "Three sons for Nebraska." He looked soberly at me. "Wasn't that always Pa's dream? Instead, he got three small graves." He sighed. "At least, Lizzie gave him grandsons to keep his dream going." His knuckles drummed the table for a few seconds. "Lizzie thinks the new one will be a girl."

"When is she due?" I looked for a lap bump on the tired woman in the photo.

"Late fall, I think. She's hopin' all of you can make it for Christmas this year. George has doubled the size of the house, and they even have a shingled roof now. No more snakes in the roof, Jess."

He chuckled and turned to Tallie. "Did your ma ever tell you about the rattler she killed in our soddie loft?"

Tallie's eyes were wide as saucers. She looked from me to Mitch and back to Charlie, shaking her head.

"She pulverized it with an iron bed warmer. It could have killed us while we slept."

Killing a rattler with a bed warmer? The thought made my stomach churn. I smiled thinly when they all regarded me with new admiration.

After Mitch shuttled Tallie up to bed, Charlie dug a

bottle out of his duffel bag. "The sutler gave me this," he explained, "after he showed me his strange footwear. He seemed to think I knew where they came from. Wanted to know if I could fetch more of them. He said he got his pair from you, Jessamine."

"Oh really? Mr. London must have me confused with somebody else," I said, biting my cheek.

"I never saw such ugly shoes, Jess. Purple, they were, but London assured me they were passing comfortable, and insisted I bring this to you."

I checked the label on the bottle. Kentucky bourbon. John London's feet must be feeling *very passable.* "Well, his mistake; our gain." I snickered, and went to the cupboard for three clean mugs. Charlie, I soon learned, could hold his liquor no better than I could. Before long, we were giggling like siblings reunited, with him providing the stories and me alternately laughing or nodding dumbly. He had an entertaining way of interpreting things, using gestures and expressions that told me he was perceptive and sentimental, maybe a little deeper than a simple farm boy. *Or maybe I was just a good audience when well-oiled?*

Mitch joined us on the porch for a birthday toast, saying little, watching our interaction rather grimly, then ultimately excusing himself. I thought he looked a little dejected when he left us, separated on the porch steps by a lantern collecting a gauzy halo of midges.

Chapter Twenty-Six
A Civilized Man

"The cornerstone of civilization? Really?" Mitch laughed. "With boar's hair bristles?"

"Well, white teeth and a clean mouf certainly make a dis-tink-shun," I mumbled as I demonstrated how to use the new toothbrushes I traded for. By wetting my brush, then dipping it in the tooth powder tin, I was able to work up a small lather.

"This works far better with real toothpaste."

"Toothpaste?"

I rinsed my mouth with a noisy gargle of water and spit into the bowl on the washstand, then gave him a toothy grin.

He came closer to wipe the wet corner of my mouth with his finger. "Does toothpaste glue your teeth together?"

"No." I grinned. "It polishes and cleans, Something new I heard about." I breathed hard against my hand, checking for the sour dregs of a night with Charlie and his bottle. "Makes breath smell better, too." *At least my head wasn't throbbing...much.*

With the intensity of a dental hygienist, he peered into my open mouth. "Does it clean up a potty mouth? That could disqualify a civilized woman, you know."

I rolled my eyes and shoved a new brush at him. "Your turn, smart ass."

As he followed my procedure, I asked how he managed to keep his teeth so white for so long.

He raised an eyebrow. "At my advanced age? I don't know. My grandfather had discolored teeth, quite a few missing, too. But then, big bellies smoked the pipe every day, and Grandfather often had a wad of *kinnikinnick* stuck in his cheek. I didn't smoke, but I chewed a lot of raw cattail stems and mint leaves."

"Big bellies? Your grandfather was a large man, then."

He gave me a look. "You don't remember Grandfather, Jess? We shared his lodge our first summer together. You once credited him for bringing us together."

The sketch of the old Indian. "Well, of course I remember him. Unforgettable," I muttered.

"That's what he said about you...when you left the village."

I was going to have to read faster to get to the village part.

A clumsy silence fell between us.

"You know, Tallie confessed to me that she hates to brush her teeth. I already gave her one of the new brushes and showed her how to use it."

"Well, maybe she will change her mind, then," he said softly. "Your brother could use a demonstration, too."

"Yes, I noticed his teeth are almost yellow."

A slow smile twitched on his mouth. "There's a subject for you to civilize, Jess."

"You don't like my brother?"

"I hardly know him. He was just a boy on the River Road, and not much older when we married and left the fort. I don't know Lizzie that well, either."

That puts us both at square one. Equalizing the disadvantage certainly worked for me.

****

Charlie's bedroll on the bearskin rug was empty when I started the morning coffee. "He ran like a chased gopher to the privy a while ago," Tallie explained when we both joined her in the barn. All but one of seven new chicks had hatched, and she was beaming like she had laid the eggs herself. While Mitch milked the cow, Tallie and I considered names.

"Too bad there aren't seven. We could name them after the seven dwarfs," I said.

"What dwarfs?"

Oh Lord, I was going to have to stop fast-forwarding, or at least censor the leakage.

"From an old German fairytale my grandfather told me." *Safe there. No way she could look up cartoons.* "Or you could name them after the days of the week, Tallie. I just think you may run out of 'F' names with all these chickens."

Her dimples popped when she gave me a quizzical look. "I guess I could try out some 'G's."

We laughed as we tried to come up with "G" names beyond Gladys and Gus. After carefully transporting the hen and chicks to a wooden crate, we added a dish of water and some feed, to separate them from the other hen still brooding on her nest.

From a conversation overheard between Mitch and his daughter, I learned there was a distinction between breakfast eggs and those that produced chicks. Rooster Frank was needed only to fertilize hens to produce chicks, while the unfertilized eggs became breakfast. In my mind, Frank was becoming more dispensable every day, though he was too scrawny to eat.

When Charlie finally joined us, I could see at once he was hung over. Mitch seemed to enjoy needling him about it while I fixed him a cup of strong willow bark tea. His blue eyes were red around the rims, and he talked in whispers, dialing down the volume of his own voice.

Charlie had consumed most of the bourbon. Knowing my limits, I had surreptitiously watered some of the bee balm growing beside the porch. Even so, I welcomed a cup of the tea that worked as well as aspirin. Breakfast took on a leisurely pace, as we all filled up on scrambled eggs and ham, and leftover peach cake washed down with cow's milk or tea.

A sudden grumble of thunder sent us all to the porch to watch rain clouds tumble over the horizon and blot out the morning sun. Laser swords of lightning cut through the sky, and the air was thick and humid. A Wyoming spring storm was finally on the burner. *So much for red sky at night or a haze around the moon!*

"Just what we need." Mitch winked, throwing an arm over my shoulder.

"A good day to lie about." Charlie sighed with relief.

Tallie tugged at his arm. "Can we play draughts, Uncle Charlie?"

His face brightened. "I brought a deck of cards with me. How about a game of Maw? Jess, you remember Pa's favorite card game. We passed a lot of stormy days and winter nights playing Maw or All Fours."

I nodded dumbly. "I need to get some bread

started, but I'd love to watch."

What I really loved to do on stormy days was curl up with a good read, wrapped in Granny's afghan, with a plate of chocolate chip cookies in close reach.

At Mitch's suggestion, we dispersed to set out buckets and containers to catch any rainfall. While they set up empty barrels in the garden and herded the cow and chickens back into the barn, I hauled the bathing boat into the yard just as the rain cut loose with a peal of thunder that rattled the cabin windows.

I debated between running through a natural shower with my new bar of soap or mixing up a batch of cookies. Cookies won. Meal planning was always innovative, and I was now cooking for four. *No take-out tacos or pizza to the rescue!*

Beans and salt pork must have been as common to the homestead wife as it was to the chuck wagon cook. I added several handfuls of dry beans to a pot of simmering water and found some cornmeal in the cupboard.

I looked up at the figure watching me chop a bar of chocolate. Charlie stood in the doorway, dripping rain like a used umbrella. His hair was plastered to his head, both arms hitched up inside his shirt sleeves, and his mouth hung open, reminding me of one of the cartoon dwarfs.

I rushed to pick up the crumpled blanket he used for a pillow. "You can leave your wet clothes on the porch, Dopey." I shoved the blanket at him.

He mopped his face and stared at me. "Dopey? Did you just call me Dopey?"

"Well, you are rather large for a dwarf." I laughed.

"Who are you?"

For a few seconds, I held my breath, then smooth as butter I heard myself say, "Why, I'm your big sister, Charlie. Leave your muddy boots at the door, please."

Chapter Twenty-Seven
Shark Bait

All Fours was a variation of Seven Up, a game I often played with Cousin Jake and Granny. Each player was dealt six cards, and trump determined by turning over a card from the unused deck. Aces were high, taking kings down to twos. Tallie picked up the card sequence fast and learned that trump would take any trick, providing it was the highest trump played. A point was awarded for winning a trick with the highest and lowest card, then the jack of trumps and also for the most tricks taken.

I thought it was a great way for any child to run some mental math, and I encouraged Tallie to keep score on paper while I finished my batch of cookies. We would have to teach Rachel how to play on her next visit. Perhaps, I could even use the deck as flash cards, having the girls add or subtract numbers.

The big cast iron stove had no glass window to watch my cookies bake, and without a watch or timer, I had to crack the oven open to determine when they were done. Charlie noticed and pulled a pocket watch out of his duffel bag, and after winding it and setting the approximate time, he handed it to me. "It keeps time when Dopey remembers to wind it." He chuckled.

I turned it over and saw that the silver casing was initialed. "*N. W.*"

"I won it—sort of—in a freak card game," he explained. "The dealer was about to call the turn when one of the losing players pulled a gun on the coffin driver, accusing him of cheating. Another punter grabbed the gun, and the shot went wild, ricocheting off a light and striking the shoe. I had a bet on the order of the last three cards and I called it right and would have won, too, but with all the commotion, and the shoe in splinters, I could see it was gaffed. The dealer knew that I saw it, too. All bets were off, and he grabbed the evidence, thinking his life was on the line. When the dust settled, he slipped me his watch, grateful for not giving him up."

Tallie turned to me with eyes round as saucers. "What did he say?"

Charlie must have read our astonished faces. He shrugged. "I think the dealer's name was Nate something," he muttered half to himself.

"You play faro often?" Mitch asked, with more than a hint of disgust.

"Well, no," Charlie confessed. "You don't hit many towns on a cattle drive, but my trail boss a few years back was something of a gamer, and he packed a heavy load of luck. He taught me how to tell when the dealer was cheating."

Except for the rain beating on the roof, the room fell silent until I took the cookies out of the oven and set the tray on the stovetop with a clatter. Only a few cookies on the edge were more black than brown. I knew faro was a favorite betting game in Western saloons, even into the next century, until roulette and blackjack eclipsed it. Everyone gambles in some way, I rationalized. *Maybe I was the biggest gambler here, pretending I could pass for Jessamine.*

Cookies containing broken bits of a chocolate bar drew raves...and a welcome diversion from the idea we were entertaining a card shark. I couldn't resist a little bow when Tallie gushed, "Ma, these are the best cookies you ever made!"

The rain drumming on the roof and sheeting the windows showed no sign of letting up. "How about a game of Maw." Charlie drew a question mark in the condensation of a window pane. "Jess, you remember how that goes. We played it enough in the soddie."

"You'll have to refresh me. It's been so long ago."

It was an easy game to learn, with the object being to win three or five tricks or stop another player from doing so. The winning "pot" was a cookie, and as the day wore on, I was encouraged to mix up another batch while I tended the bean pot for supper, adding a chunk of ham from Mary Garrett.

"I don't remember you ever cooking, Jess, until Ma and Pa died, and then Aunt Julia took over when we got to Fort Laramie."

"A domestic goddess eventually blooms—better late than never," I chirped.

Mitch had been relatively quiet all day, sharpening some knives and cleaning his shotgun and a small pistol I had never seen before. But he was listening, and now and then I could feel his eyes on me, especially when my competitive streak began to show in the card games. Growing up, Jake and I always had a running card bet—mostly over who would do chores.

The rain stopped before dusk, and we all ventured out to smell the air heavy with vapor and dripping with the fresh scent of new growth. In twos, we took turns using the privy, Tallie and I going first then checking on the new chicks that were turning into tiny balls of fluff, despite the dampness that permeated everything.

When we retired for the night, I lit the bedside lamp and pulled out one of Jessamine's journals to read. Dated 1874 on the River Road, it had been a day of rain that made it dangerous to cross the Platte River. *He helped us cross, Jessamine* wrote, *and had the right to his normal cockiness this time. He knew how to handle a team. We were one of the lucky ones to make it across. Still*—The rest of the sentence was blackened with ink.

It was clearly not love at first sight with them, and I wondered how long it would take and who would acknowledge the feeling first. From what Granny told me and what I read, both of them had ample reason for hate at first sight. Reading the journal was almost like reading an interactive novel, one that forced me to read between the lines, piecing together what I already knew.

Green Eyes peered over my shoulder. "I've never read all of your journals," he said. "Do they bring back some memories?"

I nodded, tilting the page possessively toward me. "A diary is supposed to be private. Girl stuff, you know."

"Well, I'd like to know what you thought about me then."

"Jess didn't like you very much at first."

"Well, lucky for me, she changed her mind." He put his arm around me and tickled my earlobe. "You have changed your mind, haven't you?"

I closed the journal. "You *are* very persistent." I

clucked.

"You must have noticed that I wore your Levi's all day, still damp from the morning rain."

"Impressive torture."

"You haven't forgotten our deal, have you?"

"What deal?"

"Levi's for black lace."

"I...I'm wearing them," I said slowly.

"Well, modeling them under a cotton nightie doesn't count, you know." He reached under the quilt and began to inch up my nightie.

I slapped his hand. "These walls are thin, and my brother is probably lying just ten feet outside the bedroom door."

I couldn't still the twitch of my mouth when he said, "You know, I'm really beginning to hate that card shark."

"Do you really think he's a card shark?"

"Faro is not a kid's parlor game. I've seen men lose horses, guns, everything but the clothes off their back in a desperate game."

"Maybe that's what Lizzie meant in her letter by 'saving Charlie.' "

"He's too unworldly to be a desperado. He seems more like a big kid who hasn't been long off the farm."

"Well, he has gone on a few cattle drives, and he talked about maybe trying to hire on as a sheep shearer. Last night he told me there are a few big stations around Cheyenne that put out a call for that sort of thing this time of year."

"This *is* lambing season, when all the herds also gather for shearing. He could probably make some money shearing if he has the knack for it."

"He told me he did all the shearing on Lizzie's little herd."

"Your sister only keeps enough sheep to make her own wool, just like we did."

"We did?"

He gave me a familiar long-suffering look. "You don't remember how the wolves got our sheep last fall? How could you forget such a thing? Tallie was devastated when we buried what was left of the lamb she had raised."

"I'm sorry." I tried to hide the horror I felt, as much from the act as from the new threat of exposure. This charade was getting more and more complicated, and for someone who always had command of her emotions, I was finding constant apologies as tedious as my leaky eyes and nose.

It was fortunate for me that he seemed to have a deep well of sympathy when he saw me tear up or sniffle. Maybe tears were a rare sight on Jessamine? I turned on my side to face the door and mumbled "good night," swiping a finger under my nose.

He sighed and patted me on the butt. "No goodnight kiss?"

I turned back to look into his green eyes, contrite and hopeful. "A reprise of that birthday kiss Charlie interrupted would be nice."

"You're too old for me," I said playfully. *I couldn't deny he looked pretty good for forty-three, or 168 years old if he were a fictional vampire.*

With a vampire growl, he pulled me toward him, kissing me hard on the mouth. I struggled only a little, giving in to the moment with a choked squeal.

"That's better," he whispered after a long kiss that

stole my breath. "I always love to hear you squeal, but you know, we can't disturb dear brother Charlie." He smirked. "At least not until I can fix a bolt on the door."

My gaze darted back to the bedroom door. Made of quartersawn wood, it didn't look very sturdy with its worn leather hinges. Would Charlie come to his sister's rescue if he thought she was being unwillingly attacked? Or would he think it was just two people, like he said, who "couldn't keep their hands off each other."

Chapter Twenty-Eight
A Sleep Like the Dead

I was learning there was no shortage of things to do from sunup to sundown, and "spare time" was synonymous with meal time or privy breaks. If I were to get through Jessamine's journals, I had to literally burn some night oil...providing I could tolerate the smell of kerosene. Thank God, we slept with an open window. I always did back home, and Mitch seemed to radiate enough body heat to crave the cool evening breeze that came through our window. *"Our window."* I was beginning to think like half of a couple. "Our home...Our daughter."

I made good use of tepid rain water collected in the bathing tub, using it to scrub dirty clothes with lye soap against a washboard, following Tallie's example. Together, we strung a rope line between a few stout trees and hung the clothes on the line with wooden clothespins that looked exactly like those found in any big box store in my time.

The lye in the soap put a rash on my hands and arms up to the elbows. It sent us into the woods with baskets to collect aloe and violets and mint, anything with a remedy or scent. We also found budding fiddleheads and patches of morels that seemed to grow before our eyes in the lingering dampness of yesterday's rainfall. I found a willow tree near the creek and with a pen knife cut and peeled a good section of bark to dry and shred or pulverize for future headache cures. Tallie pointed out a few wet animal tracks she thought were from deer, plus a few she was sure were made by wolves.

"Wolves? This close to the cabin? Don't they usually stay in the mountains?"

"Not when they're tracking deer," Tallie said.

What other creatures lurked in the forests and foothills that led to the mountains? *Bears? Mountain lions? A wild black stallion?* With only a penknife and scissors, we were pretty defenseless. Jessamine would have probably carried a gun, perhaps the little gun I saw Mitch cleaning.

Finn was constantly wandering out of sight with Tallie calling anxiously after him. The puppy had pulled off his splint and was scampering around with a barely noticeable limp, sniffing like a bloodhound and poking his nose into every crevice or hole he could find. Something must have nipped him in the nose when we heard a high pitched squeal that sent him back to Tallie with his tail between his legs.

Warblers and chipping sparrows flitted among the trees, and high overhead the hoarse scream of a red-tailed hawk drew our attention. In one of the snares Mitch had set, we found the bloody foot of a rabbit that had gnawed its way to freedom. Tallie wanted me to snap the trap and free the gory stump before Finn could get at it. "I think we should bury it."

I touched her cheek with the back of my hand. "Do you know that rabbits' feet are lucky charms? You could take this home and clean it up for a keepsake."

"No, Ma, I think the rabbit might come back for it.

Pa says spirit creatures sometimes do that—search for what they lost to be whole again."

"Well, he may be right. Did he also tell you that some species actually mourn their mates when they die, just like people do?"

She thought about that for a while. "Will you mourn Pa when he dies? I know he's older than you are."

I swallowed the knot in my throat and set down my basket to hug her. I wondered how many daughters worshipped their father as Tallie did. "Yes, honey, I will mourn him, but you don't have to worry about that for many, many years."

I actually didn't know when Mitch died, but I did know Jessamine outlived him to marry twice more. The fact held my conscience hostage, keeping me from full disclosure. Even if he believed my time travel story, he could be devastated knowing his beloved soulmate married twice more after he died?

I was the genetic granddaughter of Jessamine's second husband. On the other hand, if I spared him the news of his earlier death and Jessamine's remarriages, he would think I was his direct descendant, a genetic great-great-granddaughter and curse us both for an incestuous betrayal. Could a proud man who deeply loved his wife and daughter, and valued honesty and truth above all else, live with such knowledge? Taking into account his reaction to my "scandalous" underwear, I knew the answer. It was a conundrum I didn't ask for, tied up in feelings I never expected. How could I be the agent of such poisonous heartbreak? Heartbreak that could change lives, even alter the history of our family!

As the birdsong dialed down and the light between the trees became a canvas of pinkish-gold, we started back with Finn reluctantly trailing. With a heavy heart, I said a silent prayer, asking for direction that would point my pilgrim soul to the right home, in the century I was meant to inhabit.

****

With Charlie's help, Mitch had spent the day in a lodgepole pine stand, starting to clear a field for oats. "We can use the poles to fence in the garden," he announced as he washed up for supper. "And with the ground still damp, the clearing will be easier to plow."

"You really like to push your luck," I said. "Who would chop and plow with an arm stitched and pulled back into joint so recently?"

"Ironman." He grinned, washing his face and hands with one of the clean towels I took off the clothesline. "I appreciate your concern, but Charlie is a big help, and I mean to use him while he's here."

"He'll never come back again if you use him up like that."

"Well, at the very least, your brother will sleep soundly every night." He winked at me. "Think of the noise we could make while he sleeps like the dead!"

I gave him a look *he* must be surely familiar with and fought back the grin beneath it. "You are the most persistent man I've ever met."

He bussed me on the forehead. "I know a nurse with a remedy for that."

I rolled my eyes and shook my head. "You will both sleep like the dead with the agenda you've set." Before he could roll his shirt sleeves down, I checked his forearm. My stitches had left seven tiny scars, like the bird tracks we had seen in the mud banks of the creek today. He was a fast healer, I couldn't deny that. I also couldn't deny the tiny swell of pride I felt over my own handiwork. *Better than the stitching in Jessamine's quilt?*

"Well, at least my dreams will be sweeter than Charlie's," he said softly. "I doubt he'll be conjuring up black lace unmentionables."

When I thumbed my nose at him, he grabbed my hand. "What is that supposed to mean?"

I could feel the twitch in the corner of my mouth when I looked up at him. "It's a potty mouth gesture, like the finger."

"The finger. Which finger is that?" He smiled, clearly amused. "The come hither finger?"

"In your dreams"—I snorted—"where great fantasies live."

I could hear him laugh when I left our room to slice up the morning bread, brown the mushrooms in butter freshly churned, and concoct some kind of dressing for the fiddlehead salad. I was beginning to relish playing Martha Stewart almost as much as I enjoyed fencing wit with Ironman.

Everyone retired soon after supper. After washing dishes, I retreated to the porch with a final cup of chamomile tea, a lantern, and one of Jessamine's journals. She had spent the summer of 1875 in an Indian camp somewhere in the Black Hills. Whether it was by choice or not wasn't clear. Few entries described the experience until she returned to Fort Laramie in the fall and began to reminisce in detail. Meeting Mitch's grandfather must have been a highlight as he filled most of the pages, along with fresh observations of Indian customs, feasts, crafts, even their beliefs.

I scanned the diary for Mitch's name, but she had referred to him in pronouns that told me she was probably trying to forget him at some point. If I read between the lines, I could sense something had happened after she had saved his life digging a bullet out of his chest. *The same bullet that was now a keepsake in the leather chest?* It must have been a turning point in their relationship.

Saving a life, stitching up wounds, even setting an arm had to be a turning point in *any* relationship. I closed the journal and sipped my tea thoughtfully. There truly was something intimate about saving a life, something that would connect you forever to the patient. Was that what I was feeling with Mitch? An urge to protect? Sanctify?

Mosquitos drove me back inside. I skirted the sleeping figure sprawled on the bearskin rug and undressed in the bedroom. The air was damp as a sponge after the rainstorm. Too humid to sleep in underwear and shift. Mitch was sleeping curled on his side. Protecting his injured arm had become a habit in bed. I slipped under the quilt in my Victoria's Secret underwear, and in the patchy moonlight noticed the new block of wood nailed to the bedroom doorframe. It didn't look like it would actually keep anyone out. But then, after a day of farm labor, who had the energy to test that, anyway?

Chapter Twenty-Nine
Screamers

By the following week, we had a sizeable field plowed and planted to oats. Slim lodgepole pines stretched out like giant carpenter's rules alongside the garden perimeter. Finishing touches were still on the agenda, but until that could be done, we improvised ways to protect the garden from some of the flightier creatures of the night who dined there.

After relating my disappointment over the girls' summer school prospects at Fort Laramie, Mary Garrett convinced me to school the girls twice a week.

"You probably know more than any teacher at the fort," she said. "And I won't expect you to do that for nothing." Her flattery, along with a steady supply of beef and bacon, sealed the deal.

One of Rachel's older brothers brought her over to spend the next two days with Tallie and for their first "art project," I showed the girls how to make pinwheels from twigs and some of the papery corn husks we had stacked in the privy. I imagined we could intersperse them in key areas of the garden, and bank on the ever-dependable Wyoming wind to keep them moving day and night. When it became clear the project threatened our supply of *frontier toilet tissue,* we decided to build a scarecrow with pinwheel arms, instead.

We collected deadfall to build a crude skeleton,

and sagebrush and straw to plump up his body and stuff into an empty feedsack for his head. Mitch laughed at the finished project, slumping like an old man over the 'T' frame we pounded into the middle of the garden.

"He looks crucified," Charlie said, solemnly assessing the figure.

"Isn't that my barn hat?" Mitch asked.

"It had a hole in it," I said. "We thought you wouldn't miss it."

"But it's a memorial."

"To what?"

"To my head still sitting on my shoulders. If that bullet hole in the hat was an inch lower, I'd be dead as a straw man."

Tallie looked at him sharply. "Who shot at you, Pa?"

Mitch caught my glance and hedged. "Long story." He ruffled her hair. "I'll tell you later...maybe ten years later."

"Ain't scarecrows 'sposed to look scary?" Charlie said. "Lizzie made one for our garden back home and took a lot of guff because she painted a big grin on his face. The crows used him as a landing strip."

"I seriously doubt crows recognize facial characteristics," I said, prickled by the critiques. "His face isn't finished yet, and the moving hands are supposed to do the scaring, anyway."

"Impressive engineering." Mitch studied the scarecrow with his arms crossed over his chest. "Are those my trousers he's wearing, too?"

"Threadbare, beyond patching. Besides, they've been replaced by Levi's now."

"Yes, I know." Mitch winked at me. "*I* remember

that deal."

I reached up to grab the scarecrow's head and jerked it off the frame, then plunked the hat on the straw neck. "The best thing about scarecrows," I snapped, "is they're blessedly witless."

"What does she mean?" I heard Tallie ask as I marched back to the house with my arm hooked around the stuffed head, big as a basketball.

"I think we hurt your mother's feelings." I heard him chuckle before I slammed the cabin door behind me.

Jessamine's sewing basket contained a swatch of black broadcloth that was perfect for a pair of droopy eyes and a long oval mouth. I stitched them carefully on the scarecrow's face and held the head at arm's length, admiring my needlework. *Nobody viewing "The Screamer" would criticize this scarecrow again!*

****

The McGuffey readers and the dictionary came in handy when making lesson plans for the girls. For every hour spent reading or figuring math by flashing cards from Charlie's deck, I alternated with more practical activities geared to the times.

After our art project with the scarecrow, we mixed up a batch of soap, using some of the collected rainwater. Jessamine must have made her own soap, as I discovered a blotchy recipe in her cookbook for the typical lye bars. Pretending to know what I was doing, I improvised the recipe by adding a decoction of crushed violets and lavender, which not only smelled good, but added a faint tint to the finished product. Even Mitch seemed to appreciate my cleverness when he smelled the pan of bars still curing.

What we lacked was paper and a good supply of pencils. I could see why schools favored slates and chalk for centuries. The paper industry was still new in the West. I knew the Fort Laramie sutler carried foolscap, writing paper and slates, and when the soap was cured, I angled for another visit to the famous trading post.

With more chicks born from the second brooding hen, we had a surplus of chickens to barter with, along with eggs and my lavender soaps. Charlie eagerly volunteered to drive the wagon when Mitch decided finishing the fence was a priority. I could see Charlie needed a break anyway. I couldn't help feeling sorry for him. He was no Ironman.

"You've been a big help to Mitch," I told him once we cleared the rising creek water, and I could unclench my fists to wave to the girls who also stayed behind. "With his arm, he couldn't have done the clearing and plowing without you."

Charlie grunted. "He's even more of a taskmaster than George. I don't think I'm cut from that kind of cloth, Jess."

"What cloth is that?"

"Farming. I know it was Pa's dream for all of us. Land. Cash crops. Independence. I just don't fit in that scheme like Lizzie and you." He sighed.

"What would you rather do, Charlie?"

"I don't know. I always wanted to be a trapper or a soldier, but there ain't a lot of call for either of them anymore." I could see the defeat in the slump of his shoulders as he held the reins loosely between his knees. He glanced at me sideways. "You got any ideas?"

"There'll always be the military, Charlie, as long as there are wars."

"The Great Rebellion ended twenty years ago. From what I can see, the Indian Wars are a thing of the past, too. Military posts like Laramie are turning into lumberyards or civilian settlements. There's nothing to fight over anymore."

"You'd be surprised," I muttered. *Give it another twenty-some years.*

"What did you say?"

"What about teaching, Charlie. That's always a noble profession."

He laughed. "Jess, I didn't even make it through sixth grade in Arapahoe. George and Lizzie needed me on the farm. You're the only one of us who graduated high school. Even Lizzie was short-changed there." He snorted. "Besides, who can live on a teacher's wage?"

"You'd be surprised," I muttered again. *Give that another hundred years.*

We rode in silence for several minutes, while I mentally ticked off all the possibilities for an uneducated man in either his...or my century. I could think of more opportunities in *my* time, but they all involved hard labor, and none of them had much to do with farming or ranching.

"You're still young, Charlie. Once you fall in love, you may want to settle down and change your mind about homesteading."

He made a hissing noise that sounded like a curse. "Love ain't the problem. Women jest don't take to me"—he shrugged—"or maybe I don't take to them."

"Oh." I chewed my lip, thinking what that might imply. *More than a century needed for that one!*

"Then you have been in love?" I pressed.

"Not with the right person." He snorted.

"Well, maybe the heart has its own standards, like water seeking its own level. What may be right for some is all wrong for another."

"Did you know when you met Mitch that he was the right one?"

"Noo," I said slowly, thinking of Jessamine's journals. "I think that took some time to work out."

He smirked at me. "It didn't take all that much time. You weren't even twenty when you wed, I recall."

"Umm, that was young," I said half to myself.

At age twenty, I was buried in books or chained to my computer in my dorm room when I wasn't in class. Any relationship or thought of romance was the farthest thing from my mind ten years ago. Until this summer, that had never changed.

"Well, maybe love doesn't respect time tables, Charlie, and you *are* still young. I don't think you were raised to live alone."

He reached over to pat me on the hand. "I owe a lot of that raising to my big sisters—you especially, Jessie. I'll never forget the way you protected us and stood up for me when we lived at the fort."

I swallowed hard, trying to imagine what he meant. Three orphans making that trek from Nebraska to Fort Laramie to start a life with relatives they never met must have been metamorphic, indeed. Jessamine's journals didn't reflect any personal altruism. Survival must have been a normal way of life for my nineteenth century ancestors, the challenge of it taken for granted. When he squeezed my hand, I covered his with my free hand and squeezed back.

****

Lucky for us, John London was off the post on business when we arrived. I spent the last hour of our journey trying to come up with a plausible excuse for why my brother—who had supplied me with purple Crocs—couldn't possibly supply the sutler with more of them to sell. Another man, sporting sergeant's stripes, seemed to be in charge of the trading post, with the help of John Jr. who appeared to know more about his father's business than the sergeant. I recognized Mrs. London, rearranging a shelf of bolted fabric, and made a beeline for her with my soaps.

She seemed wary at first, but after smelling the lavender and commenting on the color, she warmed to my proposal and made a generous offer, tabulating it on paper. She also allotted me twelve cents a dozen for the eggs and fifty cents for each chick. Charlie and her son moved the caged chicks to one of the outbuildings in their backyard menagerie, where chickens, pigs, goats and a new supply of lambs resided—all for sale.

I had enough money to trade for slates, pencils, and chalk, and a small sheaf of paper as well as a yard of netting that I planned to use for future soap wrappings. With money left over, I bought some licorice drops for the girls and gave the change to Charlie. With a grateful smile, he promptly left the building as I continued to browse, checking out the scant supply of tableware. Plenty of tinware. *No porcelain teacups.*

After waiting on a new customer in a rather silly looking bonnet—who nevertheless bought two of my soaps at double the cost I was allotted—Lucy London approached me again. "How soon can you make more of your soaps, Mrs. Mitchell?"

"Please call me Jess." I smiled sweetly. "Well, it takes a good two weeks to properly cure the bars, and I only have one pan dedicated to use, and I've been so busy…"

"I'll give you two more pans to use," she said quickly.

I hesitated. "I don't know if I'll even be…"

"And a bucket of hog grease."

I sighed dramatically. "Well, I might be able to have some ready in a few weeks if you could give me a couple more items, on credit of course."

She smiled broadly. "I think I could do that."

Her face turned skeptical when I showed her the hat I wanted, then sent her son out to the backyard menagerie to collar a lamb. Doing business with the London family was certainly rewarding I reflected.

Charlie was nowhere to be found. I strolled down the boardwalk with the new hat pulled low on my brow, hoping Elizabeth Burt or some of the tea ladies wouldn't recognize me in the trousers I wore. My new family was used to seeing me in my preferred outfit, but I had forgotten that the women on the post, even the laundresses, wore skirts like a uniform.

The smallest house on Officer's Row was between Doc Brechemin's house and Old Bedlam. With a typical overhung porch and a swing, the white frame home was just as Jessamine had described it in her journal. I could almost visualize the three orphans standing at the door twelve years ago, introducing themselves to cross-eyed Julia, the aunt they had never met before.

The stone arsenal where the ordnance was kept was behind the house. I wondered if Charlie had stopped by, feeling nostalgic, but something stopped me from opening the picket gate and advancing to the door. I was a trespasser, an intruder out of step, and in this place—the last place I had been when I fell through time, I didn't know what might suddenly trigger something to send me back. My heart skipped a beat. *Did I even want to go back?*

A bugler standing beneath the flag sounded one of the daily calls as I ambled around the parade ground on the boardwalk, looking for Charlie and stopping now and then to mentally catalog details of the buildings that no longer existed in my time.

With a population of probably five hundred souls, Fort Laramie—with even more amenities—had to be larger than most 1886 towns in Wyoming. The parade grounds could have been a town square, with homes and businesses surrounding it. For some people, it was home for most of their life. Sergeant Leodegar Schnyder, the ordnance sergeant married to Jessamine's aunt Julia had served at the post for thirty-seven years before he retired. *Oh, the history he must have seen unfold here!*

Hand-lettered playbills were posted on some of the doors of the Administration Building, boldly announcing "The bard's premier theatrical comedy—*Much Ado About Nothing*—starring Kitty Boyd and Steve Mizner. Reserved seating available."

I laughed. Rehearsals must be going badly. No dates for the play were listed, maybe because an audience was always assured.

The Laramie River that nearly circled the post was running high after the recent rain. I could see the deterioration in the worn footbridge that no longer existed in my time. Planks scarred by wheels and hoof tracks creaked under foot, and beyond the bridge, half a dozen teepees perched like giant highway cones on the sparse terrain. A few old Indians sat hunched before one of the lodges, sharing a smoke. *Big bellies?*

As I passed the bakery, the scent of freshly-baked bread reminded me that I had packed a small lunch for Charlie and me, and I hurried back to our wagon, thinking Charlie would be hungry, too, and waiting there. The soap pans Lucy London promised were already in the wagon, along with an adorable lamb with button eyes, just finishing up the last of our sandwiches.

Lamb Chop greeted me with a little bleat that sounded more like a burp. I climbed in the wagon and let him sniff my hand before I began to pet him, and that's when I heard the scream.

The wagon rocked when Charlie jumped into it, released the break, and set the horses off with a quick snap of the reins and a loud "Haw."

I managed to grab the lamb as we toppled backward in the wagon bed and rolled against the side as we bumped across the King Bridge. The lamb was nearly as frightened as I was, bleating into my eardrum until I pinched his nose and nearly strangled him.

"Can't stop," Charlie yelled back. "Hang on, sis."

I bounced like grease on a griddle, hanging onto the lamb and the lip of the wagon until he began to slow down a mile outside of the Post, after checking back to see we weren't being followed.

"Jesus, Charlie, what happened," I yelled, kicking the back of the bench seat. "Have you gone mad?"

Eventually, he stopped, and when he turned around, I could see he had a cut over his left brow, and his eye was beginning to swell shut. "Wanna tell me what the hell happened to you?"

"You don't want to know," he mumbled with his head in his hands. "Let's just go home."

After a long silence, he asked if I brought along anything to drink. The crock I packed was miraculously unbroken, but it had popped the cork in the wild ride, and the lamb was lapping up the milk that had puddled in the wagon bed.

"Looks like you're going to have to fight for a drink," I said.

"That would make twice today." He snorted.

"Your eye is going to need some care. Want me to drive?"

He wiped his sleeve against his brow, and when he saw the smear of blood, he began to cry. I managed to tether the lamb in the wagon and jumped into the seat beside him. He cried against my shoulder while I patted him awkwardly on the back.

"Nothing can be that bad," I said, shocked at his dramatic explosion.

"I'm not...I can't be who people expect me to be," he sobbed.

Welcome to my party. "What in God's name were you running from?"

He sniffed loudly, pulling himself together. "Everything. Nothing."

"Well, now that that's all cleared up, I'm going to drive us home." I removed his neckerchief, folded it into a thick wad, and ordered him to hold it on his brow.

"Here's a thought, Charlie. Just be yourself and damn what others expect."

"That's easy for you to say, Jessie. You've always been so sure of who you are."

I laughed bitterly. *Dear boy, if you only knew.* I pulled the bag of licorice drops out of my pocket and shoved it at him.

"Help yourself, but save some for the girls," I said a little more kindly.

He popped a drop into his mouth and offered me one.

"I can always pass on licorice. I just thought the girls might like them, and you did mention licorice drops you once coveted from your...er...from me."

He looked at me as if I was the one who hit him. "But you always loved licorice."

I shrugged. "Well, tastes do change, when you grow up, Charlie."

I had never driven a horse wagon in my life, but after mastering the stick shift in my new Honda, I thought driving anything else had to be easy. I gripped the reins like a steering wheel, gave the "haw" command, and prayed the horses would cruise-control their way home. Charlie sat hunched over, seeming to focus on the road blurring past. Aside from the pounding hoof beats of the horses, the rest of our ride was punctuated by an occasional bleat from behind.

Chapter Thirty
Thrones and Phones

The lamb and licorice diverted all attention from Charlie's shiner. Pulling his hat low, Charlie busied himself unhitching the horses and leading them to pasture. When the lamb balked and bleated as Tallie lifted her off the wagon, Finn crouched into a deep growl, ready to protect his mistress. Rachel intervened, picking up the puppy to hold at sniffing distance from the lamb, until scents were exchanged and hostility forgotten.

Mitch and I watched them skip toward the barn. "The lamb was thoughtful, Jess. I just hope it doesn't attract wolves."

"I didn't think about that. Can we keep it in the barn at night?"

"If I know our daughter, she will want it in the house 'til it's grown."

"Did you knock some sense into your brother?" Mitch smirked. Charlie's eye hadn't escaped *his* notice.

"Not my work, but I think Charlie's problems won't be solved in a simple bar brawl."

"The enlisted men's club at the fort isn't open to civilians, if that's what he was about."

I shrugged. "We parted ways when I gave him some change, and he wasn't forthcoming about how or why he got hurt when I saw him again."

Something kept me from telling Mitch about the wild ride and our conversation on the way home. His opinion of Charlie was already tainted, and even if he knew Charlie wasn't my real brother, he might not understand the commiseration I was feeling for him.

"Hmmm, I take it your soap made a good barter, then?"

I couldn't contain my enthusiasm, turning toward him as we carried the school supplies into the house. "It did, and Mrs. London ordered more, even gave me enough pans and grease to triple the lot. All I need is more lavender and mint, or anything else that would make an aromatic decoction."

He congratulated me with a tight squeeze. "A clever wife is a fearsome thing."

"That sounds like something Jane Austen would write." I chuckled. "By the way, I have something for you, as well." I stood on my tiptoes to transfer the new straw hat from my head to his. His eyes sparkled when he smiled down at me. He hadn't shaved since yesterday morning, and his new whiskers gave him that roguish look I found so attractive.

"What's this for?"

I returned his smile. "Why, it's for keeping the sun off your face, and maybe diverting any stray bullets that come your way, now that the scarecrow copped your old hat." I could tell that he was touched. For a few seconds, he just stared at me, with that lazy grin I found so disarming.

"I have a gift for you, too." He put the slates and pencils on the table and guided me toward the bedroom. "I want to show you something."

When I hesitated, his face clouded over. Taking my

215

hand, he tugged me toward something shrouded in sheeting against the far corner of the bedroom. Like a magician unveiling a masterful trick, he pulled the sheet away to expose a wooden box about three feet tall, with a hinged lid.

"A shoebox?" It reminded me of the hinged bench seat Granny had ordered for our porch, to store boots and garden clogs before entering the house. Only it was half the size.

He opened the lid to expose the top, with a hole in the center.

"A planter for the porch?"

Undaunted, he chuckled. "It's an indoor throne for the queen of my heart. Have a seat, Your Majesty." His hand swept up to close my mouth. "No more hiking out to the privy at night, or when it storms outside."

"It's a port-a-potty." I gasped.

"A clever name." He smiled. "I sanded it and sealed it with varnish. The bucket inside, too."

I had all I could do to keep from laughing at the primitive object of such obvious pride.

"Of course, it needs a day or two in the sun to dry completely," he said. "What do you think?"

"I think it belongs in a bathroom," I choked. "It isn't meant to be kept in a bedroom."

He pushed his hat askew to scratch his head, frowning. "Well, maybe I can enclose the end of the porch into a water closet. I just thought maybe you'd like the convenience inside."

"The porch sounds like a great idea...more accessible for everyone that way," I said.

He rubbed his chin. "I probably don't need it as much as you and Tallie. Most men, like dogs, are happy to find a tree or bush."

"I'll have to remember that...next time I look for medicinal bark." I bit my lower lip to keep from laughing.

"I know it's crude, but until we can afford a better facility, I just thought you might...You do like it, don't you?" Wide green eyes searched my face for approval.

Unexpectedly, I welled up again. "Truthfully, I've never had such a thoughtful gift, from anyone."

He grinned like a schoolboy.

I swallowed hard and made it to the porch, conflicted by a sudden urge to laugh...or cry.

****

The evening wasn't cool enough for a small fire in the fireplace, but the light and ambiance it gave off made it worthwhile. With fresh air from open doors and windows, we were sated after a fish fry dinner, all quietly engaged in a domestic tableau. I had treated myself to a foot bath and enjoyed the feel of the bear skin rug beneath my naked feet as I sat with one of the journals open on my lap.

The slates worked well for the girls doing math and spelling, stretched out on the rug beside their ever-present guard dog. Charlie was unusually quiet, playing solitaire with his deck of cards on the table. When the girls asked how he got his shiner, he told them one of the horses thumped him when he bridled and hitched them to the wagon. He gave me a pointed look, and Mitch caught our exchange, but said nothing. Since we didn't have ice, I told Charlie the creek water was still cold enough to create a wet compress for the swelling, but he waved his hand against the idea.

"I'll take my licks for what I deserve," he muttered.

Tallie gave him a puzzled look, then turned to me. "Can we sleep in the barn tonight, Ma? Phyllis needs company on her first night here."

I laughed. "Phyllis, Tallie? You know that Phyllis starts with a P, not an F."

"It does?" She frowned. "But it sounds like an F word."

"We have the Greeks to thank for some of our English words and spelling. Photo and phone also sound like F words, but they begin with ph, too."

Rachel, who usually let Tallie speak for her, piped up. "What's a phone?"

"A telephone lets you talk to someone...miles away...or in the next room." My pantomime of a phone call, pretending to dial and speak was suddenly the focus of everyone's blank stare. *Surely, Wyoming had heard of the invention by 1886?* All eyes were on me, waiting for elucidation. "Watson, come here!" I finished lamely, seeking some shred of facial confirmation that told me I hadn't lost my mind. "Does Alexander Graham Bell...ring a bell?"

Tallie rolled her eyes at Rachel, and both girls looked to Mitch whose forehead was wrinkled with concern. Thankfully, Charlie came to my rescue.

"I did read something about that in the *Cheyenne Tribune* when I arrived at the fort. The sutler had a few old newspapers lying around to wrap stuff in. Apparently, there are some of those *telephone* machines already operating in the East, and he was showing an advertisement about it to his son."

"They'll come to Wyoming...eventually." I sent Charlie a grateful smile. "The West always gets wind of these things last, you know. Why, I'll predict that someday every home, even out here, will have a telephone."

Satisfied, Tallie and Rachel bent to their slates once more, but I could feel Mitch's eyes on me, and I shifted in the chair, uncomfortable as always under his silent scrutiny. I found my place in the journal I was reading and leaned over to absently scratch Finn between the ears.

Chapter Thirty-One
A Breed Apart

Making bread was becoming a daily routine, with two men and growing children to feed. I was even beginning to enjoy the chore that filled the tiny cabin with a yeasty aroma. Using the sour dough starter Mary Garrett had sent over with Rachel, I mixed enough for several loaves after Frank's alarm woke me in the morning.

Charlie was escorting Rachel back home today, and Tallie was riding along with them. I gave both girls some reading assignments until we could resume lessons later in the week. Rachel was clearly not up to Tallie's level in reading or spelling, but they were almost even in math.

It was agreed that Finn would stay behind, and he whined from my arms as we watched them ride out of sight. He was growing fast, and his limp was barely noticeable when he scampered about with all his puppy curiosity. As usual, I finished my morning cup of coffee on the porch, this time under a pair of sullen eyes.

"She'll be back home in a few hours," I told him. "You can be *my* bodyguard today." He looked up at me with his trusting blackberry eyes, then tried to nip the hand that offered consolation.

Mitch was already in the fields, working on irrigation ditches. In exchange for any land parceled out as part of the Desert Land Act, he explained it was important to keep our pledge to divert creek water to irrigate more cropland.

"Besides a very hot summer, the almanac predicted a very cold winter this year, so a good harvest would be important," he told me at breakfast.

There seemed to be no end to the chores expected to manage a successful homestead. The upside of all the hard work was a sure cure for insomnia. The sharp edge of exhaustion guaranteed a good night's sleep. *Helpful, especially, when one shared a bed with a naked man who radiated heat in more ways than one.*

Before I could take a reading break, I mentally checked off my chore list. Inventory supplies in the springhouse, weed garden, wash clothes, gather soap supplies, prepare meals. That didn't account for any time spent preparing lessons for the girls or attending to my personal needs.

I had gone weeks without another bath, and though I brushed my hair every night, washing it every two weeks with an egg yolk—as Tally did hers—my scalp was beginning to itch, along with other body parts. On a whim, I grabbed a towel and what was left of the bar of milled soap, heading for the sunniest expanse of open creek. Without the shade of trees, the water would obviously be warmer there. Tallie had directed me to the spot when she found me boiling water for a quick sponge bath and made the suggestion.

"Why don't you just bathe in the creek where you wash clothes in summer, Ma?"

"Great idea," I had responded with a leaping heart. "Help me carry some wash?"

I was able to follow her without appearing I had no

idea where we were going. As a matter of fact, I was getting pretty good at covering up what was regarded as my "tragic memory loss." Reining in twenty-first century expressions and memories was a great deal harder. Besides the phone gaffe, I had to backpedal a raft of convoluted lies when I once commented that a bolt of thunder sounded like an *airplane* in trouble.

I waved my hand through the green creek water. It was still colder than bath water and raised some gooseflesh at first, but if I didn't mind sharing a bath with water weed and darting minnows, it would do. With guaranteed privacy, I felt safe enough to undress down to my black bra and panties. In my Torrington closet, I had beachwear far skimpier than these.

I waded slowly into the stream and splashed a little water on my chest and shoulders. With the warm sun beating down on my back, the cool water *was* refreshing. I waded into the deepest part, feeling the muddy bottom squish between my toes as the water rose to my waist. Holding my nose, I bent to wet and lather my hair, massaging every inch of my scalp. I then scrubbed my face and neck and felt the suds slither into my bra and tickle my breasts.

After unhooking the bra to lather the inside, I slipped off my panties and washed them as well, then laid both on a large, flat rock to dry. Yellow threads of soap slid over my body and melted into the water as I resumed a thorough body scrub.

I could hear the chipping sounds of a meadowlark and floating on my back, eyes closed, hair drifting about my shoulders in a leisurely rinse, I felt a serenity I hadn't known since I gave up yoga. Trailing fingers over my hips, I settled the bar of soap in the hollow of my navel and spread my arms in the water. There was something liberating, maybe even erotic, about splaying naked in a cool wilderness stream. Kissed by the sun above, listening to the hum of nature that surrounded me, I wondered if this was a glimpse of heaven—washed clean, open and unashamed, thinking of...nothing.

When I heard the splash, my eyes flew open. I hadn't thought of sharing the stream with anything but fish or water bugs, but I remembered this was free range country, and Garrett's cattle could have wandered near, or even an intrepid deer or beaver. I didn't count on a two-legged animal with green eyes.

"The water nymph lives again." He smirked, wading toward me in water that barely reached his thighs. "Can we share the soap?"

I curled under the surface and meekly handed up the bar. "I...I thought you were in the..." I waved my hand limply toward the fields, trying not to focus on his dangling nakedness.

He began vigorously soaping his chest. "I needed a break and came back to the cabin for something to eat. The dog led me here to you."

Shading my eyes with my hand, I could see the little snitch poking his nose into some creeping buttercup draped over the bank. On the rock beside my drying underwear, Mitch had stacked his boots and clothes.

"I...I didn't hear you come. How, how long have you been here?"

"Long enough." His searing look gave me chills. He reached out to push a wet strand of hair behind my ear. "You're still as beautiful as you were twelve years ago when I caught you bathing in another river."

With his head slightly cocked, he searched my face, hoping—I supposed, to find some sign of enlightenment there.

"Maybe more so, Jess. You weren't naked then." His eyes fell to my breasts, cradled by the water, my nipples dark and taut in the cool exposure. "You would never know that you've had two children." *Busted for perky?* I quickly crossed my arms over my chest.

His thumb skimmed the side of my face and traced the outline of my gaping mouth before he leaned over to kiss my ear. I held my breath until he whispered, "Wash my back."

He handed me the soap and turned around. Dumbstruck, I slowly ran the bar along broad, sun-burnished shoulders, feeling his muscles twitch down the taper of his back to his tight buttocks, trying in vain to imagine I was washing a window. *Right. An opaque window, smelling of sweat and earth, muscles pulsing under my hand?* My mind was racing with my heart. *Twelve years ago?* Twelve years ago I graduated from high school. Prom night. Jimmy Potter. The bet.

"You can put some muscle into it," he said.

The soap slid out of my hand and disappeared into the water. He turned when he heard me cry out, and we cracked foreheads groping for the bar in the river bed. My eyes stung from the impact and loosened the stinging tears that already hung on my lashes.

"Are you all right?" He pulled my hand away from my forehead and peered into my filmy eyes. His long fingers brushed my forehead before he gathered me into his arms and held me tight against him for a long moment. "We seem to be repeating history. We knocked heads once before, too."

I could feel the solid length of him, warm and comforting in the cool water with my breasts flattened against his chest, his legs anchoring us like trees rooted in rock.

"You came to me, leaped into my arms, and told me you loved me," he continued in a voice oddly strangled. "And then we made love for the first time. Remember that?"

He pulled away to peer into my eyes, pleading for confirmation when he shook me a little. "Tell me you haven't lost *that* memory, Jess."

The dam, already cracked and leaking, finally burst.

"Not her. I can never be her," I cried. "Why won't you believe me? Nobody...God...nobody could ever live up to her...even if they wanted...desperately wanted..."

I was gasping, choking on my sobs, hysteria mounting. I struggled to push him away, slapping at him, slapping at the water. My heart was pounding in my ears—drum beats slashed by strident yelps. Finn, barking in the distance, churned up my dizzy panic. The light was fading, the sun dissolving.

And then I felt muscular arms surround me again, his heart beating against my hands crushed between us, and the solid warmth of him radiated into me like sunshine.

"Icamna," he whispered against my throbbing temple, his voice deep and comforting. "The Sioux call it a cold storm in life's currents. You've lost your way. The concussion, babies lost. Too many changes. But you will...you will survive this."

I could feel his breath in my hair, his deep voice

break with emotion. "*We* can survive this. I vowed once to protect you always, love you always...only you. I meant that, Jess."

He pushed me to arms' length, taking my hands in his and kissing each palm while his own filmy eyes never left my face. "You are the strongest woman I ever met. Whatever you think has happened to your...your firesteel..." He caught his breath and his jaw twitched. "It will return. Just tell me...*show me*...that you still want me."

I could see hope and torment swirl behind those beautiful, mesmerizing eyes, his lashes starred by drops of water or tears that must have mirrored my own. I swiped my hand under my nose and sucked in my breath, feeling my heart clutch. *Was I having a heart attack?*

Maybe I *was* Jessamine, and this was all a dream or *icamna,* as he called it. How could I doubt the conviction of such a man? Was there another man as bright and faithful, so patiently caring? His eyes saw only Jessamine, his wife, his *soul mate.* Jessica Brewster didn't exist. Maybe she never did? *Could history be changed?* I shivered now more out of fear than cold and wanted to stop thinking and just melt back into the serenity I felt before he shattered my privacy, before he shattered my life. I was too tired, too weak to fight what neither of us would ever understand.

"God help me." I clasped him around the neck, giving him my mouth,

I kissed him with a desperate hunger that matched his own and could taste salty tears on my lips, maybe his, maybe mine. A deep growl welcomed my response, and our tongues began to twist together in a slow dance that ignited other movement between us. A hand slid down my back to cup my buttocks, bringing me even closer with a sudden splash of water.

When his other hand hooked me behind the knee and wrapped my leg around his waist, I instinctively straddled him with both legs. Hungrily, he kissed my eyes, my face, my throat and when I arched back, he bent over me, holding me adrift on the bed of water. When his mouth found a nipple, my body spasmed like a fish on a hook.

I must have screamed when I felt a cool rush of water plunge inside me. It was painful and exhilarating all at once, and I began to tremble all over. He stopped suddenly, and in a hoarse voice groaned "Mitawin" against my ear.

I thought he had lost his footing when we began to drift, and I could feel myself tip backward until I felt a solid carpet of moss beneath me. Halfway up the bank at water's edge, I was smothered by more kisses, and when he began to move again, my stomach knotted with impulse, and my hips began a painful nudge that rocked into deeper movements, more groans and slippery sighs, ending in a battery of mutual shudders that tore deep growls from both of us.

For what seemed painfully long and not long enough, we held our fleshly connection, restoring our breath while I clung to the solid warmth of him until the pounding noise in my ears finally distilled to the sweet, simple trill of birdsong. *Or was that my heart?*

"Welcome back," he breathed, against my temple.

He carried me up the bank and wrapped me in the towel I had brought along. I was still trembling when he blotted me dry everywhere and brushed any residual dirt or grass from my back, as he would a small child. He pulled his shirt across my shoulders and tied the sleeves with a concentrated frown before he touched my forehead with his.

"Are you okay? It's only been months, but you...you were like a virgin."

It was Jessica Brewster who processed those painful words. *Oh God*. When the realization sank in, I was too numb to even laugh. I *was* a virgin. Maybe not technically, but I had never been with a man since prom night. Jimmy Potter had taken my virginity on a fifty dollar bet in what might have been considered date rape if I had been any more inebriated.

The emotional price I had paid for that night fed my self-imposed chastity. *No man was ever going to touch me again!* After Jimmy, I was determined to die a spinster and the legacy of the Calling Stone would die with me. Now here I was, trembling in the aftermath of making love with a nineteenth-century man I had known for two months, a man who had the distinction of being my great-great grandmother's devoted first husband, married to her more than one hundred years before I was even born! How could this happen?

"I'm going to hell." I sagged against him.

A deep chuckle rumbled in his chest. "For what?"

I looked up at him, gulping back dry sobs. "What...what just happened."

He laughed out loud as he wiped my nose with one of the shirt sleeves. "Hell will be a crowded place if that's a criteria, especially if one does '*what just happened*' with one's husband."

"But you're not...you don't...how could you possibly understand." I sniffled.

"Well, my grandfather always told me *women* were a breed apart and hard to understand, especially during their courses. Are you…?"

"No!" I could feel the burn creep up my neck.

He gazed at me thoughtfully for a long moment before he broke away to dress. When I turned my back, I could hear him chuckle again.

"You're right about one thing. I don't understand all this sudden shyness." He chucked me under the chin. "You've blushed more in the past two months than you have since we met. Is your Irish Catholicism making a comeback?"

I shook with a fresh onslaught of tears—verging into laughter—verging into hiccups.

He studied me again, hands on hips, his dark brow cocked. "I think you've hit a crying jag, my love. Grandfather may have been right."

He picked up my clothes, his touch lingering on the black underwear, then stuffed them in my boots and handed them to me.

"I'm going to carry you back to the cabin, give you a nip from the jug, and put you to bed," he announced. "You can weep into a long afternoon nap. Maybe you'll even dream of your loving *husband*." He winked.

****

I fell asleep with tears on my pillow and woke maybe an hour later feeling drained and sore. My towel was draped over the bed rail beside his shirt, and Tallie's pup was curled up on the rag rug beside the bed. Stretching my limbs, I wiggled my toes and made a snow angel under the cool sheets. Though my hair smelled of creek water, it felt wonderful to be clean again, a feeling that flashed sudden memories of a warm soak in an acrylic bathtub, clean linen, body talc, and summer oranges.

Would I always have such memories, missed in my new life? *My new life?* Something had changed. I washed my face and blew my nose fiercely, barely recognizing the face I saw in the mirror. *Jessica or Jessamine?*

I pulled on my dry underwear and the old nightshirt I had colored deep yellow. Taking Mary Garrett's advice, I used bloodroot and scrapings of wild plum branches to set the dye, hoping the process might work as well for infusing my soaps with color. Tied with a sash belt, the shirt was cool and comfortable as a summer robe.

The bread dough had risen well over the edge of the pans, hanging in scallops like snow on a roofline. I trimmed the pans and made a Pillsbury Dough Boy with globs of excess dough, juggling room in the oven for all to bake while I planned the rest of our evening meal.

When I heard the distant whicker of a horse, I knew Charlie and Tallie were home again and for some reason, I checked my appearance once more in the bedroom mirror before greeting them. My eyes were still a little red, but I saw something new in them. *Was it noticeable?* Would they be able to tell *what just happened?* Again, I splashed my face with cool water and ran the brush through sleep-tangled hair. Squaring my shoulders, I smiled at the face in the mirror, and the brave smile I saw in return gave me the courage to face my family. *My family.*

Chapter Thirty-Two
Winds of Change

Like the pungent winds of spring replacing the dry heat of summer, change was everywhere. With irrigation ditches completed by Mitch and Charlie, the garden was finally running with cucumber and bean vines, and root vegetables were sending up leafy evidence. Red and orange tomatoes hung like ornaments on evergreens, corn was already knee high, and a sea of oat stubble swayed in the new field.

Barring any storm, all livestock but the cow and the new lamb were kept in the outside paddock at night. We could always count on a dry wind by day and a desert breeze by evening, but rain was still scarce and didn't materialize again, even after threats of dark clouds or grumbles of thunder. The almanac was delivering on its prediction of a hot, dry summer.

Charlie was still with us, sleeping now on a makeshift bed in the barn. "Cooler there, with the barn doors open," he assured us. "And I can keep watch on the animals, or at least hear should anything alarm them."

With all the work Mitch saddled him with, I doubted any "alarm" but Frank's could stir him from sleep. He had missed his opportunity to shear sheep in Cheyenne, but it didn't seem to bother him. Mitch was happy to have his labor in the fields, and I was happy to have him chaperone Rachel and Tallie back and forth between the Garrett spread and ours. Charlie didn't seem to mind that, either. Whatever his secrets and faults, I found him eager to please and slow to complain. In some ways, he reminded me of Jake.

He was even cultivating friendships with some of the Garretts, a prospect I found hopeful, for his sake. Though I didn't know any of the Garrett boys, I felt Charlie needed to expand his social circle outside of the family. In truth, we *were* family. I might have been the token alien, but still, I was a descendant—just on the wrong end of time.

Perhaps the greatest change of all came between Mitch and me. Our tryst in the creek didn't erase my guilt entirely, but it seemed to unlock whatever restraint I had left for a physical relationship. I still didn't seek his affection, but I no longer fought against anything he offered. And what he offered was always generous and considerate. I had no basis for comparison, but I thought being married did have its recommendations.

We no longer slept turned away from each other at the far edges of the bed. Except for nights when the air was stagnant and sticky, we were spoons in a drawer, me on the inside, taking comfort in the feel of his heart beating against my back and his breath warm on my neck.

Like the walls of Jericho, the barriers I had constructed twelve years ago—if not completely down—were at least two thirds lower. Though he made me feel safe and cherished, often telling me he loved me, something held me back from returning the same declaration. My throat constricted at such opportunities, triggering a flash in my mind's eye, like a spam warning on a computer screen, "Don't go there." Sometimes I pictured Jessamine in Granny's old photo of her as Camille, young and smiling dreamily, as if she alone knew the secrets of love.

Yet I woke to desire when his mouth or his hands roamed my body, sparking a network of quick-fire pulses that spiraled through me, distilling into misshaped moans and squeals. It must have been enough for him. He didn't question my ineptitude or complain about my lack of invention. I thought perhaps a man who viewed nature the way he did would view lovemaking the same—natural, a release as fundamental as vitamins to good health. But somewhere, in my overload of rationalization, a tiny new thought was beginning to sprout. *Maybe...just maybe...there was something an "accidental wife" could do as well as the original?*

Even after Charlie moved to the barn, I slipped the wooden bolt on our bedroom door. I worried about impromptu noise that might travel up to Tallie's loft. But Tallie was also a sound sleeper, impervious even to the snuffling of her guardian angel who always slept at the foot of her bed, his mouth open slightly in a black-lipped doggy grin.

I always patted Finn and bent to kiss Tallie's forehead when I checked them before turning in myself, and each time my heart quickened with a maternal feeling. My view of her as Granny's future mother...or even the link to her natural mother was also fading fast.

****

With Rachel and Finn, Tallie and I ventured farther and farther from home, picking wild berries and mushrooms, digging for wild camas root and turnips, gathering moss and bark, wildflowers and anything else that held a pleasant scent or transforming dye that could be added to my soaps. Rare honeycombs were especially prized, providing us with a soap additive as well as a natural sweetener for syrups and raspberry jam. "Botany lessons," I called them, when in truth the teacher in this case was probably less informed than her students. *But I was learning.*

Mitch and I made another run to Fort Laramie with more eggs and my new batch of soap, half colored and scented by berries, half gritty with oatmeal. After they cured in the sun, I wrapped each bar in netting tied with a short piece of false nettle twine. Lucy London was delighted by the presentation, commissioning me for more of the same when I explained soap containing honey and oatmeal was especially good for complexions.

With the proceeds, I was able to pay off our lamb debt and beyond normal supplies, even pick up a few apple seedlings to plant, and stock up with chocolate bars for making my popular version of chocolate chippers. *Bite me, Suzy Homemaker!*

Chapter Thirty-Three
The Emigrant's Washtub

It was Mitch's idea to bundle up our dirty laundry and a washboard, thinking we could make a detour on our way home from delivering my latest batch of soap to the sutler. In my time, I knew about the reservoir and the warm springs near the town of Guernsey but wasn't aware of the old tag the fort had dubbed the springs. *The Emigrant's Washtubs* were aptly named for the service the hot springs once gave to Oregon Trail caravans that stopped there to wash clothes or bathe.

Torrington was probably thirty miles east of the springs, and in all the years I lived there, I had never visited the historic site, probably because it was on private property and permission had to be granted by the family who owned it. In 1886, however, there was no town, no dam or nearby golf course, and certainly no bridge across the North Platte. But with a dry summer, the river was low enough to ford easily in the spring wagon.

Anxious now, I leaned forward, hanging on to the edge of my seat over a bumpy ride. I could see a few scattered crosses and broken wagon debris that bordered what Mitch pointed out as the famous Oregon Trail, rutted from use. He pulled up sharp and set the wagon brake at the crest of a sizeable hill. I climbed out of the wagon and walked to one of the weathered crosses to read its inscription. *Eliza James, 1852.* Mitch joined me and respectfully removed his hat.

"What do you suppose killed her?"

"It could have been anything. Cholera always seemed to be the most contagious. It doesn't give her age, but unless there was an accident or attack, I imagine most of such grave markers belong to the very old—or the very young." He looked at me. "It was a long haul to the West Coast. We were lucky to make it from Plum Creek to the fort back in '74."

I swallowed hard. Jessamine's journals were testimony even to the dangers of a more disciplined freight caravan. Her entries reflected them all. Storms, drought, raging rivers, steep hills, broken wagons, even death in a matter-of-fact record that held scant mention of the man who stood beside me now. Guarding her emotions well, with only a few hints of the exasperation she must have felt, she had resisted his charms far longer and more easily than I had.

Still, she must have impressed him. Hiding her gender and embracing the challenges, was it any wonder he admired her as "the strongest woman I ever knew." *Would her shadow stalk me forever?*

Hand in hand, we scanned the valley and distant hills below us. Visible tracks made by thousands of wagon wheels during the great migrations west cut a lasting trail into earth and sandstone.

"That trail," he pointed out, "is the monument that belongs to people like Eliza who are buried beside it. It will be here long after wooden crosses are sawdust in the wind."

In my time, those ruts were *still* sharp. I knew he was right, and unable to speak, I squeezed his hand.

He pointed to the left. "The springs are about a mile from the bottom of this hill. We've never come here with a wagon, so I thought you might enjoy this view of the valley. There's a cliff further up that has signatures and dates etched into it, just like our names are etched in Chimney Rock."

He gave me the pointed look that had become an unspoken replacement for *Do you remember?* "Maybe it'll take a thousand years for that memory to erode." He sighed.

When I found my voice, I could only say, "Makes one feel rather insignificant, doesn't it?"

We scanned the view in silence, immobile as the rock we stood on, while the wind danced in our hair. With the vast blue expanse of sky above and the sun shining on his burnished face, his eyes sparkled green as emeralds, reminding me of my first glimpse of him on the boardwalk at Fort Laramie. I anchored an arm around his waist, and he leaned over to kiss the top of my head.

****

Assorted boulders bleached by the sun circled the largest spring we found. I stripped down to my black underwear, covered by a loose shirt, and found a niche between rocks. The water was a cerulean blue, and I calculated the temperature at about 85 degrees—too warm for fish, bugs, or even water weed. It even *smelled* clean. Mitch laughed at my squeals of delight when I churned my feet in it. With the washboard between my legs, I vigorously scrubbed our dirty clothes with a new brush and a bar of my latest scented soap. Hoping they would be dry before we returned home, I spread the cleaned clothes over the sun-warmed rocks rimming the pool.

After unhitching the horses and leaving them to roam free in a grassy pasture, Mitch joined me, marveling at how fast I was working.

"Bathing incentive." I tossed his Levi's at him with a sliver of soap in the pocket. "You can help," I ordered. "Maybe if you see how hard it is to get the knees clean, you'll take more care in keeping them out of the dirt."

He cocked an eyebrow. "Woman's work. I was hoping to take a long bath here."

"My hope, too. Maybe we should have brought Tallie and Rachel along to scrub clothes while we bathe?"

He grimaced. "That would end our privacy, and any other plans I had." He looked around. "I'm just grateful this place isn't as popular as it once was."

"Other plans? What other plans could there be for a giant laundry tub?" I smirked.

He looked up, shading his eyes against the overhead sun, and I could see the corner of his mouth twitch. "Well, we've got plenty of time and lots of clothes to dry before we leave."

Hooking his thumbs on his belt, he gave me an impeachable leer. "A warm bath, trading back scrubs, something would come up, I'm sure."

"Then you know all about incentive. Start scrubbing." I chuckled.

"Bossy woman," he grumbled.

I was able to finish several shirts before he finished the Levi's, complaining how hard it was to get out the stains. "Someone should invent a machine for this work."

I laughed out loud. "Somebody did. Laundromats haven't cleared Wyoming customs yet."

"Laundromats?"

"A place where washing machines breed." I smiled.

"Yuk yuk," he said, giving me a fish eye.

"What did you say?"

"Your word...*very funny*, you once told me."

We exchanged grins. There was nothing wrong with *his* memory—or his wit. I grabbed the Levi's to rinse and watched the blue water instantly darken around them. It occurred to me that even in an automatic washer, loads were sorted, and the dials or digital buttons adjusted to accommodate the heaviest or dirtiest laundry. Hot water on the frontier was not produced with the turn of a faucet or the push of a button. Lightly soiled items were probably washed first in hauled and heated water, the dirtiest items last.

At my suggestion, Mitch filled the buckets we brought along with water from the spring, and I packed them with the dirtiest socks and Tallie's trousers.

I jumped in the pool to maneuver the linens and sheets, swirling them around me like a human agitator until I reeled with dizziness. The water was deeper in the center of the pool, where I could definitely feel the bubbling spring tickle my feet. Mitch mimicked my squeals until I gave him the finger, whereupon he couldn't strip fast enough to cannonball into the center of the pool with a huge splash that showered my hair and thoroughly soaked the shirt I wore.

"Bath time." He chortled, taking the sheet from my hands to let it bubble and float on the surface. He helped me out of the wet shirt as well and whistled appreciatively at the infamous black underwear he found so alluring.

"Don't you think they need to be released, too? I mean, all laundry belongs in the laundry tub, as long as we're here."

"I can agitate them where they are," I teased, doing a playful sprinkler dance across the pool.

He came at me like a shark, pulling the water with cupped hands until I was forced to back into the rocks behind me. His hair was long and loose, shining blue black in the overhead sun, and his eyes sparkled with mischief. He hadn't shaved in two days, and silvery drops of water glistened in his beard and over his sun-browned shoulders. I threaded my fingers through his hair and settled my hands on his shoulders while his fingers fumbled behind me to unhook the bra.

"A conspiracy of women had to invent this contraption," he growled. Frustrated, he jerked it apart, popping the hooks, then cupped my breasts with his hands, raising the nipples to a hard peak with his thumbs. My head fell back against a smaller rock when I moaned, and he bent to run kisses along my neck. The warmth of sun, water, and lips was intoxicating, and I shuddered with the effect.

"I love when you do that," he whispered. "I love to know my touch can still rouse you."

His fingers slid down my sides, over my hips, and hooked my panties. When he sank to his knees in the water, like a knight paying homage to his lady, I put my hands on his shoulders and stepped out of them. He stood up with his trophy, and I laughed when he twirled it like a flag, letting them fly off his finger with a little war whoop. The water was crystal clear, bluer than the sky above, and when I looked down, I could plainly see the proof of his considerable arousal.

"I love you," he murmured hoarsely in my ear. He drew back to look at me then, and I knew at once he expected me to utter the same fervent declaration. As always, something held me back, but body language had become an acceptable replacement for what I still couldn't say.

I smiled, looping my arms around his neck and rubbed my cheek against his whiskers. When he took me in his arms, the niggling little voice in my head always turned silent now. My shameless body told me one thing. My struggling conscience had lost the battle to tell me another.

When I felt his fingers grope me beneath the water, every trace of conflict was dismissed. I had discovered a body language to love that involved triggers and a range of telltale sighs and involuntary groans, like the one creeping up my throat. Like a secret panel opening at the touch of a button, my legs moved to accommodate him.

This wasn't at all like our first encounter in the cool creek. A warm bath had always been a sensual experience for me, but sex under warm water was elevating that experience to pure ecstasy. His hands sailed the curves of my body, finding every trigger that set my heart pounding in my ears like waves crashing on a rocky shore. My nails dug into his back, pulling him deeper as I slid against the slippery rocks at my back.

"Oh Lord," I screamed, and my voice came back to me in hollow echoes, joining his deep rumble as the sounds of lovemaking broke against the rocks that surrounded us. We were slowly sliding beneath the surface, pulled by the spring or our own heedless footing and tactile distraction. His mouth covered mine as we sank below the surface and tangled like thrashing eels until I could feel his shuddering release as his breath poured into my mouth, and we floated upward together, breaking the surface.

Gasping, I thought I had lost at least three of my senses, and I grappled at one of the boulders, feeling as washed and beaten as one of the shirts draped there.

Mitch was hanging over another rock, catching his own breath, with his eyes closed, his long hair a curtain of water running down his face and shoulders.

"Are you all right?" he panted, flinging his hair back when he got his footing and hoisted me onto a small ledge.

I felt boneless, dizzy, trembling with residual flutters. When my heart and lungs recovered enough to push words out of my mouth, I gave him a crooked smile. "Just missing gills."

"That doesn't always happen," he panted.

"Near drowning? I should...hope...not."

He laughed and hooked my wet hair behind my ears before he planted a kiss on my forehead. "I think the French called it *la petite mort.*"

Understanding a few French words, I blinked.

Settling beside me, he took a few deep breaths, stretching his arms and legs wide, then gave me one of his half grins. "I think I told you how the nuns in St. Louis tried to teach me some French, but I had a hard enough time learning English and their ritual Latin. They had a great library at the academy, and when I stopped running away, I was even allowed to choose what I wanted to read."

I moved closer, and his arm dropped over my shoulders, his fingers parting wet strands of my hair. Maybe because I couldn't talk about my own past, I always enjoyed prodding him about his. "And what did you choose?"

"Probably not what you'd think? I was seventeen. I scanned the shelves for every French novel I could find."

I gaped at him. "They had those in a nunnery?"

"Well, not in plain sight, for sure. I think I started at the top of every shelf, working my way down, looking for false covers, but I did abandon my search whenever I found something that held my interest."

"Tell me"—I smiled—"what claimed the interest of a teenage boy looking for lust?"

"Well, there was a lot of European and English history, sagas of war, some science. I couldn't read French, but I did find a lot of diagrams that were interesting, mostly medical texts or books a farmer might find informational." He chuckled.

"So you learned about 'the little death' from diagrams?"

"Well, no. One of the white boys at the Academy was French and trusted to work in the library the year before he left. 'Frenchy,' the rest of the boys called him. He could translate the few French novels we did find. One of them was called *Les Liaisons Dangereuses*—four volumes of letters, all about love and betrayal among immoral French nobles of the last century. They were quite descriptive."

In the back of my mind, I thought I remembered a costume drama that won a few movie awards.

Dangerous Liaisons was one of those movies that spawned generational remakes, like *Pride and Prejudice.*

"Hmmm, and I thought Jane Austen was titillating romance."

He nudged my leg. "Well, I don't suppose anything we read could be as titillating as making love in a warm pool of water on a beautiful summer day...surrounded by rocks and buckets of dirty socks."

I had to laugh, picturing Jake's hot tub on his deck, and the two of us buzzed by wine, sitting in bathing suits surrounded by wet towels and smelly gym clothes, trying to recover from our short run to the park and back.

"I must confess I'll never think of *any* washtub in the same way again."

He squeezed my shoulder. "I think we should do our laundry here more often, or maybe test out *all* the warm springs in Wyoming." He grinned. "There are others, you know—beyond the Bows to the south and northwest. And even beyond the Rockies, there are some unbelievable springs, deep and clear in every shade of blue. Geysers, too, spouting from the earth among waterfalls and canyons that would blind you with awe."

"Yellowstone, you mean?"

"That would be a good name for it, I guess. I saw it as a boy, but I've always wanted to take you and Tallie there. The timing was never right." He rubbed the side of his nose. "Do you think maybe we could leave your brother in charge of the homestead for a few weeks? That is, if he stays the rest of the summer."

"That might be more than Charlie could handle," I

said thoughtfully. "He has a lot on his mind already."

He made a rude noise. "Gambling, you mean—or maybe girls?"

"Definitely not girls," I said. "I don't think Charlie is wired for girls."

He looked at me sharply, and I could see my meaning slowly dawn on his face.

"Charlie?"

"Does that bother you?"

"Does it bother *you*?"

"Not as much as it bothers him right now. He feels lost and tormented."

He sighed. "I knew a man in Grandfather's village who was like that. He dressed like a woman and made crafts instead of war. Grandfather explained to me the night sun came to No Water as a boy and offered him a bow or a woman's pack strap. He chose the strap."

"Whatever happened to him?"

He gave me a narrow look. "You met No Water. He was at our campfire many nights. Didn't he accompany you back to Fort Robinson when you left the village?"

I did not remember reading anything in the journals about an Indian named No Water, and had skipped the references to Fort Robinson in Nebraska.

I shrugged, calling up one of my pat excuses. "That was, it was so long ago." Quickly, I put the train of thoughts back on track. "But I don't think Charlie wants to dress as a woman. He just wants to be accepted, no matter who he loves."

His hand gently fondled my ear. "Well, I don't think anybody can control who they love. We couldn't. I had every reason to hate all whites when my mother was killed. You had every reason to hate my people when your grandparents were killed."

Was he referring to the battles? He must have felt me stiffen. The only "grandparent" I ever knew was Granny Lou, but in Jessamine's shoes, I was beginning to understand why it may have taken her so long to succumb to his charm. This was an era filled with war and lawless violence over land, gold, even the right to live a dying lifestyle. Interracial love was probably frowned upon more in his century than mine, and same sex love was a taboo that hadn't even reached debate status in 1886. In my century, with some states beginning to recognize equality in marriage, Charlie might have felt at least he wasn't the missing piece in a jigsaw puzzle.

"Did Charlie tell you about his, er, his preference?"

"Not exactly, but that shiner he got was not from a horse thumping his eye. Something happened at Fort Laramie when he drove me there. I guessed his secret on the way home."

Mitch screwed up his forehead in thought and stared at the sheet adrift in the bubbling currents of the spring. His hand left my shoulder and under the water, I felt him grope for mine. When he brought it up to his mouth, pink and shriveled from the warm water, he ran his lips over my knuckles and sighed, with a tender glance at me. "You're a good sister, Jess."

For a few minutes we were silent, lost in thought, absorbing the sunshine and the feeling of utter contentment in the warmth that gloved us. There were some feelings that could never be altered, even by the strongest will—or the force of legislation. Maybe love was one of them.

"Are we done here?" he finally said.

"Just the buckets to finish, and we both could use a good scrub."

He dropped his head and closed his eyes. "Well, I'm spent." He sighed, with a lazy grin.

I laughed. "Mr. Darcy would never admit that."

He opened one eye to look at me. "Was his wife a clever redhead?"

"Lizzie was very clever. I don't think she was a redhead, though."

Laughing, he kissed my knuckles again.

While I started working on the socks, he soaped his body and washed his hair. When he stepped from the pool to pull on his britches, I stole a glance at his naked body. There was little slope to his broad shoulders, one slightly higher than the other. I wondered if this was because of the dislocation. The little scars on his forearm were visible against his deep tan, bird tracks, like the reverse image of a tattoo. The scar on his chest was also silver white, not nearly as symmetrical as my tiny stitches.

He was lean, yet muscular, with long legs that were surprisingly hairless, given the patchy hair on his torso that still glistened with droplets of water. I always thought male anatomy in college textbooks was exaggerated, but in three-dimensional color, after a warm bath, I had to reverse my opinion. Discounting the scars, for a man of the times who was pushing the top edge of his life span, he looked pretty amazing.

Chapter Thirty-Four
The Birdwoman

I handed up the sheets for him to drape over nearby bushes, and when he left to bring back the horses, I started my own bathing routine, soaping my hair first, then using the suds that trailed down the rest of my body, and finally dunking to rinse off before I collected my floating panties. Circling the pool, now bubbling with a smattering of suds, I looked for my missing bra, reaching down when I slipped on the melting bar of soap.

"This what you look for, missy?"

Startled, I popped up to see a portly woman dangling my bra in one hand with the other clamped on a covered basket at her hip. She had short black hair that curled around her face like a feathered cap, dark eyes, and a wide smile showing a gap in her front teeth. She reminded me of a Russian nesting doll, the largest one in the set.

"Yes, that's mine," I said, embarrassed in my nakedness to have to reach for it.

She studied the bra for a moment, then winked when she tossed it to me. "Very nicely."

When I saw the hooks were bent, I grabbed a dry shirt from the rocks. "I'm sorry to take up all this space." I gestured and climbed out of the pool to gather up whatever was dry. "You've come with laundry, too?"

Her laugh was deep and short. "Just need to soak my feet and wash Digital."

"Your digits?"

She laughed again. "My bird." Opening her basket, she reached inside to pull out a large black bird and tossed it into the pool. "Digital."

I shrieked more out of surprise than fear. The bird began to flap around in the pool, seeming to glide on the water as it splashed, making the most unearthly raucous.

"He like warm pool." She plopped down beside me and pulled off her short boots. "I like for sore feet."

The stench hit me like a slap on the face. Her feet were like the gnarled brown roots of a tree I had once photographed at the Shirley Basin on a school campout. Her toenails were thick and yellowed by fungus.

"Are your shoes too small?"

"Feet too big for old time shoes." She sniggered.

"Do you live around here?"

"Here and there."

"You don't talk like anyone around here."

"Not many speak like me." She studied me with a directness that made me fidget. I craned my neck to look around her, searching for Mitch. *The horses must have wandered far in the valley.*

I pulled a few socks out of my bucket, nervously scrubbing them together before she stopped my hands and pulled one onto her ample lap.

"I tell your fortune," she announced with authority. The bird, having had enough of the water, jumped onto a rock and began to preen his feathers with an odd cooing sound.

Again, I looked for Mitch.

"Your man will return so soon." She flipped my hand over to examine the palm. "You have water hand—long fingers matching palm make you emotional, strong minded." *Her* fingers were surprisingly long and straight, adorned with several rings, three of them with colored gems as large as a Truman dime. She wore a gaudy crucifix that hung nearly to her waist, and her arms jingled with thin metal bracelets as she ran a finger across the width of my palm. "Heart line is also strong for love, but chop lines make big tears."

I had never had my palm read, or even glanced at newspaper horoscopes, thinking it was all mumble-jumble nonsense that preyed on the insecure. Granny told me once the wife of one of our presidents actually directed his itinerary by how the stars aligned. I also thought science fiction and fantasy were aptly named—fiction and fantasy. At least I used to think that.

She called the deep straight line a half inch below my heart line the *head line,* telling me I was a realist. *Much better,* I thought, suddenly intrigued. Tickling my palm, she traced a few more crossed lines.

"Rosamund see very big decisions you make in life." One of the crossing lines extended nearly to my wrist with two bracelet lines arching upward to meet it. She sighed deeply, and her sudden frown made my heart skip a beat.

"What is it? What do you see?"

"You have a strong fate line, but again, many little chops in it."

"What does that mean?" I was getting irritated and flexed my hand to relieve a sudden cramp.

"Much confusion in your destiny." She ran a fingernail across my wrist in a cutting motion. "This very bad." She traced the blunt arrow that nearly joined the vertical line above my wrist.

"Tell me," I demanded, growing a little alarmed.

She folded my fingers into my palm and looked away, muttering something about lines often changing with age.

"Please," I coaxed. She had my full attention, and I could clearly see that she struggled now with indecision.

She gently released my hand and stood. The bird at once flew to her shoulder, and two sets of narrow black eyes peered down at me, blocking out the sun above. "What I see is pain and death. You risk life having boy child unless you go back."

My stomach churned. I wanted to laugh. Instead, I stared at her for a breathless moment, searching her eyes for doubt or trickery. I opened my hand and studied the lines she referenced. *Were palms like fingerprints—different on everybody?* She had been right about almost everything else. Changes, indecision, emotional traumas. But a *child? A boy child?* My head was beginning to throb, and I felt suddenly chilled. I wanted to sink back into the comfort of the warm water. Where the devil was Mitch?

A large dragonfly hovered over my shoulder, and I shooed it away with a splash of water. When I looked up, the Birdwoman was gone. I rose, feeling stiff and awkward as an old woman, myself, and scanned the horizon for any sign of her. After I finished dressing, I climbed one of the hillocks to get a better view. Mitch approached from the west, walking between the two horses, with a hand grasping each headstall. I waved to him, then slowly swiveled direction. The only other movement I saw was the gentle sway of treetops in the ever-present wind.

"Did you see the old woman?" I asked while he hitched the horses back to the wagon.

"What old woman?"

"I think she called herself Rosamund. A fortune teller. She read my palm."

"A fortune teller?" He chuckled. "More likely a laundress from the fort."

"She didn't bring any laundry, just a big black bird in a basket, and she threw it into the pool, and it splashed and raised the biggest ruckus. Surely, you must have heard the echoes?"

He stared at me with bemused skepticism. "Did you nap while I was gone? Fall into a dream? The horses were a long way from where I left them."

I showed him the large black feather I had found swirling in the pool. It perfectly matched the blue black color of his hair.

Chapter Thirty-Five
Where There's Smoke…

Palms up, my hands felt like flat fossil rocks nesting in my lap. I stared at them on our way home, studying the lines and cross lines etched there. I knew palmistry had existed for thousands of years, but was it a true, dependable science, or merely an almanac of the mind, stabbing at the future, confirming the past?

Mitch tried at first to make light conversation but gave it up when he saw how distracted I was. "I take it you didn't like the reading the old woman gave you. Did she confirm your fears about going to hell?" He chuckled again.

"What? Oh, she didn't go that far. She didn't see me living happily ever after, though. She didn't see me living long at all."

He turned on me, his jaw twitching. "Jesus, Jess, you don't believe all that crap, do you?"

"She was right about some of the things she told me."

"Like what?"

"Like being emotional, yet realistic, many changes in the past...and the future."

"That could apply to almost anyone. Standard predictions, I'd say."

"But fingerprints are individual. Nobody has the same fingerprints. Don't you think maybe hand prints are like that? Based on size, lines, and marks?"

"They may be individual, but how can you credit the interpretations as absolute truth?"

"How can we credit anything as absolute truth," I mumbled. "It seems unreal to me, even being here."

"Where did you expect to be?"

"Not living in a log cabin in Wyoming with a husband and child."

I could see his jaw popping. "Is that something you regret?" he said softly.

A bubble of emotion caught in my throat.

He pulled the wagon to a stop and turned to me anxiously. "Well, is it?"

I shook my head, unable to find my voice. He picked up my hand and roughly massaged it with his own, like he wanted to erase the lines I feared.

"Jess, if I could give you more—a better house, an easier life, the children you want, I would. I would give my life for you. Surely, you must know that by now. You and Tallie are the sun that shines in every storm we face, the only constant that makes everything real for me. And I don't need anybody reading my palm to predict that will *ever* change."

My lashes were damp with tears when he moved my hand to press against his heart. He may refuse to believe that I was an imposter, not the wife he knew and loved so well—but the Birdwoman knew. She knew I was out of place and time.

"You will risk your life...unless you go back."

Go back? She had called her bird "Digital." Did anyone of this century use that word or even know what it meant? I had to find her, confront her. Maybe she knew what happened to Jessamine, what would happen to all of us?

Mitch needed a wife he deserved—not a great pretender—even if it meant sacrificing my own happiness. Because in the depths of my realist heart, the truth lurked. The truth I was so reluctant to put into words. *I was deeply in love with him...and the honest and simple life he offered.*

Still unable to speak, I gently retrieved my hand, and my chin quivered when I braved a smile. I turned my face, unable to trust myself from blurting out the confessions that would only break his heart, even if it might lighten mine. How could I tell him I was not the soul mate he thought I was, not the talented woman— damn her—who would outlive him and marry twice more.

We rode on in silence, each of us lost in thought, until the air changed.

It was a wispy gray finger, like the tail of a comet purling in the sky. We both smelled the smoke before we even noticed it. I could see Mitch trying to calculate the source, and the more distance we covered, the faster he drove the horses.

"It's coming from our place," he cried, and a chill of fear jolted through me.

"Maybe Charlie is burning sagebrush."

"Let's hope so." He snapped the reins and called out to the horses as the wagon lurched into high gear. I wedged myself closer to him and braced my feet, holding onto the edge of the seat as we bounced along the primitive road.

When we rounded the last bend in the road, we could see the flames shooting from the barn. The horses were galloping by now, with Mitch snapping the reins as he braced in a stand while I gripped his leg, steel-hard with tension.

The pastured horses whinnied when they spotted us, the Appaloosa running the fence line with the red mare and pony close behind. I couldn't see the other animals or any sign of Charlie or Tallie. Surely, they would have seen our wagon dust and heard Mitch shouting at the horses.

We both leaped from the wagon when he was able to brake about one hundred feet from the barn. I immediately shouted for Tallie, panicking when I heard no response. The fire was confined—mostly to the front of the barn and the roof—but dry hay in the mow made quick tinder, and the wind was driving flames into a pitched firestorm.

"Look in the house," Mitch yelled before we parted in opposite directions.

"Be careful," I yelled back, as he ran toward the barn. Once inside the house, I screamed for Tallie, scrambling up the loft steps on all fours. Her room was empty, the bed still neatly made. I threw open her window to scan the yard and woods beyond. Calling again, without response, I rocketed back to the barn.

Mitch had pulled out saddles, tools and bags of feed, dumping them into a pile several yards behind the barn. With a tarp he wielded like a matador's cape, he was shooing some of the chickens away from their smoldering roosts.

"She isn't in the house," I yelled above the growing snap and roar of the fire. He shook his head, gesturing likewise at the barn.

Orange flames were now snaking across timbers that outlined two thirds of the structure. Thunderclouds of smoke belched from the roof and two small windows. We both screamed into the dense smoke for Tallie and Charlie, until I thought I heard a feeble bleating.

"The lamb. Could she be with the lamb?" I cried, and our eyes locked with terror.

Mitch dipped the tarp in the outside water trough and pulled it over his head. "Stay clear, before the barn collapses."

"No!" I grabbed his arm. "You can't go back in!"

For half a second, our eyes met in shared fear and determination. Nothing would stop him from saving his daughter if he thought it was possible, and he would die trying. He shook me off and disappeared into the heavy smoke pouring out the back door. I could hear him choking out Tallie's name, and I filled a bucket with water and began to follow him until the smoke and heat drove me back. Helpless, I stood as close as I could to the door, screaming his name. If he couldn't see me, I hoped he would at least come to the sound of my voice. *Oh God, please, please let him hear and come back to me!*

In what seemed like an eternity, he shot like a cannonball out of the door, chased by the flaming remnants of the tarp. He raced to the water trough while I doused the tarp with my bucket of water, and when he plunged the lamb into the water, there was a loud hiss...and the sickening smell of burnt wool. His face and arms were blackened by soot, and his hands in the dark water looked pink as patches of loose flesh rose to the surface beside the lifeless body of Tallie's lamb. When he splashed his face and neck with the water, I could see some of his hair and brows were singed. He sputtered with relief and shook like a dog before he fell into the circle of my arms.

"Not...there," he choked. "She's not inside."

He shuttled me back from the driving heat, still gasping and coughing as we stood together watching the barn roof collapse and a new geyser of flame roar up to consume it. I looked around and was relieved to see the cow in the distant pasture, unscathed and still as a statue chewing her cud. The horses had stopped running and were clumped together, snorting and shaking off the ashes that had begun to drift over them.

Once he caught his breath, Mitch drove them further back. I had read about freed horses sometimes running back to their stalls in a burning barn, but our horses knew the security of the barn only in the worst weather.

Chickens didn't have horse sense, however, and I watched with alarm as they tried to find their burning roosts and perished in running balls of cackling flame.

We fell back further as skeleton timbers collapsed, and the heat spread through the air, even warming the ground we stood on. Helpless and stunned, we watched the fire grow and subside, like the ribbons of a sunset, fading into a last, furious glow. The wind was blowing southeast, sending sparks and ashes into the fields, thankfully, away from the house. In a daze, we moved to stamp out the sparks that flew into the garden, grateful to see only the scarecrow had taken most of the damage there. His head and arms were gone, but his screamer face was still intact, drooping over his charred chest.

"Tallie must be at Rachel's," I said, and he nodded. Our hope was confirmed when we saw the Garretts' buckboard and several riders flying down the road toward us. Tallie jumped from the wagon before it stopped and ran into our waiting arms, and we all cried with relief while Finn circled our stronghold, barking in frenzied excitement.

Rachel and her parents joined us while the Garrett boys unhitched lathered and nervous horses from our own wagon and led them to the creek for a drink.

"We came as soon as we saw the smoke," Mary apologized. "It was all downwind."

"What started this?" Henry asked, gaping at the inferno.

Mitch wiped his sweaty face on the remains of his scorched shirt, and stared at his hands, red and swollen. "It was burning when we got back. There was nothing anybody could do."

"Did you get all the animals out?" Rachel cried.

"There are casualties," Mitch muttered, looking sadly at his daughter. "Some of the chickens are lost, and…I tried to save the lamb."

"My lamb." Tallie fell into my arms, burying her face in my chest.

"We can get another lamb, honey." I hugged her tightly, resting my chin on the top of her head. "I'm just glad you're safe. Where's Uncle Charlie?"

Over Tallie's head I noticed Mary throwing an odd look at her husband. "Charlie brought the girls over and ate lunch with us, but when Rachel invited Tallie to stay overnight, Charlie left, saying he had someplace to go. We thought he meant here."

Mitch and I exchanged puzzled looks. "He wasn't here when we got home. When we couldn't find Tallie, we figured they were together."

"Maybe he went to the fort for something," Mitch said.

With a sinking feeling, my hand flew to my mouth.

Chapter Thirty-Six
Beneath the Ashes

Barn embers smoldered for two days. We watched from the porch of the cabin as the glow blossomed and faded in the intermittent wind. The privy enclosure Mitch had been building at the end of the porch became a new shelter for the five remaining chickens and three chicks that survived the fire.

When blisters popped on Mitch's hands, I rubbed them with aloe and loosely wrapped them in linen strips. I could tell he was in pain, but I couldn't stop him from helping Tallie bury her lamb beside the one wolves had killed last year. Tallie fiercely declared she would never raise another lamb or eat mutton as long as she lived. Almost nothing was left of her dead chickens to bury. She added a beak and three claws she found to a box of her keepsakes, which also included the lamb's bell collar.

I convinced her to put the bell on Finn, to keep better track of him, as he was starting to wander out of sight. He always came when called, but his curiosity took him farther from home as he grew to resemble a black and white fox terrier, with short floppy ears and long legs and tail. Mitch thought he might make a good rabbit hunter one day, even with the slight hitch in his leg.

Like snow in summer, white ash seemed to blanket

the ground. I worried about blotches of ash damaging garden vegetables and spent the next two days earnestly dusting and watering the plants that had survived. Mitch quartered off a small area with a coil of rope he had managed to save from the fire, bringing the cow close to the cabin. A frontier home without a cow, I was beginning to understand, would be like a grocery store without a dairy section.

We walked around like zombies, dealing with the losses in quiet restraint, fearing what we would find in the heap of barn ash when it was finally safe to search the debris. Charlie had not returned home yet, and one of the Garrett boys who had checked at the fort told us he wasn't there either.

Three days after the fire, what I dreaded most, I gleaned from Mitch's expression when he took the water pail from my hands. Without a word, he led me back to the porch and told me to sit down on the step.

"He's there." He slowly clenched his fingers over sooty shreds of his hand wraps.

I knew at once who he meant.

"The body is beyond recognition, but this was in his hand." He gave me what was left of Charlie's pocket watch, misshapen, but with the glass face still intact beneath its silver cover. The hands stopped at 2:26. A tear glided down my cheek, and I swiped it away with the back of my hand.

"That isn't all." Mitch squeezed my knee. His eyes were filled with sympathy when they met mine. "Your brother wasn't alone."

I gaped at him. "What do you mean?"

"There are two bodies...fused together."

"Two bodies? But who?"

"Impossible to even tell the gender."

Our eyes met, and we both sighed in unison. He wasn't my brother, and I didn't know him well, but I felt his loss, nevertheless. He *was* my ancestor, Jessamine's only brother, which made him my great great-uncle. What was it Jake had said at Granny's funeral? *Grief lingers only when someone dies young or unexpectedly.* Charlie *was* young, and he certainly died unexpectedly. He also died thinking he had little hope for a happy future, and that alone was enough for tears.

"There's more." Mitch threw an arm across my hunched shoulders. "I also found a revolver in the ashes. Did Charlie own a gun?"

I looked at him, stunned. "I don't know. I never saw him with one."

"The handle and part of the barrel was melted, but I think the rest was nickel plated, most likely a Smith and Wesson .44—a Cavalry favorite."

"Where would Charlie get a gun like that?"

He stared at his feet in thoughtful concentration, but if he had any ideas, he wasn't going to share them. "I think it's best to bury the bodies right away."

I nodded, brushing away tears with my fingers, and rose to get one of the clean sheets we brought back from the Emigrant's Washtub. "I can help."

His hand was heavy on my arm. "I think I should do this alone. When all is ready, I'll fetch you and Tallie."

I pulled the German Bible off the bookcase to find Charlie's name in the dedication pages, and carefully recorded the date he had died. I couldn't read the German version of the "Twenty-third Psalm," but I vaguely remembered the English translation of several phrases. I also remembered a poem I liked that seemed appropriate, and I tried to collect the memory on paper. Charlie needed someone to speak for him. Jessamine would have done that, and right now I was the closest thing he had to a protective older sister.

He was laid to rest near Tallie's pet cemetery. Tied in the sheet, the body shroud looked small and vulnerable for enclosing two people, and it was bleeding dark ash. Each of us released a handful of dirt into the grave that sounded hollow as raindrops on a canvas roof. Mitch gave a blessing in Lakota and clutching the Bible, I led us in the Lord's Prayer while the rest of the dirt was added slowly. My voice cracked when I recited the Housman poem I had penciled on a sheet of paper, hoping I had the gist of it.

> *"Lie you easy, dream you light,*
> *And sleep fast as you may;*
> *And luckier may you find the night*
> *Than ever you found the day."*

Mitch gave me a nod of approval when I finished. Tallie was still and silent, the open grave her cynosure. Mentally, I prepared answers to the questions I expected to get about the poem I recited.

Alfred Housman was an Englishman who would be around Charlie's age in 1886, perhaps not yet famous for his haunting poetry that fed literature classes across the ocean. "When I Was One and Twenty" was one of my all-time favorites, inscribed in the notebook I had intended to use one day in my own teaching curriculum. Of course, I couldn't tell Mitch that and had to dredge up another lie to satisfy his curiosity. *Something Jessamine had learned in high school, or maybe the verse a Fort Laramie Chaplain used at a funeral?* More and more, my conscience prickled with the domino string of lies I was forced to tell.

But Mitch didn't ask about the poem. I could tell he was tired and preoccupied and probably in pain, using blistered hands to clean up the barn debris and dig the graves. I made him soak his hands in cool water each evening and coated them with aloe before wrapping them in clean bandages. He hadn't been able to shave for days. His beard was growing thick, and new lines crinkled at the bridge of his nose.

He was also calculating our losses and future needs, and perhaps that alone was more than enough for any proud man to bear. I helped where I could, shoveling ash that seemed to be a magnet for every change of clothes, offering bits of advice like practical magic, fixing favorite meals, even taking the initiative in the comforting sanctuary of our bed.

****

I was at the creek washboarding a pile of stained clothes when I saw Henry Garrett ride up, and I put my task aside to greet him. He had warmed up to me after he saw the changes in Rachel. The girls had become very close. Transporting them back and forth every few days in my teaching arrangement had become an easy routine. We were wearing a path between homes and hearts, and shy little Rachel was blooming like wild roses in summer, and finally finding her voice.

Garrett removed his hat after he dismounted, and we walked back together to the house. I told him we had found Charlie in the ashes and buried him in the woods. That didn't seem to surprise him.

"Did you find out how the fire started?"

I shook my head. "Mitch found some shattered

lantern glass in the debris, but we couldn't be sure. There was still a lot of dry hay in the mow. It could have just ignited spontaneously." I felt that was a reasonable explanation, and he seemed to agree.

"Your barn sits more in the sun than ours. That may be an advantage in winter, but not when it's the hottest summer in memory," he observed.

I waved and hollered to Mitch in the oat field, and he joined us as we all walked up to the house together. True to form, Garrett dispensed with any small talk and got right to the point.

"I know this must be grieving time, but I jest wanted to give you something to chew on," he began. "We both know that you have a sizeable water supply with the creek. I have a sizeable herd of cattle that need water to thrive, and the trickle of water I once had is a dry gulch now."

As if on cue, he accepted the glass of water I offered him, and smiling, took a long gulp that dribbled down his beard. Mitch gave me a cautious "what-now-glance" over his head.

"So here's the thing," Garrett continued. "You folks don't want to sell, but how about leasing some of your creek land or trading some water rights for a small herd of your own?"

"Is that legal? Can open range be leased?" Mitch asked.

"We'd have to check out the boundaries, but the WSGA might have some sway in the matter."

When I caught Mitch's eye with an inquisitive gesture, he explained, "Wyoming Stock Growers Association."

"According to the territorial governor, there's up to

two million cattle in Wyoming, maybe half that amount of God-damned sheep by now. The only cattle ranches that are thriving this summer are the ones with water access. I would be willing to pay you by the month—or annually if it comes to that...for your water."

Mitch looked at me. "What kind of money are you talking about, Garrett?"

"I'd be fair. Our daughters are thicker than calf splatter, and I appreciate what your missus is doing for Rachel. With that in mind, I'd be willing to spot you twenty dollars a month, or give you a good start on your own herd come next calving season. Cattle are going for four dollars per hundred weight right now. That means forty dollars on the hoof for a well-fed beefer!"

I could tell that Mitch was interested, but he tried not to show it. "I don't know," he grimaced. "Can I talk this over with my wife?"

I raised my eyebrows. All I knew about the worth of beef was that a pound of lean ground round went for roughly four dollars at the Torrington Meat Market, and a steak dinner at the hotel was maybe five times that. Considering the price of a bar of soap in 1886, I thought maybe Garrett's offer was pretty fair.

"There's money in cattle," Garrett continued. "I've made over one hundred fifty percent over the last five years." He paused to let that sink in. "There's eight cattle millionaires in Cheyenne already," he added.

"We're homesteaders, Garrett, not ranchers. We're not looking to get rich, and I don't want to chain my family to something they couldn't handle. You've got sons to help you. I'd have to hire men to do the labor you get free."

"You saying no to both offers, then?"

Mitch hedged, rubbing his chin. "Like I said, Jess and I have to talk about this."

Garrett sighed and looked at me, slightly bemused. Decisions in *his* family were not as democratic, especially where his own wife and daughter were concerned.

"Well, go ahead and chew on this. You can send word with Rachel when you're done talkin' and git down to decidin'." With that, he clamped his hat back on his head and mounted his horse to ride back the way he came, nodding to us with a look that was the back side of friendly.

Chapter Thirty-Seven
Bold Choices

We sat side by side on the porch steps later that night, just as Charlie and I once had, with a lantern between us and spirits to share. The venerable springhouse jug, saved for any crisis, medical or not, gave up its last dregs to explore the possibility of a better life.

"Well, what do you think of Garrett's proposal?" Mitch clinked our mugs together and threw back his shot.

I felt the weight of decision resting uneasy on a substitute wife. "I don't know what to think."

He looked a little annoyed. "You've never lacked an opinion before."

I had already speculated that twenty dollars a month was probably equivalent to twenty times that in my time. Maybe even more, if you took into account the goods and services that were nonexistent temptations in 1886. Mitch couldn't be clearing half that amount with bartered eggs and wood—or even an occasional horse sale. Most of the soldiers at Fort Laramie made thirteen dollars a month. *Shoot, I was lucky to get a haircut for that in my time.*

"Well, Garrett's offer for water rights could be fair," I said cautiously.

He nodded. "It would mean a steady income at

least. But what about the prospect of cattle ranching? If we could hold out 'til next spring, the cattle offer was more generous. We could eventually build a new barn, add on to the house, maybe even send Tallie to a real school someday."

"Hire help, depend on good weather, booms and busts..."

"Sounds like you do have an opinion." He smirked.

I held my hand, palm-side up. "I'm a realist, remember? I like sure things, and the cattle business will have lots of competition from sheep and sugar beets in Wyoming."

"Oh, so you can see into the future?" He gave me a sidelong glance. "Did you catch the art of prophesy from your Birdwoman at the spring?"

I chewed on my fingernail and recalled what I knew about Wyoming history and the cattle wars and oil scandals. "What if there's a hard winter, and cattle don't survive it?" *Wasn't the winter coming up historic for its blizzards?*

"Well, that's a good point. Most ranchers can expect to lose two or three percent of their herd each winter. Catastrophes offset profits in any business, though. Sheepmen expect that, too."

"Sheep have wooly coats and huddle together in bad weather."

"Garrett would probably throw me a necktie party if I decided to go with sheep. Bread isn't broken between sheep and cattle ranchers, Jess."

"Well, I didn't mean sheep were a better alternative. You have to hire shepherds and shearers for them. I just thought you liked being independent, living off the land."

"I do, but I have you and Tallie to consider." He took my hand in his and pointed up to a gibbous moon breaking through the clouds. "I want to give you both a bite of that cheese." He gave me his endearing lopsided smile.

"Actually, it's a lot of basalt rocks," I muttered.

He rolled his eyes and kissed me lightly on the temple. "You decide what we tell Garrett. I'll abide by the wisdom of my prophetic wife."

My throat was growing thick with emotion once again. In the last few days, I had lived in the kingdom of tears and fears, and it was draining the life from me—along with the constant reminders of Jessamine and my thriving attraction to her husband.

I had to make another trip to Fort Laramie to telegram Charlie's Nebraska family. Posting a letter wouldn't do. Lizzie would notice my handwriting was different from her sister's. A telegram would be succinct, without explanations I wouldn't make, even if I could. At some point, Jessamine's sister would expect a letter of details, one that skirted all the circumstances around Charlie's death and who was buried with him. That was a mystery that might *never* be solved, anyway.

I didn't know Lizzie, or how much insight she had to what she had referred to in her letter as *"Charlie's problem."* Was she close enough to her brother to know what was in his heart? Cousin Jake was the closest I had to a real sibling, and I could truthfully say I had little insight to his beliefs or conscience. I didn't even know the details surrounding his divorce.

"Incompatible," he had simply grunted with little remorse when it was over, and we never discussed it

271

again. I had never shared with him or anyone else what happened to me on prom night twelve years ago. Granny probably guessed but never brought it up. Did everyone in my family culture secrets? My life was linked with secrets, past and present. and I was caught like a fly in a spider's web, with the most deceptive secret of all.

"Let's sleep on a decision," I said, rising. "I'm going to bed."

"Good idea." The glint in his eye hid no secret of his intention.

Chapter Thirty-Eight
Résumés

Our race home in the wagon cracked two wheel spokes—enough for Mitch to worry about the stability of another long ride. A spare wheel had burned in the barn. He thought the spokes could be fixed with pine pitch and some kind of tape. When he showed me the wheel, I doubted it could be fixed—even with some gorilla duct tape, given the condition of country roads.

I remembered laughing when Cousin Jake modeled his new graphic tee last fall. It pictured a roll of the gray tape with the slogan, *Duct Tape—the ultimate power tool.* How easy life would be with an all-purpose quick mend to our problems. *Stitch and glue, paste and stick, once again, new and slick!*

We decided to ride the Appaloosa and red mare to Fort Laramie, instead, and sent Tallie to Rachel's for a couple of days. The idea of riding on the back of a beautiful horse on a summer day became less of a thrill after we set off at an extended trot. A half mile away, I was already saddle sore. It had been years since I managed a long trail ride on a pushbutton horse like Dolly. We walked the horses after Mitch realized I was struggling to keep up with the Appaloosa.

"What happened to the girl who once out-raced me from the Three Mile Ranch back to the fort?"

I thought it was safe to say that neither the red

mare nor I were conditioned to race anymore. As if she understood, the mare gave a validating whinny that made us both laugh.

"Are you feeling better this morning?"

I nodded and smiled. In truth, my roiling stomach told me breakfast was trying for a desperate escape after the jolting trot. On foot, however, I had a similar feeling the last week but chalked it up to heat stroke after hauling water to the garden, scrubbing clothes, and setting up a new batch of soap. A pot of peppermint tea and an evening foot soak in the shade of the porch was always the perfect fix, along with a good night's sleep.

Mitch had spent half of yesterday at the Garrett ranch, delivering Tallie and the worksheets I had created for the girls. Since the fire, Tallie's grief over the loss of her pets, as well as her uncle, began to breed an uncharacteristic listlessness in the child. She seemed to recover with a change of scenery, I noticed, and after talking it over with Mary Garrett, we began to alternate equal time spent at the Garrett ranch.

Mitch and I had also composed an informal contract—in duplicate—to show Garrett, committing him to a monthly stipend in exchange for water access. I was pleased Mitch had readily agreed a short term water lease was our best option. If the coming winter proved to be as devastating to Wyoming cattle as I knew it would be, the lease could be amended or nullified, and Mitch could opt for the alternative offer. That is, if Garrett had any cattle left to spare after the blizzards of 1887.

However, I knew there would always be cattle in Wyoming—more so in Mitch's lifetime. Oil and sugar beets were still future resources. After some discussion, both men had signed the agreements, each keeping a copy, and Mitch was given twenty dollars for the first month of water rights.

"This has to be in his best interest, too," Mitch told me that evening. "He fears sheep will take over the territory." He rubbed the side of his nose with a finger and gave me a crooked grin. "We rode out together to look over his herd, and I learned a lot about grazing choices and cattle types. He's serious about integrating his herd with bovines and Texas longhorns. He already sent his eldest son to Cheyenne, looking to buy some and drive them up here."

I had smiled at his new enthusiasm. "You sound like *cattle rancher* will soon be added to your résumé."

"My résumé?"

"Your list of talents."

"Herding you was my greatest talent." He pulled me roughly into his arms and nipped at my neck. "We do make a good team, don't we Jess?"

I had begun to believe he was right about that.
****

After exchanging a small bag of new soap for cash at the trading post, I went directly to the Fort Laramie post office where the civilian telegrapher had a niche and handed him the scrap of paper containing the succinctly-worded telegram Lizzie would receive:

Charlie died in barn fire July 20. RIP on homestead. Jess.

Until I received a letter back from Jessamine's sister asking for details, I had time to figure out how to respond more kindly. Not knowing Lizzie, how insightful she was about Charlie, or what her sensibilities were on the subject of his sexual preference, my head was telegraphing its own reminder; *"Oh what a tangled web we weave, when first we practice to deceive."*

The only "missing" notices posted on the bulletin board at the sutler's were for an orange tabby cat, a silver pocket watch, and a green woven cartridge belt. When I had asked Lucy London about any people disappearing lately, she gave me a curious look and then made some derisive comment about Laramie's AWOL soldiers.

"Around pay days—and summer weather—you won't find anybody missing," she said.

While Mitch was busy checking out the lumber supply and possibly negotiating for a timber exchange to replace the barn, I headed for the laundress quarters in the opposite direction and learned there was no foreign-speaking laundress at the garrison who read palms. When I described the bejeweled portly woman and her bird, I was regarded with amusement, skepticism, and pity, sometimes all three in one expressive face. Dejected, I was heading back to the trading post when a dark-skinned Indian boy caught up to me.

"You looking for a woman with a black bird?" he asked in perfect English.

"Do you know where I can find her?"

"The Birdwoman is *I'cimani.* Soldiers call her and those in her camp *Travelers.*" He pointed north, beyond the trading post. "Near the stage coach stables, you will find her wagon."

I thanked him, and his dark eyes lit up when I pressed a small coin into his palm. We had passed the stage line on the road to Fort Laramie. The Rustic Hotel was south of the stage line on the road, not far from the sawmill where Mitch had gone with both horses. The area was about a half mile from where I stood near the bakery, rooted to the spot until the aroma of oven-fresh bread made my stomach growl. I stopped in the sutler's and bought some peppermint sticks for Tallie. Sucking on one of them settled my stomach while I hiked to the stage line.

Though Birdwoman was not a laundress, she also was not a figment of my imagination...or even a dream as Mitch had teased, until he saw the feather. I pulled it from my pocket, caressing the silky edge of the vane. What the woman read in my palm, what she implied was too precise to be discounted. She knew I was not from this century. She even knew what I was beginning to suspect. She had hinted my life was at risk if I stayed. She had called me a realist, with many decisions to make. God help me, if she was even partially accurate, my fate was clear as the lifeline in my palm, and she was a key player in the choices before me.

It was the longest half mile I ever walked.

Chapter Thirty-Nine
Fine Dining

The Rustic Hotel would never pass even one star standards in my time. Made of half sawn logs with a sod roof, it had only paned glass windows to recommend it. Windows and a convenient location on the stage line. It also had stables and corrals for horses—a living diagram of the photos on display in the Visitor Center I was familiar with in my time.

When the park service hired me, I had also learned the hotel was built in 1876 by the post trader of that year. At the time, it was also supposed to have clean linens and a cook to provide meals in the dining room. Several years later, a patron complained of bed bugs, and the corral began to pollute the fort's water supply. I was probably viewing it now—only ten years old—at the height of its worst reputation. Across the road, to the left, I could see the sawmill, but before I joined Mitch, I had to find the Birdwoman.

Several active children greeted me as I approached a few bright-colored wagons and tents in the distance to the right of the hotel. Grinning, they all wore bandanas or scarfs somewhere on their body—head, neck, or waist. The girls wore skirts that seemed short for the times, showing brown legs and dirty feet. Two of the older girls sported woven ankle bracelets, their ears pierced by silver hoops. They ushered me toward a makeshift table displaying carved or beaded crafts and baskets filled with polished wooden crosses, grass bracelets, or stones sparkling with bits of quartz or amethyst.

"You see what you like, lady. We make special deal," a dark-eyed boy with curly hair invited. "All charms guarantee wishes. Come, choose for your heart." He gestured and bowed with the grace of a courtier, taking my hand in his.

I laughed. "You *are* selling charm, young man. How much are these?"

"How much coin do you have?" He grinned.

I jingled together the few coins left in my pocket, hesitating to show their worth. "I came here to find a woman with a black bird, and I'll pay gladly if you take me to her."

Looking around, the only adult I saw leaned against his wagon, nonchalantly carving something with a pocket knife. There were four wooden wagons with round roofs, painted like faded old circus wagons, with narrow doors below smaller portholes with shuttered flaps.

One of the wagons had the figure of a long-legged bird on the door.

The boy followed my gaze. "That's Rosie's wagon." He nodded, holding out his hand.

I gave him the coins I had and stood aside as he knocked on the door. When we heard a loud squawk, he opened the door and ushered me inside. The walls were painted black, but tiny pinholes of light from outside crossed the room like laser beams. When my focus adjusted, I could make out a bed, table and two chairs, a trunk and a cupboard, all decorated in colorful scrolls and symbols. The bird, chained to a perch at the far end, glared at us through eyes red as rubies.

Almost like a genuflect, the boy made a strange gesture, muttering something in a foreign language. "Rosie must be with Old Harvey."

"Old Harvey?"

"The hotel cook. Not so good as Rosie. She show him how to make goulash and halva for guests."

I thanked him and walked back with an entourage of children following me, chattering like magpies in their own language. *Travelers.* I knew the term, often interchanged with *gypsies.* How did they ever get here from Eastern Europe? Why didn't any of the laundresses know about them? *Or maybe they did.* Fort Laramie had to be the melting pot of the West. Two hundred and fourteen acres with a history of bringing together French fur trappers, Native Americans, English, Scotch, Irish, and German recruits, and now, even Hungarian gypsies. It was hard to imagine any of them coming together in "Kumbaya" combination.

The children drifted away as I approached the hotel and noticed a few people sitting outside on chairs, facing the sun. A tall man holding a small girl approached me in the dooryard.

"Were those pikers bothering you?" He frowned, with a sour glance at the retreating children. "They've been warned not to bother the guests or stage passengers."

"Why, no, they were no trouble," I replied.

"If it weren't for Rosie and the help they give us in the stables, we'd chase them all away. They're more trouble than the Injuns, always promoting or selling something."

Hesitantly, I held out my hand and introduced myself. After juggling the child in his arms, he wiped a hand on his shirt and told me his name was James Hogle and the baby was Myrtle.

"My wife and I manage this place now. Are you looking for a room?"

"No, I'm looking for your cook."

"Old Harvey?"

"Old Rosie." I smirked.

He made a disapproving noise and pushed his hat back on his head, looking me over more closely. "The cooks are fixing lunch now. You can certainly get a better meal here than in the commissary if you need a good fill-up."

"You're a pretty good promoter, yourself, Mr. Hogle. My husband is at the mill. I think we both could use 'a good fill-up' about now."

****

We sat at a small corner table in a Spartan room dominated by two large trestle tables that seated about ten people. Most of them looked more like ranch help, rather than patrons. When I peeked under the stained tablecloth on my side, I could see tomato seeds lodged in a crack.

"Not much ambiance to recommend fine dining," I said half to myself.

Mitch chuckled. "This is the only *fine-dining* place you'll find between Cheyenne and the Black Hills. And fine dining in the Hills would probably mean venison you kill and roast yourself." He winked. "After this last week, I think we deserve to splurge, especially now that we have some monthly cash coming in." I could tell the fact had lifted his spirits.

"Well, I heard the cook here has some imagination."

"Old Harvey? I imagine he's never made French fried potatoes or cookies with chocolate bits in them."

I smiled demurely. "I want to prove to you that I didn't imagine the Birdwoman at the warm springs. She's here—cooking with Old Harvey."

Mrs. Hogle interrupted us and took our order for goulash and sour dough biscuits.

"So she's not a laundress," he said, showing a little surprise.

"She's a *Traveler*, but not the stage kind. You know—a Gypsy; suave people known for fortune telling and fleecing."

"Fleecing sheep?"

"More like denuding people...of cash, according to Mr. Hogle."

"Gamblers then."

"You might say that, but I don't think they get sucked into addiction too easily."

Mr. Hogle in the flesh interrupted us this time, balancing two beers with Myrtle still attached to his hip, with her finger up her nose. When I introduced Mitch, Hogle seemed a little flustered, forgetting to offer his hand. "Enjoy your meal," he muttered in quick departure.

I leaned toward Mitch and lowered my voice. "I don't think he trusts anybody with black hair and darker skins."

"Well, I'm used to that, usually from anybody new to the West." With furrowed brow, he clinked his beer bottle against mine. "Trust goes both ways—maybe farthest of all between those we care about."

I grimaced after taking a sip. It was warm and filling, with a taste as bitter as the prom memories that made me swear off boys...and beer. "You'll have to finish this." I held my fist over the soft burp that escaped my mouth. "Beer just doesn't agree with me."

The bowl of goulash was worth our two-dollar dinner. The biscuits were feather light and the halva made with sunflower seeds and cut into bars was a perfect dessert, something neither of us had ever tasted before. I was delighted when Rosie herself delivered two cups of tea after dessert.

"Do you remember me?" I asked her.

She scrutinized my face with a wrinkled brow then took up my hand and examined my palm.

"I remember." She squeezed my fingers and glanced furtively at Mitch. "And this is the father?"

I felt the color drain from my face as I stared at her mutely. Mitch looked from her to me and back again.

"I also read tea leaves," she added, circling the rim of the teacup with her forefinger.

I felt suddenly sick.

"I have special teacups in my wagon." Her black eyes drilled into mine. "You come to me, anytime, missy. Sometimes leaves explain what palms can hide." With a knowing smile that sent a chill through me, she nodded and left us each gaping after her.

"So that's your Birdwoman," Mitch said quietly. "Is it true, what she said?"

"I...I don't know if tea leaves are better..."

"You know what I mean."

I sighed and looked away, anywhere but into the fathomless green. "I don't know yet. I can't be sure."

"You will tell me when you are sure, then."

"Yes, of course." I ventured a quick smile, scraping my fingernail over a stain on the tablecloth.

"You're scared, aren't you?"

I nodded carefully, not wanting to shake loose the sudden welling in my eyes. Other words came to mind besides scared—sick, confused, indecisive. I sat quietly, my hands folded on the table while I surreptitiously studied the bracelet lines on my wrists while he surreptitiously studied me. I was truly relieved when he finished his beer in one long gulp, planted some money on the table, and took my arm to lead me outside, out of the cloying drift of hops and garlic and into fresh air.

We walked in silence to a copse of trees where the horses were tethered. Before he untied them, he took me in his arms and pressed his lips against my forehead.

"I know how you feel, Jess, and you're not alone. It scares me too, maybe for another reason." He held me away and peered into my eyes. "I swore once that I would always protect you, and I meant that, but there are some things beyond my control. I can't step in to go where you have to go. No man can do that when his wife gives birth. I can't take on your pain and disappointment when it doesn't work out, but that doesn't mean I can't feel what you feel. I thought my heart would break when you almost died after our son was born."

He pulled me tightly against him until I was sure I would suffocate from his body heat or the heady scent of beer on his breath. My legs went limp as the ground began to quiver beneath my feet. I looked up when I heard the rolling thunder, but the sun was still shining through the trees. Then it appeared over the bend in the road, the Deadwood coach hurtling toward the stage station, the driver reining in six lathered horses who knew they were close to the oasis that ended their long run.

We watched the station come to life with stick figures running to meet the coach that squealed to a stop as a cheer went up from passengers inside. Happy, I supposed, to be stopping at the end of a jolting and dangerous ride. The very thought of it propelled me to a nearby bush where I delivered myself of the best goulash I had ever eaten.

We watered the horses in the Laramie River, and I waded in to wash my face and neck but stopped short of drinking from it myself. Mitch had a canteen of spring water he offered me, but it was warm from the sun. Nevertheless, I swished it in my mouth and spit it out, at least diffusing the taste of gall from my stomach.

"Poor baby." He helped me onto the mare and squeezed my leg with a worried glance.

We rode home slowly. I pulled my hat low over my eyes and pulled the neckerchief I wore up to my chin, hoping to absorb the silent tears that slid down my cheeks and tickled my neck.

Chapter Forty
True Confessions

Somewhere between Fort Laramie and the homestead, the battle in my head came to the only end game a realist could make. Emotionally exhausted and physically stiff after the long ride, I felt drained to the core and must have looked it. After dismounting, I leaned against the mare's neck and closed my eyes, burying my forehead in her silky mane while I clutched her cheek strap. As if tunneled through a fog, I heard a deep voice come at me, the words slow and precise, and then I was moving toward the cabin in slow motion, drifting without using my feet.

"Are you all right, Jess?"

He was carrying me, just as he did three months ago, onto the porch, through the door, setting me gently in the rocker.

"I'll make you some mint tea," he said. "That always worked before."

Numbly, I watched him, pouring filtered creek water from the gallon jar we kept on the counter into the kettle, lighting the stove, and rummaging through the cupboard for tin cups and the canister of tea leaves. He glanced up at me from time to time, with a worried smile, making small talk about the long day, long week, the need for more tea leaves. He was wearing the Levi's I had given him for his birthday, and I noticed they were a little tighter and faded now from wear, still dusty on the seat from our ride.

When the tea kettle whistled, he pulled it off the stove without using a hot pad on the handle, and I smiled as he cursed and shook his fingers, then made some deprecating comment about healing hands and his talent in the kitchen.

He handed me the warm cup and stood with his back against the fireplace, cradling his own cup as he smiled down at me. I took a long gulp, savoring the minty taste and smell that always revived me.

"I almost forgot something." He set his cup on the mantel and hurried out the door. "Be right back."

My hands were uncommonly cold as I cradled the warm cup on my lap, and I wiggled my bare toes in the bearskin as I began to rock, feeling suddenly very old...and very frightened about what I knew I had to do. I could hear the chickens cackling from their new roost on the porch, raising the volume when Mitch vaulted past them.

He was hiding something behind his back. "I got these at the trading post for you and Tallie, and forgot I had them in my saddle bag." He produced two oranges he proceeded to juggle before me with amazing skill. "I know how you said you liked them, and the Trader doesn't get them all that often. These were the only two I could find that weren't bruised."

When I began to sob, his concentration broke and one of the oranges dropped with a thud and rolled across the floor. "What now?" He frowned. "I thought you'd like some fresh fruit, Jess."

"I'm not Jessamine," I cried.

He looked at me sharply. "So we're back to that

287

again? I assumed the identity crisis blew over when we began to make love again."

With the heels of both hands, I rubbed my eyes and stared at him. "Oh God, I never was Jessamine. I...I can't ever live up to the pedestal you put her on."

He looked slightly pissed, slightly amused, turning the orange over and over in his hands. "You certainly look like her," he said quietly.

"My feet are bigger," I mumbled.

He made a noise ripe with sarcasm. "So who do you think you are?"

"I'm Jessica Brewster."

"Jessica, huh?" He carefully set the orange on the mantel and leaned against the fireplace, crossing his arms. "Then how did you come about replacing my wife...Jess...ica?"

I took a deep breath and gulped down the rest of my tea, concentrating on my cup, unable to meet his eyes. "I work at old Fort Laramie and was at this living history tea party, and, and then I was on a boardwalk that wasn't there before, and you, you were leaning over me, and everything was different—the buildings, the trees, the people...the year." I looked up to gauge his reaction.

His jaw was tight as a drum, his eyes narrow. "The year?"

I gripped the ends of the rocker arms, digging my fingernails into the wood until I could feel my hands cramp. "I drove to work that morning in my red Honda hybrid. A car—a car," I exploded, my voice rising shrilly, "with four rubber tires and an instrument panel that looks like something on an airplane, and I had my cell phone on the console—a cordless phone that could connect me with anyone on the planet, and I wore my purple Crocs—rubber sandals that molded to my big feet." I was screaming now. "The tea party was at Fort Laramie, a hundred and twenty-six years from now."

He was breathing heavy, still drilling me with his eyes; his whiskers—even the hair on his arms—seemed to bristle with electricity.

The orange and both family photos leaped to the floor when he slammed his fist on the mantel, and his harsh laugh made me cringe.

"Christ, you do have some imagination...Jes-si-ca." He spit my name tersely, pronouncing each syllable. "You know, if you were saying this shit a hundred years ago, you'd be burned at the stake."

Hot tears were raining down my cheeks, skidding off my chin, melting in my mouth. I gulped, staring at him, imploring.

"I *tried* to tell you this before. I can't...I can't expect you to believe me, but it's all true." I was choking on half-sobs that caught in my throat like barbs. "You...you must have guessed. I know you...you noticed I knew things...said things..." I took a deep breath and cleared my eyes with an impatient sweep my hand.

"Bras and black lace bikinis—all are common things in my time. Even the 'F' word you found so, so offensive is...is as common as indoor plumbing...and you don't have to be a...a whore to say it."

He began to pace, his jaw popping with the rhythm of his breath and the beat of my pounding heart. He stopped suddenly and pulled me out of the rocker, digging his hands into my shoulders.

"If you believe all this, how can you deny your

289

own child? What the hell are you going to tell Tallie?"

I tossed my head and a sharp wail cut through my throat. "Oh God, you still don't believe me." He was startled when I pushed him away, angrily blurting. "I love Tallie—how could anyone *not* love her—but she is not my child. I've never had a child. I never *wanted* one!"

Everything about him was clenched in anger as he stared at me, his teeth, his jaw, his fists. I backed away, shaking now from the storm roiling in his eyes. Fighting for my own control, I squared my shoulders and lifted my chin.

"Tallie and I are linked through ancestors. Her daughter left me Jessamine's journals and the Calling Stone and, and a basement full of boxes…" I took another deep breath, choking on the truth I knew would damn us both. "I was born in 1982," I shouted. "Do you hear me? Nearly one hundred years from now!"

His face crumbled, then turned a deep red, and even his hair seemed to spike with voltage. He lunged at me, slapping me hard across the face. I cried out and dropped to my knees, bending over the core of my pain. I thought for a minute he was going to kick me, but I heard him stamp out the door, yelling what sounded like an Indian war cry that went on and on, until I clamped my hands tight over my ears and heard only the mewling of my own voice and the brittle snapping of my shattered heart.

When I pulled myself up to the door, I watched the dust trail that led down to the creek, watched him splash across and take up the road beyond, riding the Appaloosa as if he were chased by the hounds of hell.

I crawled into bed like a wounded animal, and

hugging the feather pillow to my heaving chest, I buried my wet face in Jessamine's neatly-stitched quilt.

Chapter Forty-One
Phoenix Rising

I woke to a familiar sound, a little more garbled and hoarse, definitely not the clarion call of a proud rooster. For a minute I lay still, dazed and confused, taking in my surroundings. Through the paned glass window, the morning light flashed six perfect squares on the wall of pegged clothes across from the bed. The wash stand, the mirror, the kerosene lamp, the throne, they were all there, touchstones of the room I had slept in for months. A room dominated by a bed I had shared...with guilt and undeniable ecstasy.

I padded over to the corner to use the throne, then washed my hands and face before glancing in the mirror. My eyes were red and swollen, and I could almost make out a stained handprint on the right side of my face. I waggled my jaw painfully, then held a wet cloth against it. The pain was nothing, nothing compared to the heaviness in my chest and the rumbling in my stomach. *Nothing more than I deserved.*

I rushed outside in bare feet and retched beside the porch. The sun was lighting up the sky, promising a bright blend to the dark grief that was my justice. Birds began their morning song, mingling now with hoarse, intermittent crowing that caught my attention once again. It had been more than a week since the fire, and we all assumed the rooster had perished with most of his harem. I stepped off the porch and walked around the cabin, still dazed, but eager to find something solid, something resurrected from the shambles of my life.

His tail feathers were short and singed. He was thinner, his wattle gone, and the red comb on his head was charred and leathery, but otherwise, he was intact. I held out a handful of chicken feed, and he rushed to peck it out of my hand while I ran my hand over the ridge of his backbone. The hens couldn't see him, but they knew he was there. I could hear them cackling like little witches from their makeshift roosts on the porch.

Only two eggs from the surviving hens told me that routine takes a vacation—post trauma—even with dumb animals. Yet, there was comfort in routine, a natural tranquilizer that made me believe life would go on. I needed to know that, needed to know breakfast eggs and chicory coffee would fortify me for whatever came next. And if I didn't have to think too much, and could just let life swirl around me in a stupefied state, I would survive the minute, the hour, the day, maybe even whatever fate lay beyond. Like Frank the rooster, I could rise from the ashes to crow again. I found my shoes and went to milk the cow.

****

Tallie returned home later in the day, chaperoned this time by Mary and Rachel, with Finn announcing their arrival in the dooryard. Mary and I exchanged glances, each of us telegraphing angst in a single look. Tallie greeted me with a bright smile, then skipped off with Rachel to lead the horses to the creek.

"What happened now?" Mary mounted the porch and could see my face more clearly. "You look terrible."

I nodded, trying to summon a thin smile. "It's all finally catching up with me, I guess." *In for a penny, in for a pound, I had become so damned good at massaging the truth.*

"What about you? Is it the girls?"

She snorted a little. "The girls are always a joy and comfort. Henry left this morning for Cheyenne. It's been ten days since our oldest boy Jed left to see about getting some bovines, and we haven't heard from him since."

I invited her inside for a cup of coffee. "Is that unusual? It *is* nearly a hundred miles away." *Without a cell phone, no easy way to track and communicate at a distance.*

"Jed was supposed to ride to Fort Laramie to catch the Deadwood Stage to Cheyenne. Henry told Jed to telegraph the fort when he reached our contact at Abney's Livery in Cheyenne, and relay back how many bovines we could get. Depending on the number and arrangements, we would decide whether he needed drovers to bring them back here. Our nineteen-year-old, Luke, went to the fort the other day to see if there was a telegram waiting." She took a tiny sip of coffee, then added some sugar from the bowl on the table and stirred briskly.

"So was there a telegram?"

"'Twas, but not from our boy. Abney said he couldn't hold the bovines for us any longer." She stared at me through worried eyes that held her own tears at bay. "Luke checked at the Fort Laramie stage station, and nobody there remembered seeing Jed or his horse."

I chewed my lip. "Could he have decided to ride his horse to Cheyenne?"

She shrugged. "Henry said with all the money I sewed into his waistband, it would be safer and faster for him to take the coach. We both thought a lone rider could get waylaid more easily, but Jed told us he was a grown man now, and if we trusted him enough to make deals, we should trust he could fend off any attack with his pistol."

In the back of my mind, something niggled at me. "What kind of pistol did he have?"

"I hate all guns. Henry knows that, so he keeps all their hardware in a gun safe in the barn. All I know, it was a big pistol, Smith—something."

"Smith and Wesson?"

Mary shrugged again. "None of the other boys liked it. Luke even claimed it gave him a rash on his hand when he used it once. Why do you ask?"

Mitch said the gun found in the ashes of the barn was nickel plated. My earlobes always turned red from nickel plated pierced earrings. Luke and I probably shared a common allergy to the mineral. My stomach lurched when I took a sip of coffee that suddenly tasted like dishwater. I swallowed hard, ignoring the question.

"Wasn't Jed engaged to be married this fall?"

She sighed deeply. "Well, that's probably why Henry sent him on this mission alone. His girl, Emily, broke the engagement off a few weeks ago, and Jed was so disjointed Henry thought his brain was going cork-dry."

She opened her mouth to go on, then caught herself and worried her lip for a few moments. When she lowered her voice, she looked at me shyly. "Can you keep a secret?"

I nodded once, almost afraid of what I would hear

next.

"I heard Henry yelling at Jed one afternoon when they thought they were alone. Henry was goading him to act like a man, and when Jed began to cry, Henry must have felt guilty for riding him so. He told him he could go alone to Cheyenne for the bovines—if he pulled himself together. Then he said...then he said something, I can scarce believe..." She gave me a look of such pitiful sadness, I had to blink. "I'll never forgive him, Jess. He told Jed he'd allow him some extra money for...for The House of Mirrors."

"The House of Mirrors?"

You know what that is, don't you?" She wiped her eyes on her skirt. "The girls there are just a classed-up version of them that cribbed at the Three Mile Ranch. Henry told him after a few dips of his wick, he'd soon forget Emily."

Dips of his wick? I chewed my lip again, this time to keep from smiling. I was familiar with the history of the ranch, just three miles from Fort Laramie. The notorious buildings that remained were put on the National Register of Historic Places, like Fort Laramie. Prostitution was legal in Wyoming well into the twentieth century, and Cheyenne was once famous for its brothels, even had a street designated for them— probably where The House of Mirrors was located.

I reached out to take Mary's hand and offer my silent comfort with a firm squeeze. I couldn't think of anything to say that might give her hope, suspecting as I did what really happened to her son. This was something Mitch needed to know about. As if cued by my thoughts, Tallie interrupted us.

"Where's Pa?" She stood at the door with Rachel

close behind, holding a bucket of acorns gathered from beneath the bur oak.

I gave her the most believable answer I had already prepared. "Wood detail for the fort. He may be gone a couple days."

Lying to Tallie pained me more than lying to anyone else, for some reason, and I automatically crossed my fingers behind my back, hoping this one didn't count. Mitch would be back. As angry as he was with me, he would never abandon his daughter, especially if he thought he was leaving her care in the hands of a lunatic...or a witch. I forced a smile of reassurance. *Lunatic, liar, imposter, fornicator.* If I ever flew back to my own century to lead a normal life, it would only be a holding pattern. I was convinced more than ever I had solid reservations in the Netherworld.

Chapter Forty-Two
Return of the Native

The pony cart wasn't much bigger than a wheelbarrow with two rickety wheels that screamed for the need of oil. Watering the garden while snacking on the last of the raspberries, Tallie and I heard the cart approach long before it hit the crossing. I recognized one of the gypsy boys from the camp near the Rustic Hotel, driving a shaggy pony with a long switch. I also recognized the sorry looking Appaloosa gimping alongside the cart.

Dropping our water cans, we ran to intercept it, and the closer we came, we could see two long denim-clad legs dangling from the rear of the cart. Tallie's scream stopped the squealing cart in its tracks, while my heart shimmied up to my throat. Mitch's head was propped at an angle against his saddle in the bed of the cart, his eyes closed, his bearded chin on his chest, with the saddle blanket thrown over him. The smell was overpowering.

"Is he, is he dead?" I managed to sputter.

"Dead drunk," the boy snarled with disgust. "Rosie told me the spotted horse would lead me here. I help you unload him at the house."

With her hands covering her ears, Tallie ran behind the squealing cart, while I managed to halter the App and lead him to pasture. His coat was dirty and stiff as brush bristles, dried from a lathered run. He smelled as rank as his master but managed to trumpet a thin whinny that got an immediate response from the little herd greeting him at the new fence line.

With clumsy effort, we managed to haul the dead weight out of the cart and lay it flat on the porch. I told Tallie to fill every bucket we had with creek water. The boy tagged along with her, no doubt hoping to get a drink and water his pony, still hitched to the wagon and heaving a little from the long trek.

I unbuttoned Mitch's soiled shirt and tore it loose at the arms, then pulled off his boots and Levi's, tossing them into a pile in the yard. He moaned a little once freed of his clothes. Naked and inebriated, Ironman didn't look so tough. Especially with his eyes closed and hair and beard matted with puke. Finn began to lick him on the face but backed away with a chastened look that almost made me chuckle. Out of consideration for Tallie, I got a towel from the house and draped it over his torso.

The first bucket of cold water on his face shocked him into consciousness. He sputtered and cursed, and his head jerked up, then bounced back with a thump against the porch deck.

"Serves you right, you bastard."

The boy laughed while Tallie gaped at me in shock.

When I splashed him with another bucket of cold water, his eyes opened a slit, and he tried to rise on his elbows, shaking his head with effort. With my bare foot, I pushed him back down, and he grabbed for my ankle protesting, with a string of curses that included the infamous "F" word.

Again, I squelched a chuckle when I glanced at Tallie's shocked face. "Sweetie, why don't you make us a pot of coffee," I told her. "I'll scrub him down before we put him to bed." She had probably never seen her father—nor anyone else in this condition. Come to think of it, neither had I, but *my* can-do instincts were kicking in. Tallie tearfully disappeared into the kitchen, and I turned to the boy who obviously was not shocked by anything he witnessed. He told me his name was Rigo.

"Do you know any good remedies for a hangover, Rigo?"

The boy grinned and shrugged. "Pacal, maybe?"

"What is pacal?"

"Soup, made from stomach of sheep or cow, with plenty of garlic and pepper."

"Well, we'll skip that cure," I muttered. *Though a dose of garlic might seem like Ralph Lauren aftershave on him just now.* I studied the body sprawled at my feet, muttering half to myself, "Just what were you drinking?"

"Rosie give him *slivovitsa* at campfire," the boy said.

"Rosie, the Birdwoman?"

He nodded. "Your man came at Rosie like a big wind, but she calm him down good."

"I see." I wondered just how Rosie accomplished *that* feat. "Well, I thank you for bringing him back home. Can I get you something to eat or drink? We have bread and ripe tomatoes, maybe a glass of milk? Oats for your pony?"

Rigo ate everything we offered but especially favored the milk. The condition of his teeth told me milk was probably not a staple in his diet. He fed his pony oats by hand and turned her loose to drink from the bucket of water we set near the porch.

I washed Mitch with a rag and soap, scrubbing out a lot of pent up frustration and disgust, which proved to be dicey when I had to dodge his flailing arms. Another rinse with a bucket of creek water, this one warmed a bit by a pot of boiling water, and the smell was almost undetectable, unless you came within a foot of his open mouth.

Before Rigo left, we had Mitch propped up against the house, drinking black coffee and glaring darkly at us all. When I offered to help him rise to go to bed, he mumbled he didn't need my help and holding his towel protectively at his waist, he struggled to rise, took two steps, and folded like a jackknife, losing the towel. We managed to pull him back up, and this time he cooperated enough to make it to the bedroom before collapsing on the bed. I tucked the quilt around him, threw up the window to freshen the air, then changed my own tainted clothes after taking a cursory sponge bath.

I fixed a light supper for Tallie, both of us eating without much appetite or conversation. When she finished the dishes, she trudged up to the loft without her usual goodnight kiss. I settled for the night on the bearskin rug with my pillow, wishing the familiar chorus of night crickets could drown out the sound of a buzz saw coming from the bedroom.

Chapter Forty-Three
A New Deal

Mitch slept through Frank's abbreviated morning alarm. Again, Tallie was unusually quiet during morning chores and breakfast, and feeling drained myself after Mary's disclosures and tending Mitch, I understood why. Her father was her hero. I didn't know what kind of relationship she had with Jessamine, but once again, I felt responsible as a substitute mother. Wasn't there a catch phrase or physician's code in triage—*First Do No Harm?* Or maybe it was something missionaries were taught as a priority. At any rate, I felt this special nine-year-old—who was destined to become the mother of my beloved Granny Lou— needed some kind of solace for the changes in her life.

Changes I had brought on. *I was her missionary,* ad litem.

"Honey." I patted the bench seat beside me. "Come sit down." I put my arm around her thin little shoulders and hugged her against me. She looked up at me with wide green eyes, paler than her father's, which added to her innocence, and my own trepidation. There was more to mothering than I ever imagined. My stomach fluttered a little, maybe anxiety, maybe the morning nausea that was growing worse. My own life was inundated with *maybes*, and the desperate need for my own personal missionary—or guardian angel.

"Tallie, your pa loves you very much," I began, and her eyes instantly moistened. "What you saw yesterday was...well, just not typical of him. Sometimes, when life gets too complicated, we make choices that make us sick."

"Like Pa was sick yesterday?"

"Exactly. You know, when you cut your finger or scrape your knee, you try to heal the wound and take away the pain with ointment and a band aid."

"A band aid?"

"Something to cover the wound, like the wrap we put around Finn's leg."

She nodded solemnly.

"Well, sometimes grownups use liquor like a band aid to fix what wounds their heart. Your pa did that, but the fixer poisoned him and he got sicker. Rigo was nice enough to bring him home to us, so we could heal him in a better way."

"But why did you call him a bastard, Ma? I know what that means, you know."

I tried hard to keep a straight face as I focused on her upturned chin.

"What do you think it means?"

"It's an ugly shaming word that means he was born without a pa, right?"

I tapped the tip of her nose with my index finger. "You're going to be a formidable woman someday, Tallie. There isn't much that gets by you."

"Rachel heard her brother Jed call their pa that once, and he got whipped for it."

"Well, sometimes, in the heat of anger our mouths work faster than our heads. That was wrong, Tallie. I was angry with your pa, when I should have been more understanding."

"Do you still love Pa?"

Navigating around the lump in my throat took a moment or two. "Maybe too much." I nodded. "But even love has expectations."

She looked at me quizzically.

"Like you and Finn, Tallie. You expect him to come when you call him, and when he takes off after a rabbit and doesn't listen to you, well, you get angry. I've heard you call him a dirty dog, and I've seen you push him away when he tries to lick you with doggie remorse."

She began to smile. "I never can stay mad at him, though."

"And that's because you love him and understand his instincts. We all make mistakes, big and little ones, but that doesn't make us bad people or *dirty dogs*."

Her freckles seemed to collide when she wrinkled her nose again. "Well, I could never stay mad at Pa, either."

"Good to know, Tallie." I gave her a hug, and when she chained her arms around my neck and gave me a resounding kiss on my cheek, tears flooded my eyes. I quickly brushed them away with the back of my hand. "Where is that dirty dog, anyway? I haven't seen him this morning."

"I'll go find him, Ma." She wore her favorite tan corduroys that had been handed down from one of the younger Garrett boys, and she hiked them up and ran out the door with her usual can-do enthusiasm. I brushed another tear from my face and sighed deeply, holding my head in my hands.

"Thank you for that."

Startled, I looked up to see Mitch standing in the shadows against the far wall, fully dressed. His shirt was buttoned wrong, his hair mussed like a dark cloud around a face finally reflecting the age of a work-worried man of forty-three.

"You heard?" I asked.

He nodded. "Aside from your artful lying, you *might* make a good mother."

"Then you believe what I told you...who I really am?"

He crossed the room, poured himself a cup of coffee, and sat heavily down across the table from me. Close up, I could see dark circles around his red-rimmed eyes, the furrow between them deeply etched. He held both hands around his cup, as if drawing energy from it. "I still find it hard to believe." He looked up at me with a terrible sadness. "It might have been easier to digest if you simply told me you *were* a witch—or even the green ghost of Fort Laramie."

I snorted, lightly rubbing my temples. "You think I find it any easier to believe? Imagine an unmarried spinster recreating history at a tea party where she works, and suddenly finding herself living that history...with a husband and child who just happen to be her own ancestors? And if I didn't look like Jessamine's clone, I probably wouldn't have been able to pull any of this travesty off."

I caught a brief flash of sympathy in his eyes. "I do owe you an apology, I suppose, at least for yesterday. Did I...did I hurt you?"

Instinctively, my hand flew to my cheek. My arms were bruised from deflecting several solid hits when he flailed at me on the porch, but I rolled my eyes and said nothing.

We both sighed, taking noisy sips of coffee to keep from looking at each other.

"What is a clone?" he finally asked in a small voice.

"A look-a-like, taken from DNA..." I stopped myself. "Do you really want to know about the future?"

He shrugged. "Only the future of my family, but I'm afraid to ask."

"The family does well. No murderers or horse thieves among us." I smiled weakly. "And some of the women, especially, live long full lives."

"Jessamine?"

"Jessamine, too. I imagine she has merely traded places with me and is also baffled by our time-travel switch."

"Then you think you might be able to switch back again?"

"If we could figure out how to do that." Our eyes finally locked. "You want that, don't you?"

When his face crumpled with torment, I knew the answer and turned away. "Of course you do." *How could any man with a wife so perfect and so talented not welcome her return?*

"I don't want Tallie to know about this," he muttered after another long silence between us. "She wouldn't understand, and you *have* given the performance of a lifetime pretending to be her mother and...and my wife," he added with a flush. "I only ask you to pretend longer...until we get all this fixed." He paused before adding, "Pretend being Tallie's mother, I mean."

I could feel the rise of emotion in my chest. "Yes,

maybe I missed my calling and should have become an actress instead of a teacher," I said a little too sharply.

"You were a teacher?"

"I planned on it but took a job with the state park service, when I couldn't find a teaching position."

"The park service?"

"Fort Laramie is a National Historic Park Site...in my time. It's missing many of the buildings you know, but some, like Old Bedlam, were reconstructed, and it's all a living museum now. History protected and preserved. The past enlightens the future." I snorted. "Even the Three Mile Ranch is a protected Historic Place in Wyoming."

His mouth twitched at that. "Of course, hardscrabble and proud of it; that's Wyoming."

"There will always be cattle and sheep in Wyoming, but maybe not as many as now. Savage competition among the ranchers will spark a brief war in Johnson County in a few years."

I looked at him, wondering if he even knew or cared where Johnson County was. I was nervously recounting what I knew about Wyoming history, maybe still trying too hard to convince him I was finally telling the truth.

"And eventually," I finished, "there will be a Wyoming sugar beet industry and oil fields, complete with a government scandal over the drilling."

He closed his eyes and snorted ruefully. "I don't want to know about any of that. I'm a simple man, living a simple life."

I snorted again. "Uncommon maybe, hardly simple." I came around the table and found myself reaching out to correctly re-button his shirt.

His jaw twitched a little when he gazed down at my trembling fingers. "I could say the same about you, Jess." His face colored again. "Should I still...call you that?"

"Well, that's what my Cousin Jake always calls me. It *is* short for Jessica, you know."

"Then, do you agree...to pretend...a little longer...for Tallie?" He held his hand out, and I took it hesitantly. For a few seconds too long, we held fast, our eyes meeting only in a quick glance to seal our new commitment.

After telling Mitch what Mary Garrett had related about her son and his revolver, we came to another mutual decision that tweaked the truth. We could speculate but didn't really know if the body we buried with Charlie *was* Jed Garrett. And even with speculation, we would never know how or why they died together in a flaming barn. Disappearances seemed to be common around Fort Laramie, more prevalent actually, in the whole western frontier.

A couple of old saws came to mind: *What's done cannot be undone*, and *what you don't know can't hurt you.* Some things were better kept secret, for the sake of all concerned. I thought ruefully that sometimes silence is the kinder mouth that swallows the deepest hurts.

Chapter Forty-Four
Lost and Found

Mitch and I spent the rest of the morning attempting to avoid each other. I kept to the house; he disappeared outside. When I did catch sight of him as I gathered a few garden vegetables for supper, he looked miserable, sitting on a tree stump beneath the bur oak, holding his head like it might roll off his shoulders. I knew he had to be nursing a terrible hangover.

He seemed grateful when I approached him later with a mug of willow bark tea and an egg sandwich. "Have you seen Tallie and Finn?" I asked, hand to brow, sweeping the horizon.

Staring at the sandwich in his hands like it was a foreign object, he moaned as if in pain. "How do I explain my behavior…"

"Your daughter will forgive you for anything."

He looked up at me hopefully, and in the dappled sunlight his eyes had the same innocent cast I had seen in hers this morning, though still pink around the edges. "Is that another surefire prediction or just your best guess?"

"Your crown may be tarnished, but you'll always be the king in her life," I assured him.

"You do have a way with words." He took a gulp of the tea, then poured some on a bandana he tore loose from his neck and pressed it over his eyes.

"Have you seen Tallie?" I asked again. "Normally, she doesn't miss a meal, and it's well past noon."

He shook his head, finally eating the sandwich.

"Finn must be giving Tallie a good chase this time. I'll go find them." Giving up a tiny bit of resistance to gloat, I added, "We'll need to find more willow bark, anyway."

Frowning, he finished his sandwich in a few big bites and wiped his mouth on the bandana. "I'll look too." He stood rather clumsily, and his face blanched a shade while he steadied himself against the tree. "We can fan out and cover more ground that way." He looked toward the woods.

****

After about an hour searching for any sign of Tallie or Finn, I headed back, thinking maybe Mitch had found her, and I'd find them both back home waiting for me. I had never ventured far from the cabin by myself, and every little rustle of leaves or warning call of a bird set me further on edge. This was the wilderness, and I had nothing with me for protection but a small knife in a basket filled with sprigs of yarrow and several new shards of willow bark.

Mitch was back already, loading his shotgun and a smaller handgun at the kitchen table. He had a knife laid out also, a wicked looking thing half stuck in a beaded scabbard I had never seen before. "What did you find." I dropped my basket in sudden alarm.

"Wolf tracks." He frowned without looking up at me.

"Are you sure they weren't dog tracks?"

"I'm sure," he snapped. "I came back only for this, and my horse."

"I'm going with you."

He shook his head. "Somebody needs to be here if she gets back. *When* she gets back," he amended quickly.

"I'm going with you," I repeated more loudly.

"She's not your child."

I flinched. "But I love her, too," I said softly.

He stared at me for a moment, his jaw still popping before he picked up the small handgun and slapped it into my hand. "Can you shoot this?"

"Of course," I lied, thrusting my chin at him.

"All right, then pack up some food, while I saddle the horses. This ain't no picnic," he added, "but if I know Tallie, she will be hungry when we find her."

Oh God, please let us find a hungry child, I silently prayed.

****

By the time we started out, the sun was already dancing below the tallest tree tops. Mitch pressed his lips into a loud whistle that demonstrated how we could keep in touch without using a gunshot if we became separated on the trail. I tried to imitate him, but my whistle came out like the last wind of a dying canary.

He grimaced. "You don't know how to whistle?"

I knew what he was thinking. *Jessamine could whistle.*

I can bake chocolate chip cookies, I wanted to retaliate, but instead I asked if separating was necessary.

"We'd have a better chance of finding her if we fanned out—at least a few hundred feet or so," he conceded, then gave me pointers on what to look for— broken branches or twigs, foot or paw prints in mud or

311

sand, patches of clothing. "What was she wearing?" he asked.

"Tan corduroys and a yellow shirt, I think."

"Yellow. That'll stand out, unless we come to fields of tickseed."

I knew we were heading southwest, toward the foothills of the Laramie Mountains between Fish Creek and the Laramie River. Mitch didn't think she would cross any water, even if the hot, dry summer made an easy portage.

"She would cross anything," I argued, "if she knew her dog was on the other side."

We traveled slowly, sometimes riding, sometimes walking to see the advantage of both elevations, and if I could no longer see Mitch or hear him call Tallie's name, I did hear his whistle loud and clear when he was out of sight. I called out too, until I was nearly hoarse, but my only response came from the crows that did a good job telegraphing our presence.

The light was fading as the sun dipped behind the mountains, turning vertical shapes into silhouettes that swayed in the rising breeze. When Mitch began to whistle several times in a row, I reined the red mare to follow the sound and joined him at a dry gulch.

"I think I picked up their trail." He knelt to point at several prints in the sandy soil. He distinguished the elongated heart shapes of a deer track with the similar, but more concave prints of a pronghorn. "It's a deer crossing, but there are other prints here, as well."

My heart quickened when he pointed out the paw prints, and the heel mark of a small boot. "Finn and Tallie!" I cried.

"The paw prints are too big for Finn." He looked

ahead to a visible trail of tramped down grass. "They came this way, though." His expression was tense when he gave me a leg up onto the mare. "I want you to stay horsed, close to me now, don't speak unless you must, and if I give you a signal, turn back to the cabin. Can you find your way back?"

The fear I heard in his voice accelerated my own racing pulse. "I'm not going back without you and Tallie."

Looking up at me, he sighed. "I'm thinking of the two of you, Jess."

It took me a moment to understand what he meant, and when he asked once more if I could find my way back, I pointed vaguely in the direction of the setting sun. Without another word, he squeezed my leg and re-mounted the Appaloosa with a little effort. I could tell both horse and rider were still *under the influence.*

We rode into a grassy meadow that rose in elevation and gave us a clearer view of the mountains to our right. He slowed once to skirt around something on the trail that looked like matted cigar stubs.

"What was that?" I whispered when I rode up beside him.

"Wolf scat." He ignored my gasp when he rose in his stirrups to search the horizon.

Before long, we came to a scattered pile of bleached and cracked bones. My heart was beating fast, though I could tell they were animal bones. I wanted to call out Tallie's name again, but Mitch's posture and grim silence told me to keep still. He was the native woodsman, trained young to read signs and react appropriately. Because of his condition, I could tell he was concentrating extra hard, using every sense common to prey and predator alike. I slipped my hand inside my pocket and felt the little gun that rested against my thigh, hoping I would be able to use it if I had to. *If I had to. Yet another first!*

When we came to another small clearing, I could see a bloody fresh kill this time, and a patch of white fur sticking up from a pile of dirt and leaves. I thought I was going to be sick. Finn was black and white. My eyes darted over the killing site, searching in vain for a patch of yellow—or tan corduroy.

Mitch reined up beside me to whisper that we were being observed. Then I heard it. The distant yipping of a dog and I could feel relief race through me like a current of electricity. *Wherever Finn was, Tallie had to be, as well.*

As we raced toward the sound, I had the uncanny feeling we had an entourage, and in the deepening shades of dusk, I could see the tall meadow grass sway and part in parallel lines that flanked us. The yipping grew louder, turning into a cacophony of whines, barks, and howls that couldn't possibly come from one little dog.

Mitch aimed his shotgun at something ahead of us. He had looped his reins around his saddle horn, and when the shot rang out, the Appaloosa flinched, breaking stride for only a second before launching back into his gimpy gait. When I screamed, all hell broke loose. Three wolves came after my mare, nipping at her long tail, sending her into a panicked gallop that rattled my teeth. I heard more shots, followed by more yelps.

"Use your gun," Mitch yelled at me.

I had all I could do to keep my seat and stirrups, fists paralyzed around the knotted reins I had buried into the mare's flying mane as I rocked in the saddle. Two more shots rang out, followed by more high-pitched yelps.

Somehow, I managed to saw the reins back to my hips, trying to stop the mare with a voice edged in panic. Remembering what my riding instructor once told me about checking a runaway, I dug my heel into her flank and pulled the left rein to the cantle until her shoulder twisted and we veered, dropping to a lope, then a trot that became a fast walk that bounced me in the saddle like grease on a griddle. When she stopped suddenly, I lurched forward, clasping my arms around her neck to keep from falling. We both heaved, gasping for breath.

Mitch was nowhere in sight when I recovered enough to move on. Following the sounds of more yips and whines, I soon found myself interrupting a Mexican standoff. The mare was sweaty and still huffing when we approached a large oak that had fallen against two other trees, all leaning like dominoes over a tangle of roots that looked like the petrified arms of a giant squid. Something moved in a dugout between the arms, and I heard the distinct tinkle of a bell. When I urged the mare closer, I could see the black and white head of Finn emerge from the dugout, wearing the lamb's bell around his neck, his pink tongue hanging out the side of his mouth.

He whined in greeting and probably would have come to me, but crouched ten feet away—half hidden in the brush—Mitch commanded him to stay and wonder of wonders, the dog obeyed. With his gun in one hand, loose reins and the wicked looking knife in the other, Mitch moved only to glance in my direction, as he tersely ordered me to halt and stay horsed.

I wasn't about to argue, but I felt for the gun deep in my pocket and slowly pulled it out with a shaky hand.

At the edge of the clearing, two wolves crouched, equally tense with bared teeth and sharp claws representing *their* arsenal. One was nearly twice the size of the other, maybe five feet long, black with a gorget of gray fur at his neck. If it wasn't for his yellow slanted eyes and sharp teeth, he might have looked like a very large, very intimidating German Shepherd. The fresh carcass of a dead animal lay a short distance away.

"Where's Tallie," I hissed.

He nodded toward the dugout. "She's alive. I'm out of bullets, but they don't know that."

"What are we going to do?"

"They prefer to attack moving targets," he whispered, "but will respect an equal show of threat."

"You want me to snarl back at them?" I said, stupidly.

He gave me a fierce sidelong glance. "I want you to shoot the one that doesn't attack me."

"Shouldn't that be the other way around?" My hand on the gun was shaking uncontrollably now.

"Oh God," he swore.

Either God answered with a grumble of thunder, or more wolves were telegraphing their presence in the brush. Sheet lightning lit up the sky above the mountains. It hadn't rained for several weeks on the plains, but from our porch we had often watched the night sky flash behind the foothills and mountains. Heat lightning was not foreign to a Wyoming summer. *Oh yes, yes, let there be rain,* I willed, certain now that I detected the sharp smell of ozone in the air.

Muffled yips and a small voice in protest came from the tree den, and all eyes centered on a small furry gray pup wriggling past Finn to run toward the two crouching wolves. With a mixture of awe and relief, I watched the smaller wolf nudge the wolf pup, then clamp teeth delicately around its neck and trot off with it, leaving the black wolf standing his ground alone. There were more yips and whines in the distance, followed by a meaningful howl, communicating what I imagined to be some kind of pack family reunion.

The only live wolves I had ever seen were in a zoo, demonstrating only laconic behavior from a man-made enclosure designed to look like a set from the wilderness. Wolves in captivity did not behave—or even resemble the wolf that threatened us now.

Whether it was the electricity in the air or just feral instinct protecting what was theirs, whiskers stood straight as boar bristles on both alpha males—still staring at each other through slitted eyes; one pair yellow, one pair green. Every muscle in Mitch's jaw was taut with concentration. He had dropped the reins, and his hand now gripped his knife so tight I could see corded veins run up his arm. Miraculously, the App remained still as his master, with ears pinned to his head, revealing his own tense warning.

I thought I saw the wolf's head lift an inch or two, and when it thundered again, deep as a growl, I wasn't sure if it came from the wolf or the mountains behind us. Silver and blue streaks split the sky, followed by a loud crack that jarred us all, and my mare became skittish once more. I leaned forward to run my hand along her lathered neck, whispering, "Easy girl," and when I looked up again, the black wolf was gone.

In a flash quick as the lightning, Mitch spun around to pull Finn out of the den and reach for Tallie. Whimpering, she clamped her arms around his neck and buried her face in his chest. Her red braids were tangled with leafy debris, her yellow shirt and pants streaked with dirt. Before she clamped her legs around his waist, I noticed one of her boots was missing.

"Is she hurt?" I cried.

We both frantically examined her, checking for blood or broken bones. Claw marks had shredded one of her sleeves, but the scratches on her arm were superficial. No bites or broken bones. I touched her forehead but felt no heat. Her eyes were dull and half closed, and she was dry gulping for breath, her dusty face streaked with tear runnels.

When Finn wedged between us to lick her bare foot, she focused briefly and in a tiny voice, whimpered, "We found a puppy."

Mitch opened his mouth to say something, but after a warning look from me, he merely sighed. "Let's go home."

Chapter Forty-Five
The Teacup

We traveled slowly, protected, I thought by the rain that sent wolves and wildlife into sheltered retreat. With no moon to light our way, Mitch relied on his innate sense of direction and whatever sign he could read through a steady veil of rainfall. He took off his shirt to wrap around his daughter, melted into his chest on the Appaloosa.

I wasn't about to remove my shirt, but I hovered over the dog that curled around my saddle horn. *Chastened,* I thought, if his doggy intellect even comprehended the trouble he had caused. His nose was deeply scratched, but the rain washed away residual blood, and I thought it would heal with only scars—if he kept it clean and gave up probing into random holes and wolf dens.

I could imagine the scenario that might have taken place. Tallie on Finn's trail, Finn chasing a rabbit or deer into wolf territory, child finding dog, both finding "puppy" in wolf den, shelter under siege from anxious parents. After the amazing standoff I just witnessed, I had a new understanding of how all parents—wild or domestic, with two legs or four—shared the same protective instincts when it came to their progeny.

Finn might have kept the wolves at bay for a short while, but I shivered with the thought of what we might have found if we had come even thirty minutes later. *Bloody bones cracked and piled amid tattered bits of tan corduroy and red and white hair?*

Tallie was asleep when Mitch carried her to bed. She sighed but didn't wake while I took over to undress and wash her lightly with a flannel rag. Finn watched me intently, and when I finished tucking her under her quilt, he jumped up on the bed to lie beside her. Too late, I wiped each of his paws and whatever dirt remained on his ears and mouth, but I could still detect the musty scent of a wet dog mingled with something pungently wild. I gave him a grudging pat on the head and kissed Tallie's forehead before I left them.

Mitch had seen to the horses and brought our wet blankets and saddles inside. In the flickering light of a Betty lamp, he bent over a saddle, wiping it down with something that kindled the smell of oiled leather.

"Is she all right?" He looked anxiously up at me.

"Sleeping like a baby." I smiled. "She's as tough as…as her father. No worse for wear, I'd guess."

He closed his eyes and sighed with relief, paused, then added, "What about you?"

"Just wet, but I'll probably feel worse tomorrow." I rubbed my backside.

He rose and came to me, putting his hands on my shoulders. "I want to thank you for all you've done for Tallie. None of this must have been easy for you."

"Tallie is easy to love," I said. "I can see how natural it is to…to want to protect a child." *Your child,* I wanted to say.

His hair was still damp and shiny, pulled back now into his usual queue. The flickering light from the lamp played with shadows over his face, and I could see his eyes had lost their strain after a wash of rainwater. Still, I couldn't mistake the troubling indecision I saw in them now. Something more was on his mind.

He broke the weight of silence between us. "The gypsy gave me something for you." He went to the fireplace and to my shock, worked a stone loose at the base. From the cavity behind it, he removed a small bundle wrapped in a colorful scarf, and set it on the bearskin rug. "Come, open it."

I knelt on the rug across from him and nervously began to untie the scarf, my heart quickening as I could feel the shape of the object so well protected. The blue and white teacup clearly mended, with several hairline cracks radiating through it, and missing its handle. I turned it upside down and set it on the rug between us. The word "Mitawin" throbbed there like the answer found in a crystal ball. *My wife.* He had called me that several times in the throes of passion. But the word wasn't meant for me, and the woman who it inspired came between us, large as life. The room seemed to reel about me, and I closed my eyes against the dizziness that engulfed me and listened to the drum of the rain on the roof and the metronome in my heart.

"Jessica." I could hear his deep voice break.

Jessica. He was calling my full name, not Jess or Jessamine or even the word on the bottom of the cup. *Jessica.* The one word that possibly meant he believed me.

"I found it in my saddlebag this morning and hid it, until I could decide."

I opened my weary eyes and lost myself in the dark sanctuary of his. "Decide what?"

He picked up the cup, clutching it in both hands.

"Decide whether to smash this to pieces...or return it to you." His face reflected the pain I felt. "The gypsy said you would know what to do with it."

I took the cup from him, and with hands shaking, wrapped it in the scarf and set it aside. Still shaking, I offered him my hand in thanks, and he clasped it in both of his before slowly raising it to his lips. His eyes were soft and filmy as he gazed at me with a look that pierced my soul. When I reached up to cup his chin, his eyes snapped shut as he dropped his head to capture my hand between his cheek and shoulder, giving up a low groan. I took his hand and held it to my tripping heart.

"I love you," I whispered, and he responded instantly to what I knew he once longed to hear, pulling me into his arms with a long and desperate kiss that made us both wince.

He carried me into the bedroom, and we undressed quickly in the dark. I could hear our damp clothing drop against the plank floor like sodden leaves peeling off the branches of a rain whipped tree. I was the tree, soft and stripped of the hard core that guarded my heart. I fell onto the bed, naked and open to his touch, refusing to think about whom we were, the future or the past.

"No guilt," he whispered as he bent over me.

"No blame," I added.

And with our hands and mouths, we found every trigger that urgently transported us into a void stripped of doubt and damnation. As if choreographed to the music in my heart, our bodies danced in harmony, paying fierce homage to everything we could never put into words. And after our climactic throes rippled into a sense of overwhelming peace, I knew at last what it was like for me—*Jessica Brewster*—to be a woman loved only for myself.

The rain had stopped, and a sickle moon filtered light through the window, enough to read the serenity in his eyes as we faced each other in silence. "I love you," I whispered again, and he closed his eyes and pulled in a deep breath.

"Do you hear me? I will never love another man."

He reached for my hand and pressed his mouth into the bowl of my palm, his eyes traveling over my face like a blessing. "Yes, you will," he said quietly. "You are a woman who needs to love."

With his finger, he traced the heart line on my palm. "This is long and deep," he said with a sad smile. "Maybe that means you will love deeply."

"Oh, I do," I whispered, turning to snuggle into the curve of his shoulder and reach up to kiss him tenderly behind his ear. For a long time we just lay there, holding hands and staring at nothing while memorizing breath and scent and the luxury of being lost in our own time.

Chapter Forty-Six
Fictional Osmosis

When his arm came around my shoulder to adjust the pillows, we sat up to lounge against the headboard. I took his palm in hand and traced *his* heart line. "Yours is forked. What do you think Rosie would say about that?"

He peered down at me. "She *did* read my palm after sedating me with some vile tasting liquor. I was already too drunk to remember everything she said, but I do remember she told me I was a lucky man to know two great loves in my life."

He kissed my temple and pushed a loose strand of hair behind my ear. "Do you know any man in your time who had two women—a man who split his soul with love for each?"

I thought about it for a minute. *Dr. Zhivago, a favorite old movie classic came to mind. He was torn between his wife and mistress and ended his life with neither, dying of a heart attack within reach of his long lost love.*

"I don't know anyone who ever talked about soul mates. I thought most girls were silly to talk about their love life, so I never paid much attention to their chatter. I never had a close girlfriend—or even a real boyfriend—so the only way I learned anything about romance was from fictional osmosis, I suppose."

"Fictional osmosis?"

"Well, yes, absorbing the romantic life of a character in a book or movie is vicarious time travel for the heart. It's also a lot safer. You can enjoy the ride and close the book, or leave the theater with no personal heartbreak."

"Were you so afraid of heartbreak?"

I twisted a little to look at him. "I was orphaned young. Maybe losing people you love at an early age does that. Betrayal will also make you cautious." He was sympathetic, but not overly shocked, when I told him about Jimmy Potter and the bet that took my virginity on prom night.

"Some things do not change over time or culture." He sighed. "Growing up in Sioux camps, I knew boys who plotted to bed comely maidens, and the more protected the prize, the harder they tried." He smiled at the memory. "After a girl's womanhood rites, she was constantly chaperoned by old women, and sometimes, the girl even wore the ropes."

"The ropes?"

"Around her waist and between her legs...guarding her virtue."

"Like a chastity belt?"

"You could call it that."

I sniffed. "Oh, that must have been awfully uncomfortable."

"Among my people, I think making war came a lot easier than making love. Hot blooded braves were able to expend a lot of...well, maybe more honorable energy in battle. And if they excelled in bravery, they drew the attention of a maiden and her family protectors." He nudged me with his foot. "So you see there were few options to peel a plum, so to speak. Indian birth rates were always very low, children considered a gift."

I twisted again to smile at him more directly. "And how many plums did you peel?"

Even in the thready moonlight, I could see his color deepen a little. I didn't want to bring anyone else into our bed but had to ask him the single question that had plagued me since the first time we made love in the creek.

"Am I...did you notice many...differences?"

He knew at once what I meant. "Do you really want to know that?"

I nodded.

"You are enough alike in things that mattered. I think love blinds the eye to things that don't matter."

"Like bigger feet and smaller, er, other assets?"

He chuckled when my eyes dropped to my chest. "There are other differences, but I reasoned most were caused by a concussion that drove your memory loss."

"Physical looks aside, I don't have any of her talent."

He seemed surprised. "You are both strong minded, opinionated, curious...it isn't hard to see you swing from the same family tree, though tears and blushes never came so easily…"

"But I can't make quilts or shoot a gun, or even whistle!"

His mouth curled in amusement. "Learned accomplishments, not talent."

I held my breath, wanting him to continue, at the same time dreading to hear the nuance in his voice that lifted cherished memories of *her*. He knew which comparison piqued my curiosity most of all.

"She was not inhibited when we were...alone. Your—uh—your inexperience stunned me at first. Then I dismissed it as rejection of me, or of what was feared most. Her mother had several miscarriages and six children, but only three who survived. Her father wanted sons, and she assumed all men shared that desire. Failure always came hard to Jessamine, especially after our son was born dead."

"I read about some of that in her journals. She almost died too, didn't she?"

He sighed, and there was a look of distance in his eyes. We were talking about her in the past tense, as if she *was* dead. But if history couldn't be changed, she would be back, and they would have time together again. Jealous as that made me, I couldn't tell him she would outlive him to marry two more times. It would break his heart. If, as he said, I was a woman who needed to love, he was my counterpart—a man who needed to love, as well.

After an awkward silence, I asked him how he came to be so well-educated, hoping for a happier recall.

Propping himself on one elbow, he stretched on his side and flashed his trademark smile. "Nuns. You know about the St. Louis orphanage run by nuns. After my mother was killed by soldiers in a raid on our village, I was taken there by a remorseful general. It took six years to strip away the savage"—he snickered—"at the behest of my white father."

"You knew your father, then?"

"He knew *I* existed, but I learned *his* identity only when I left the asylum after I turned eighteen. I was given a letter and one hundred dollars from David

Mitchell. He had been a Superintendent of Indian Affairs when he met my mother, and he had a wife and several all-white children who didn't know of my existence."

I rubbed his arm. "What happened to you then?"

"With a new pair of boots, a horse, and the gift of a name, the Indian prodigal returned to his grandfather's village, now part of two worlds—belonging to neither."

"So you never met your father?"

I could hear the click in his knotted jaw when he looked away. "His letter made it clear that a happy reunion was never on his agenda. I imagine the money substituted for any guilt he felt."

"I'm so sorry, Mitch." I gently traced my fingers over the little pink scars on the inside of his arm. *Would they fade with memories of "the nurse" who stitched him up? Or would it become a timestamp of our summer together?*

"Do you really want to know all this?" He frowned.

"If...if I am pregnant, I would like to know more about the father of my child."

I held my breath when his hand cupped my stomach and our eyes met for an instant before he looked away. I pulled his chin back. "Didn't we agree—no blame, no guilt?"

"I *did* think you were my wife."

"I know you did. And I thought I'd never be able to forget that I wasn't."

Our eyes met again and held in mutual anguish, unspoken words hanging in the balance.

When he found his voice again, it was soft, almost apologetic. "I never believed in magic or even simple coincidence. But six years of education by Catholic nuns taught me to believe that the white man's God was no different from my grandfather's Great Spirit, and the origin of life was sacred to both." He paused to pull in another deep breath, then continued a little hoarsely, "I vowed that if I ever had a son, he would never measure his worth by what one hundred dollars could buy."

His gaze probed mine. "Are you certain, do you know for sure you are carrying my son?"

Even as intimate as our exposure was, I could feel the pointless heat of a deep blush creeping up my neck. I knew the logistics, but I had never discussed anything so personal, even with Granny. "I…I don't know all the signs, but I…I haven't had a monthly here, and I do feel queasy every morning."

His hand squeezed my breast, and I winced at the tenderness I felt there.

"That's a sign," he whispered. He took up my hand again and circled my wrist with his long fingers. "Drunk as I was, I do remember the shock I felt when the gypsy told me your life...and our child's," he added softly, "would be at risk if you stayed here."

His forefinger traced the bracelet line inside my wrist. "Who can say if palm reading isn't a science? You've told me things that will happen that are impossible to imagine, leaving me few choices. Are you a witch?—telling the truth?—or just plain crazy?"

This is crazy. I almost chuckled at the irony. Anchoring my forehead against his solid chest, I could hear his heartbeat, strong and steady, while unstoppable tears filled my eyes once more. *I never used to tear up so easily.*

"I won't let you risk…"

I felt his chin on my head, and the shuddering breath he took when he couldn't go on. We were both weeping now, wrapped in the silence of the night and the warmth of our embrace.

The room grew darker as clouds stippled the moon, and we made love again, squandering time, slowly savoring all the ways we could touch and feel, give and take, lose ourselves in the timeless rhythm of a fantasy that had begun without intention, but must end with it. When he reluctantly slipped from me, I felt hollow as a soap bubble, fragile and adrift. Only the hoot of a night owl brought me back to the touchstone of where I was, somewhere between hard reality and the solace of his arms.

There was nothing left to say. We slid easily into a familiar spoon position, and as always, I took comfort in the feel of his steady heartbeat against my back. His hand usually rested on my waist or hip, but this time he cupped my stomach.

"Our end is his beginning," I heard him whisper. "He will be the link that bridges our time." When he drew in a quick breath and kissed me on the soft spot behind my ear, I covered his hand with my own and thought I felt a tiny flutter, like the wings of a butterfly deep beneath the cup of our hands.

Chapter Forty-Seven
The Last Sunrise

I don't know if I slept at all, but my eyes opened to a subtle change of sapphire light fading slowly into gray. After slipping gently out of his arms, I dressed quickly in my black underwear and the chemise and blue dress from Fort Laramie, then ran a brush through my disheveled hair without looking in the mirror. In the pre-dawn light, I studied him, still lying on his side, clutching my pillow now, like a memory of me. His dark hair fanned starkly against the white of his own pillow. The sideburns and beard I had found so attractive had grown in the last few days, covering his chiseled jaw. With his green eyes closed, he looked vulnerable, dark lashes feathered against his cheeks.

I didn't need to see the green. It was locked in my memory, every shade that changed hue with light and emotion. I had memorized them all, along with the musky smell of him, leather and sweat, and a new mingling of our heated sex in the tangle of sheet that twisted around his long legs. His chest was exposed, and the dark hair that shadowed it rose and fell with his breath. I remembered the first time he held me in his arms. Though troubled and scared, I felt undeniably safe in that snug harbor. Even in sleep, his mouth curved slightly into the tiny half grin I had grown to love. I gently brushed away his hair and feathered a kiss behind his ear. A responsive twitch at the corner of his mouth told me I had sealed his dream.

I tiptoed out of the room, closing the door quietly behind me, lit the iron stove, and put on the teakettle. While the water heated, I crept up the loft steps.

Tallie was sleeping almost in the same position as her father. Instead of a pillow, one arm locked around her little black and white dog. Finn, with a crippled leg and now, a scarred, swollen nose—the saved treasure of her heart. With her green eyes closed, all resemblance of her father was lost, but I could see in the shape of her mouth the promise of her own daughter, my beloved Granny Lou. I kissed my finger and touched her softly on her lips, choking back a sob when—like her father—she also smiled in dreamy response.

I placed the porcelain teacup on the table, beside the baskets of vegetables and herbs I had gathered early yesterday. *Only yesterday?* It seemed like a lifetime since first I entered this room. I looked around. Nothing had changed in four months, nothing to mark my presence here except for the dried herbs and flowers that hung in bundles from the fireplace mantel, ingredients for soap or recipes that needed spice. One wall was also lined with Tallie's artwork and penmanship papers. I smiled at the intricate drawings of her pets, all names carefully scripted beginning with the letter "F." She probably had her mother's talent for sketching. Jessamine's talents were many. None that I could think of had passed down to me, in spite of what Mitch thought.

But still, I couldn't discount the nuggets of self-discovery and education I had accumulated in the last four months. I had learned about natural dyes and making soap, inventive cooking, and had a surprising capacity for adapting to a primitive lifestyle, if you could stretch that into a talent.

Most of all, I had learned to love in the first person, with clarity and joy, and saw the wilted heart of a self-possessed thirty-year-old spinster blossom in the summer sun. The same timeless sun that had beat down on generations of my family, and would do so until the end of days. And with "the gift" growing beneath my heart, I knew our family legacies, like the sun, would shine on another generation. Maybe not through the women in our family, but through a changeling.

I cradled my stomach, still flat as a board, but I knew he was there, and I knew the Birdwoman was right. My child *was* a boy. Mitch's son—who would never measure his worth by the value of *any* amount of money, if I could help it.

I filled the mended cup with the last of our tea leaves, and before the kettle could sing, I took it off the burner and poured in the hot water. Carefully, nearly blinded by tears, I carried the cup out to the porch, to watch the sun rise over the mountains.

Chapter Forty-Eight
Redux

Fish Creek, August 2014

I drove my Jeep Cherokee into the clearing and parked beside the silver Escalade already there. When she saw us, the Realtor quickly closed her notepad and gathered up a few papers after tucking a dark sweep of hair behind her ear. She was overdressed for a walk in the country, wearing designer jeans and expensive western boots with a stylish scarf draped softly about her neck. The sun glinted on her silver earrings and when she smiled, I thought she could have just stepped out of a toothpaste commercial.

Jake looked at me and wiggled his eyebrows in approval. "Do you think she's single?"

I laughed. "Check her fingers, or better yet, just ask. That might clue her in to your interest."

He gave me one of his long-suffering looks before I reached behind me to open the car seat and gather up my eager child. Once outside, Jake took the baby and hoisted him to his shoulders, with a mutual cry. "Whee!"

I pinched the baby's chubby leg and told him to hang on tight to Uncle Jake. His face lit up, and with both hands, he promptly gathered handfuls of Jake's hair, giving him two blond horns—an image opposed to the suave look Jake probably wanted to present to a single woman with great teeth.

"Whee." He laughed from his new perch, showing all of *his* even little baby teeth.

"Meredith Morgan," the Realtor said, offering a hand to each of us. "And this must be your baby."

"Just mine," I corrected, introducing Jake formally. "We're related, but we aren't a couple."

Her surprise seemed genuine. "My assumption. When you called about this property, I thought maybe you intended to build a ranch out here...you and your husband."

"My husband is dead," I said, maybe too succinctly. "I didn't think there were any requirements here for ownership. If you're worried about my income..."

Her smile wavered only an instant. "Oh, no, I'm sorry, I didn't understand. It's just, well this land has been in public escrow so long and is still relatively primitive and remote. I just figured nobody but another rancher would even want it."

"Another rancher?" We stopped on a rickety footbridge that funneled into a rather overgrown deer path running up the slight incline. She handed me a listing sheet with all the pertinent data, explaining what *wasn't* on the sheet, I presumed.

"This land was an original homestead once, then became a cattle ranch." It reverted back to the state when the family matriarch died, back in 1950, I believe. Wyoming Park Service planned a campsite here, but nothing ever came of that, so eventually the acreage was divided up to sell off bit by bit. This acreage and two smaller plats near the foothills are all that's left of the original hundred acres."

I glanced down at the stagnant creek beneath the bridge, trying to pinpoint where I had washed clothes in the heat of summer. The water was muddy brown now, and the channel had narrowed, maybe even changed course over more than a hundred years. I drew my bearings from a large flat rock, and with a sudden jolt, I was flooded with the memory that could have been the day I conceived—the day that altered my life forever.

"Jess, are you all right?" Both Jake and the realtor stared at me. "You look like you've just seen a ghost," he said.

I loosened my grip on the bridge rail and pulled myself together, taking my sunglasses out of my pocket. "Just a headache coming on. I should have worn a hat, the sun is so bright here."

"I have some bottled water in the van," the Realtor said.

I waved the offer off. "How far does the property line extend from here?"

"There was once a house farther up, toward the treeline, and a large barn." With her left hand, she pointed, and I noticed there was no ring on her third finger. Jake noticed it, too and threw me another brow-wiggling look.

"What happened to them?" I asked.

"Both might have been dismantled for the wood. Wood was always at a premium around here. There was part of a stone fireplace still standing, though, when I first got this listing."

"I would think this land would be prime," I said. "With a creek running through it, wouldn't it be a perfect setup for cattle or sheep."

"Well, yes, but to be perfectly honest this plat hasn't been an easy sell. There were rumors and a local mystery that fed superstitions about a jinx."

Jake snorted. "Well, if that's why the price is so affordable, I say bring on the jinx."

The baby giggled when Jake whirled around and did a few deep knee bends, making us all laugh.

"What's his name?" she asked.

"We call him M.C., for Mitchell Charles."

"Mitchell, is it? Well, maybe that's a happy omen. I believe Mitchell was the last name of the original owners." She flashed her winning smile.

As she led the way up the deer path, I heard her say, "I don't think you can ever make wise choices based on rumors."

"I agree completely," Jake said, leaping ahead to keep up with her.

"What sort of rumors?" I asked.

"Well, an original barn here burned down in a fire that took the life of a visiting family member. As the story goes, he was buried on this property, but years later, his body was exhumed to be taken to a family cemetery in Nebraska. When the bones of two bodies were found in his grave, along with a rusted pistol, foul play was suspected."

"Sounds like the makings of a great mystery novel," Jake said. "Who was the second body?"

"Nobody knows. There's always been stories of disappearances and ghosts linked with Fort Laramie, and then when the original owner disappeared—"

My stomach lurched. "What do you mean—disappeared?"

"I think it was sometime before the turn of the last

century. The ranch was becoming pretty prosperous when the owner went deer hunting in the mountains one day with his dog and was never seen again."

We arrived at a gray weathered picnic table, and I sat down heavily, suddenly wishing I had taken the bottled water I was offered. My heart was beating wildly.

"Never seen again?" I repeated breathlessly.

"There was a huge search, but neither body—dog or man—was ever found. It was like the mountains swallowed them up."

Jake noticed me flinch. "That *is* wild." He moved the baby to his lap.

Stiffening his body into a projectile, my son loudly commanded, "Down." On the ground, he checked his balance for a moment, then began to toddle over to a patch of dandelions, and bent to pick one with his dimpled hand. We all watched his sure-footed navigation of the rocks in his path, as he brought the flower back to me.

"Mama," he said with a toothy grin, melting my heart as always when he looked up at me with his innocent green eyes. I was glad the sunglasses hid my own eyes as I sniffed the flower and threaded the stem into the hair behind my ear.

"What a clever, handsome child," the Realtor said. "How old is he?"

"Nineteen months," I said, softly adding, "The image of his father."

Jake threw me a worried look. I had tried to tell him what had happened to me because of Granny's teacup, but he thought they were the ramblings of an injured brain. He had faithfully visited the hospitalized woman he thought was me—in a coma after crashing my red Honda into a tree near Fort Laramie. Ultimately, it *was* me, not Jessamine, who woke in the hospital as the celebrated survivor of room 212. I was declared *a miracle* and sent home two days later.

The *real* miracle was my pregnancy, which needed a creative explanation. But artful lying had become a specialty in the four months I was gone. I fudged the dates and told Jake I shopped at a sperm bank for a donor to insure the family legacy after Granny died. I knew that would be easier for him to swallow than the impossible truth. I could hardly fault Jake for his doubt or feel guilty over such deceit. If it hadn't been for the baby, I might have thought I *was* crazy or an accident victim coming out of a dream-riddled coma.

The pregnancy *was* difficult, ending early in a caesarian that could have ended badly over a hundred years ago. Mitch's son was the "gift" he declared it to be—my link to another lifetime, and as long as I could hold him in my arms and gaze into his father's eyes, I knew I had a piece of them both as long as I lived.

"If you don't mind, I'd like to stroll around the property." I handed my son back to Jake again. "I am dressed for it." I indicated my old boots and Levi's.

They both seemed a little startled by my sudden abruptness, but Jake winked at me over the baby's head, and before I was out of earshot, I heard him deliver a pickup line to Meredith after asking if he could call her "Merry." *Go for it,* I chuckled to myself.

The fireplace had lost its shape in a rough pile of stones, some heavily covered by gray lichen. What was left of the blackened hearth stone was partially buried and the oak mantel was missing. I took a deep breath, imagining what it had looked like just a few years ago...years that had somehow morphed into several lifetimes. That last night Mitch and I sat on the bearskin rug before this very fireplace, separated only by a blue and white teacup that would tear us apart forever.

I dropped to my knees on the ground, aligning myself to the same spot I had taken, facing the haunting image I could picture sitting before me in that emotionally charged scenario. *I love you,* I told him. Three words I had never uttered to any man before or since. Three words I might never voice again—except in a dream.

Remembering something, I crawled over to the base of the fireplace and wiggled some of the rocks that were still intact, hoping it wouldn't bring the rest of them crashing down on me. When I found one that seemed looser than the others, I carefully tugged it away from the cavity it concealed and was surprised to find a piece of paper there, yellow and brittle with age. I opened it carefully, and read the faded script.

"Love has no end, only beginnings." In smaller letters, almost as a postscript, he had added, *"Teach him to whistle."*

I didn't know whether to laugh or cry as I folded the note and slipped it into my black lace bra, then plucked the little dandelion from my hair and sealed it in the hidden cavity. When I thought I could move again, I walked to where I imagined the porch would have been and tried to align my sight with the last one I had of that 1886 sunrise. I could still see the distant mountains, but everything nearby was overgrown, tangled with briars and native sage.

The bur oak was still there, majestic in its new

height, gnarled and thickened with age, its scalloped leaves as green and wind-rustled as I remembered. Already it had survived wood shortages, a barn fire, and winter storms for at least one and a half centuries—its mighty arms reaching now in grateful supplication. Once, it sheltered a kissing couple, little girls collecting acorns, and a chastened man lamenting honor lost in the eyes of his daughter. Would the tree live long enough to shade my great grandchildren?

When I closed my eyes, I thought I could hear the cackle of chickens, the distant bark of a dog, and the soft whicker of a horse. I could feel the dry wind brush my face, tinged with the scent of beebalm and lavender that once grew beside the porch. Then I smelled something else, something sealed in my memory forever: musk and leather—*his* scent.

Jake and the Realtor were engaged in the playful art of flirtation when I returned to the picnic table. "You've got a sale," I told Miss Morgan.

They both stared at me, cautious and surprised.

"It feels like home already." I smiled dreamily, visualizing the site for a new house with a great view of a mountain sunrise.

"Home," Mitch's son repeated, laughing when I lifted him into my arms and tickled his ear with a feathery kiss.

If you enjoyed *THE ACCIDENTAL WIFE,*
the following pages contain
an extended excerpt from its companion book,
THE ACCIDENTAL STRANGER,
available soon from The Wild Rose Press, Inc.

He melted into the shadows, drawn to the sound of another human voice. He had never come this far, never dared to put himself in such danger. In the spangled light of sunset, he watched her bend over the child, like the graceful arc of a bog violet. She was singing a ditty, and the happy tune drifted in the wind, tugging at his heart. He closed his eyes and tried to remember his mum's voice, light as faerie strings, singing to him so long ago. When life was simple and true, but for the want of food.

No hunger now. Not in the physical sense. There were always rabbits, fish from the river, even deer he might hunt with the primitive bow and arrows he carved four winters ago. He hungered more and more for the sights and sounds of humanity, even the touch of another living creature. For a while he toyed with the idea of finding a pet he could tame—maybe a bird or even a stray wolf. Anything to break the isolation and spend the lonely hours. But a pet might give away his presence, put him at risk.

The woman set the child on the porch step, then demonstrated how to hold hands, palms together, fingers pointed in prayer position. Blowing between her cupped thumbs, she produced a weak sound. The child mimicked her and made her laugh. She was tall and when the wind whipped her thin shift against her body, he could see that she was slender...curved in all the right places. Her hair was lank and loose on her shoulders, as if she had just washed it. He couldn't make out the color. In the fading glow of sunset, it looked purple.

The child stood, teetering on the step with arms forward, reaching out for her. *Too daring for a girl—yet*

1

the long hair made him wonder. With a high-pitched whoop, he—or she—flew into the woman's arms, and they twirled in a circle, laughing in harmony. Another sound that cut into his memory; like the sweet chords of the cruit his folk played.

The house was made of stripped logs, with an eyebrow porch that looked like it ran around two, maybe three sides. Well-built…new, judging by the patina of the wood. *Where would such logs come from?* Wyoming pine stands, even in the Bows, were plundered for miles around the fort. Finding such uniform logs without going a great distance…then hauling them to such an isolated spot…? He stroked his beard. Not even a wagon or barn in sight.

Maybe he was drifting again? Conjuring up the visions he missed, the undeserved comfort he craved, even as a watcher. His mum had visions. With her last breath, she told him he would find his people living in wooden houses with glass windows and fenced yards.

He patted his chest, feeling the secret pocket that held the fading image of his father. His father in uniform. It was a good thing both his parents were gone now. The shame of knowing their son… He caught his breath. Best not to go there.

A shrieking night hawk diverted his attention, soaring high above him. The woman must have heard it, too. She looked upward, shielding one eye like a salute, her gaze drifting toward him. He crouched deeper in the thicket. She was real, no faerie hallucination.

He checked his bearings, marking a path for the quickest retreat. When he heard a door slam shut, he held his breath and listened for footfalls. Nothing but the night wind ruffling through the sage. When he looked up, the porch was empty and yellow light—like the eyes of a demon—poured from two of the nearest cabin windows. He crossed himself, then crept slowly away, like a phantom of the night.

He would be back.

A word about the author...

Born and raised in Milwaukee, Wisconsin, Carol Ann Johnson Fosdick was hooked on writing at age ten after winning a contest. She has freelanced for over thirty years, writing for local and national publications, with stories in three anthologies, including Minnesota's *Blossoms & Blizzards*, and a Prentice Hall Literature Series. Her writing dreams are forged on a country hilltop in Rochester, MN, with husband, family, and a menagerie of wild and domestic animals.

http://cjfosdick.com

Thank you for purchasing
this publication of The Wild Rose Press, Inc.

If you enjoyed the story, we would appreciate your
letting others know by leaving a review.

For other wonderful stories,
please visit our on-line bookstore at
www.thewildrosepress.com.

For questions or more information
contact us at
info@thewildrosepress.com.

The Wild Rose Press, Inc.
www.thewildrosepress.com

Stay current with The Wild Rose Press, Inc.

Like us on Facebook

https://www.facebook.com/TheWildRosePress

And Follow us on Twitter
https://twitter.com/WildRosePress